A Murder For Mistress Cwen

A Murder For Mistress Cwen

Interminable

Chronicles of Brother Hermitage

by

Howard of Warwick

From the Scriptorium of
The Funny Book Company

The Funny Book Company

Published by The Funny Book Company
Crown House 27 Old Gloucester Street
London WC1N 3AX
www.funnybookcompany.com

Cover design by Double Dagger.

ISBN 978-1-913383-25-1

Also by Howard of Warwick.

The First Chronicles of Brother Hermitage

The Heretics of De'Ath

The Garderobe of Death

The Tapestry of Death

Continuing Chronicles of Brother Hermitage

Hermitage, Wat and Some Murder or Other

Hermitage, Wat and Some Druids

Hermitage, Wat and Some Nuns

Yet More Chronicles of Brother Hermitage

The Case of the Clerical Cadaver

The Case of the Curious Corpse

The Case of the Cantankerous Carcass

Interminable Chronicles of Brother Hermitage

A Murder for Mistress Cwen

A Murder for Master Wat

A Murder for Brother Hermitage

The Umpteenth Chronicles of Brother Hermitage

The Bayeux Embroidery

The Chester Chasuble

The Hermes Parchment

The Superfluous Chronicles of Brother Hermitage

The 1066 from Normandy

The 1066 to Hastings

The 1066 via Derby

The Unnecessary Chronicles of Brother Hermitage

The King's Investigator

The King's Investigator Part II

The Meandering Chronicles of Brother Hermitage
A Mayhem of Murderous Monks
A Murder of Convenience
Murder Most Murderous

Brother Hermitage Diversions
Brother Hermitage in Shorts (Free!)
Brother Hermitage's Christmas Gift

Audio
Hermitage and the Hostelry

Howard of Warwick's Middle Ages crisis: History-ish.
The Domesday Book (No, Not That One.)
The Domesday Book (Still Not That One.)
The Magna Carta (Or Is It?)

Explore the whole sorry business and join the mailing list
at
Howardofwarwick.com

Another funny book from The Funny Book Company
Greedy *by Ainsworth Pennington*

A Murder for Mistress Cwen

Caput I: A Happy Wanderer

On a dark summer evening in the year of our Lord 1068, the streets of Derby rustled with dark movements. Well, the street of Derby did. It was a large place with nearly 150 dwellings but they were crowded together and didn't really need too many streets.

In these trying times, it didn't pay to be out after dark making movement of any sort, no matter how many streets you had to do it in. The Norman overlords took a dim view of movement and tended to put a stop to it.

Many of the noises on this night were natural, as the animals of the darkness went about their business. Occasionally, a particularly loud disturbance would indicate that one of the animals of the darkness had eaten one of the others.

Different sounds told of people going about business, which was best conducted away from the glare of daylight. Such business was not uncommon in this town, despite the risk from passing Normans. Derby had an attraction.

It was an attraction very few people of the town talked about and if pressed would frequently deny even existed. It was impossible to get directions to it and no inhabitant of the town would confess to having visited it, ever. It was a source of shame and embarrassment and all of the local people would express their deep desire for it to simply go away; until they visited it under the cover of darkness. Sometimes quite regularly and for prolonged periods. The right question had to be asked of the right person in the right circumstances if a stranger were to find his way there. And it was usually a him.

The women of the town shunned the place on every possible occasion. The men only shunned it in public and in daylight and in front of the women. Nevertheless, they forbade their daughters from going anywhere near it under threat of severe punishment. Which only made some of the daughters even more intrigued.

This contradictory and blatantly hypocritical attitude explains why one particular stranger on this particular night was having a hard time finding his way to that renowned den of depravity: the workshop of Wat the Weaver.

The man rubbed his bald head in frustration as he took another mug of ale from the landlord. 'Look, I know it's here somewhere. How could I be trouble if I know it's here somewhere? Do I look like a Norman?' He did not look like a Norman. He was short and round and bald and of middle years, carrying a look of wealth about him. The Normans in England tended to be tall and lithe and armoured and carried looks of entitlement about them.

The landlord's blank face showed no sign of having even heard a word. He was considerably older and thinner than his customer and his grey pallor gave the impression that he hadn't been out of his tavern for years. He spat in a mug and wiped the inside with a rag that must have made it dirtier instead of cleaner.

'Never heard of him.'

'Wat the Weaver? Never heard of Wat the Weaver? Everyone's heard of him. Everyone knows his workshop is in Derby. I'm not asking you to take me there. I only want to know where it is.'

The landlord gestured the stranger to keep his voice down. He beckoned extravagantly and the message was more akin to "for God's sake keep your voice down". He looked around his tavern, over the head of the man with all the questions and noted that everyone was engaged in their own conversations. The arrival of the stranger had frozen the place into a tableau of silent staring and enquiry, as was natural, and every word the man spoke would be considered and commented upon for weeks to come.

That the new face turned out to be neither trouble nor entertainment soon restored the normal hubbub of discussion. That he asked about the weaver made them get back to their own business in double-quick time. No one wanted to be involved in a discussion about the notorious workshop - at least not where anyone could hear them.

Eventually, the landlord seemed content that it was safe to speak, even then it was a very low mumble. 'I couldn't say.'

The stranger was finding this very hard to believe. Surely a landlord would know, of all the people in town. He had spent what felt like hours searching every corner of Derby and, as the day ran out, the tavern was his last resort.

A whole weavers' workshop couldn't vanish, or be hidden in a relatively small place like this. It would have to be quite a big building if the volume of tapestries coming out of it was anything to go by. He knew the tapestries existed, he'd seen a few of the things and each one had been a fresh revelation. The sort of revelation he could understand people not wanting to talk about.

'You don't know?'

The landlord sniffed. 'Couldn't say that.'

'You do know?'

'Couldn't say that either.'

'Well, what could you say?'

'Have another mug of ale.' The landlord spoke quickly as his wife came to stand at his side.

The bald man rubbed his head again and quickly drank the mug he already had.

'What brings you to Derby then?' The face of the wife moved into the arrangement occasionally referred to as a smile. In her case, it looked as if all the bits of her face knew where to go, just not what to do when they got there.

She was obviously a lot younger than her husband, which might explain the sour expression her face was built upon. Of course, it might also be explained by a naturally sour disposition. She also seemed to be a bundle of energy, flitting here and there and doing three things at once while she talked. Her husband had stopped doing the one thing he seemed capable of and got a scowl for his trouble.

The stranger tried a smile but nothing changed on the wife's face. Perhaps it was stuck that way.

Her husband wore a look that screamed "say nothing". A look he directed at the stranger, making sure his wife couldn't spot it. It was a common expression in these parts and the landlord was an expert.

'Oh, you know,' the stranger shrugged, 'bit of trade.' He tapped the side of his nose.

This made the wife fold her arms across her chest like a barricade. 'Really?' It wasn't a polite enquiry.

'Can't say much at the moment but if things go well, and I see no reason why they shouldn't, there will be a very comfortable result.'

'And who would this trade be with?' the wife's demand spat from behind her ramparts.

The landlord was almost climbing off the top of his own legs at this. His gyrations and grimaces made clear what the answer to this enquiry should be. Nothing.

The stranger looked shocked at the question. 'I couldn't

possibly let on, you know, not until the deal is done.'

'You can tell me.' There was an air about this question that said if it wasn't answered things could get nasty. It was unlikely that the wife of a landlord owned her own torture chamber, but it looked as if she'd like one.

The stranger beckoned the wife to draw close and looked over his shoulder around the tavern, just to make sure that none of the crowd, eager for any sniff of news or gossip, was listening. The quality of a secret told by a stranger to a landlord's wife he'd only just met did not seem to concern the wife.

'Hawks. It's all I'll say. Hawks.'

'Hawks?'

'Hawks.'

'What? The birds, hawks?'

'That's them.'

'You've got trade with the hawks?' The wife dropped her defences and took a step back.

The stranger now gave the wife the look-upon-greeting-a-loon. 'With the hawks? Of course not. That'd be daft. Not with the hawks themselves? How would that work?'

'I don't know, do I? You're the one who said hawks.'

'And that's right. Hawks is me trade.'

'Ah.' The wife seemed very happy that she'd got it now. The landlord breathed a sigh of relief as well. 'You're a falconer.' She clearly thought that this was a wholesome and reputable trade. Compared to the weaving that went on around here, it was.

'Well, not exactly a falconer, as such.'

The look of suspicion fell back across the wife's face. 'What do you do with the hawks then?'

The man tapped the side of his nose again. 'That's the trade.'

Now the wife leaned forward and beckoned the stranger close. She too looked around, giving the universal signal that she is about to say something very interesting and that everyone nearby should try not to listen. 'You don't,' she looked again, clearly ashamed of what she was about to say. 'You don't make tapestries of 'em, do you?'

'Tapestries?'

'Shh. Yes, tapestries, of the hawks? You know, doing things.'

'What? Flying and hunting and so forth?'

'Could be.'

The stranger shook his head. He managed to give the wife a very peculiar look while simultaneously winking at the landlord. 'No. Just the hawks. Of course, people do like a good hawk tapestry. Nobles and the like. Probably some ladies out in the field with a hawk on the arm.'

'Enough of that,' the wife barked. 'We don't have any of that talk here.'

'Eh?'

A wifely finger pointed, menacingly. 'Ladies in fields. I know what you're after.'

'It was you mentioned tapestry. I don't have anything to do with tapestry. Just hawks.' He managed to look completely confused by his own conversation.

'Yes, well, mind you don't.'

Landlord and stranger exchanged the open looks of men out of their depth.

'Who you doing hawk trade with round here with then?' The wife continued her interrogation.

The man shook his head that she wasn't going to get the

information out of him by simply repeating the question. 'Can't say, mustn't say. Important though. Important people.'

'Important people? Round here? There aren't any important people around here.'

'Never know who you might come across.'

'I do.' The wife's suspicion was not dying. 'And they're best avoided.'

'May not be local,' the stranger suggested. 'Good meeting point, Derby. Very handy spot. Not too far north, not too far south. Everyone can get here nice and easy. Good spot for negotiations, if you know what I mean.'

'These important people coming here, are they?' She indicated that the tavern might need a bit of a clean if any important people were going to visit.

'Oh, no. Can't be seen in taverns. It's very confidential trade.'

'Hawks?'

'That's right. Soon as I can tell you about it you'll be amazed.'

'Really.' The wife didn't seem the type to be amazed. Not even if a hawk walked in, ordered an ale and explained the deal in person.

'Absolutely. But it's all quiet for now. Until the trade is done. Then you'll see.'

'There's hawks everywhere. What trade can make out of hawks?'

'The ones flying about are no good, are they?'

The wife looked quizzical.

'Got to be on the end of your arm, haven't they? Not going to get some hawk in a tree to just give you a pigeon or two. They have to fly off and kill them and then not eat them. And they don't just fly to sit on your glove out of choice, oh no.'

'Right.' The wife was starting to sound reluctantly convinced that the man really was here to do trade involving hawks. And also that she'd probably heard all she wanted for one day about hawks. Hawking was not something the ordinary folk got involved in unless they caught or hurt some Noble's hawk by mistake. Then they got deeply involved.

'Of course, your important person isn't going to want any old hawk. Has to be something special for them.'

'Really. Well, I expect you'll want some more ale.' She nodded to her husband to fill the stranger's already brimming mug and went back to her work.

'Hawks!' The landlord gave a great sigh and leaned towards the stranger as they were now confirmed brothers in arms, just emerging alive from a great trial. He held a hand out, 'Ernulf,' he introduced himself. 'Most people call me Ern.' He waited for a moment but got no name in reply. 'That was clever that was. I'd never have thought of hawks. How did you come up with that?'

'Simple really. It's true.'

'True?'

'Of course. I really am here about hawks.' The stranger lowered his voice. 'That's why I want to see the weaver. I don't want any of his tapestries, I've seen enough of those things for one lifetime.'

'What's he going to want with hawks? He's a weaver.' Slow recognition lit up Ern's face. 'Ah, you think he might buy one. He is rich, no doubting that. Might be the sort of thing he'd be interested in. Mind you, nobles take a dim view of anyone else having a hawk, and from what I hear the Normans are even worse. Not even old Watty can deal with that lot.'

The stranger leaned back and folded his arms. 'Old Watty

eh? Would this be the same old Watty that you've never heard of and can't say where his workshop is?'

'Ah, you can't be too careful, see.'

'Can't you?'

'Absolutely not. Doesn't do to go blabbing on about Wat the Weaver.' He even mouthed these last words so the breath of them did not pass his lips.

'I do see that now.' The stranger gave an extravagant nod towards Ern's wife.

'Yeah, well,' Ern bridled a bit. 'The weavers are a good source of income for us all but you wouldn't think so, the way some people go on about it.' He indicated with a nod that "some people" were all women. 'There's the man himself and the apprentices and everyone. Fair old proportion of our money comes from there, one way and another.'

'So you actually know the place quite well.'

'Oh, yes.' Ern now seemed happy to boast of his great friendship with Wat the Weaver. 'Wat and the other two get all their meals from me. His cook's pretty dangerous when it comes to food.'

The stranger looked intensely irritated and hissed through his teeth. 'You supply the place you couldn't say anything about? The place I've been asking about for the last hour? An hour spent drinking your revolting ale.'

'My ale's not revolting.'

'So which way is it then?'

'I could tell you, that's true. But maybe I don't want to now. After all, revolting ale's not something to have a friendly conversation over.'

'All right, all right. How much do I owe you for your delicious tankards of ale.'

'Tuppence.'

'Tuppence? For a few mugs of plain ale? What do you put in it, swans' livers? I can buy five gallons of stuff like this for tuppence.'

'But five gallons of ale don't know where weavers' workshops are, does it?'

The stranger huffed and grumbled but handed over two pennies, making sure that the remaining mug full of revolting ale stayed in his grasp.

Ern leaned forward once more. 'You take the north road for a mile and go left at the stream crossing. Up the bank and you can't miss it.'

'That's a fair way out of town.'

'Ar. There's a reason for that.' Ern tipped his head to his wife once more. 'Still don't think a weaver's going to want a hawk though.'

'Who said anything about one hawk.' The stranger filled up with his own importance.

Ern gave this some thought. 'No point having more than one hawk. How would you hold on to it?'

'You think too small, you do. It's not about one hawk, it's about hawks, lots of 'em. And the lots of people who would want lots of hawks. I've got my hands on an arrangement which could see a very nice return. Of course, it's only for the people with the money. Man like Wat the Weaver's bound to have more than he knows what to do with. I can't make this available to just anyone.' It was clear that Ern and his wife were firmly in the camp of "just anyone".

'If you think you're going to get anything from the purse of Wat the Weaver, good luck to you. He only pays the bills he owes when you can get him in a small room with no windows to jump out of.'

'He'll love this once I explain it.'

'No one ever got rich by spending money.' Ern summed up his view of the world.

The stranger disagreed. 'Spending money is the only way to get rich. And the best way of all is to spend other people's.'

Ern shook his head at this nonsense. 'No point you going up to the workshop after his money anyway.'

'And why's that? Keeps it all locked away somewhere else?'

'Nope. He's not there.'

'What!? I've spent all this time, and tuppence, to find Wat the Weaver and now you tell me he's not there?'

'Oh, not at all.'

'Eh?'

'You spent all the time and money finding the workshop of Wat the Weaver and now you've found it. You never asked if he was in.'

The stranger made some incoherent noises and looked around the room as if he wanted to break something. 'How do you know he's not there?'

'Him and the other two have gone off again. Always going off, they are.'

'The other two? There are two other weavers?'

'Mercy, no.' Ern seemed quite grateful that there weren't three Wat the Weavers in Derby. 'The other two. The monk and the girl.'

'You've lost me.' The stranger did look very lost. And quite keen to get out of the tavern, even if it did mean a walk in the dark to no purpose.

'The monk, Brother Hermitage.'

'Brother Hermitage? Funny name for a monk.'

'Ar. Young fellow and all. And he's the whatnot.'

'Whatnot?'

'Yes, you know.'

'Erm. No.'

'King's whatnot.'

'The king's whatnot?' The stranger didn't sound any less confused, but he was a little more cautious. Reference to the king tended to do that to people.

'Investigator, that's it. He's the King's Investigator.'

'Is he?' The title clearly meant nothing to the stranger, but anything with "King" in front was cause for concern.

'He is. And the three of them go off investigating. Apparently, they look into murders and so forth.'

'Murders?' If the stranger had been paddling in small waters he now fell into a very deep hole.

'I had it from one of the apprentices. The king sends for him whenever there's been a murder or the like. Our Brother Hermitage goes off and investigates all over it and that finds out who did it. See.'

'Remarkable.'

'Isn't it?'

'What the devil's he doing with a weaver then? Shouldn't he be at the king's side or something?'

'Not for the likes of me to wonder about things,' Ern expressed another of his approaches to life.

'I've never heard of an investigator before.'

'Me neither. Some new fangle or other. The things they come up with eh? It'll never catch on though. I mean, investigation of a murder's going to be of no interest to anyone, is it?'

'Unless it's you that's been murdered?' The stranger suggested.

'Hardly likely to care, I'd have thought.'

'Or your wife?'

Ern glanced at his wife with a slightly wistful look in his

eye.

'She'd want to know who killed you to get the weregild.'

'Oh. Right. Yes.'

'Must be kept busy with the Normans though. Lots of murders about, I'd have thought.'

'That's probably why they're gone again. Another murder done somewhere and off they go. Good job Wat's got lots of apprentices. Can't have time to do any actual weaving anymore.'

'You said there was another one?'

'Another one what?'

'With the weaver and the monk?'

'Oh, Cwen, that's right.'

'Cwen?'

Well, Leofcwen, if we're being polite. Which we have to be.' A slightly haunted look dropped onto Ern's face.

'Leofcwen?' the stranger repeated the name. Very slowly. 'What's she like then?'

'Young thing,' Ern explained. 'Tiny, really. Doesn't look like she'd have the strength to knock a duck off a post.'

'But she does?'

'Oh yes,' Ern seemed to shrink a bit. 'And probably rip the post out of the ground to beat the rest of the flock to death.'

'Bit of a temper?'

'Not really. A bull with a boil has a bit of a temper. Cwen's unique.'

'And she lives with the weaver?'

'She's one herself.'

'One what?'

'A weaver.'

'A woman weaver? How's that possible?' The stranger frowned.

Ern shrugged. 'Because she says so.'

'Any idea where she came from?'

'None. And if I was you, I wouldn't ask.'

'Why not?'

'Because it's none of your business.' Ern indicated that he was only reporting what the answer was going to be.

'Know when they're going to return?'

'Nope. They been gone a good while though and they're never usually away for long. We'll know when they get back; they'll send for food. Wat lets Mrs Grod feed the apprentices, but has all his own food from here.'

'Mrs Grod?' The stranger had moved from confused to utterly bewildered.

'His cook. Most reckon she was a camp scavenger who found an old cook pot amongst the dead after a battle and kept it.'

'Ah.'

'And she's never cleaned the pot.'

'Perhaps I'll wait here.'

Ern nodded that this was a good idea. 'We got rooms, but if you want my advice?'

'Yes?'

Ern nodded back to his wife. 'If anyone asks, stick to hawks.'

The stranger indicated his agreement. 'Be interesting to meet Cwen though,' he said as he supped his disgusting ale. 'Very interesting indeed.'

Caput II

Wat Wanders in.

'Well Master Stigand, still waiting for the hawks to fly in?' Ern's wife had greeted Stigand like this every morning for the best part of a week and it had not only worn thin, he could see right through it and was ready to punch whatever was on the other side.

Instead, he just smiled and gave the very fake laugh that was his daily response. The constant carping was bad enough but he was wishing that he'd never even given the woman his name. The fact that she used it in every sentence, sometimes twice, was driving him into a very bad place.

"Master Stigand, will you be wanting a meal today, Master Stigand? Master Stigand, can I ask if you want your straw changed Master Stigand? Master Stigand, do you think it will rain today Master Stigand? Only I told my husband, Master Stigand, that it wouldn't." He never knew that his own name could be so annoying.

He had considered returning the style of address, just to see if the woman would realise how irritating it was. When he discovered that her name was Angel, he couldn't bring himself to do it.

He prayed every morning that news would come of Wat the Weaver's return so he could get out of this place. After that, he prayed that something heavy would fall on Ern's wife. Something on a very high shelf that should never have been put there in the first place and about which she had complained on several occasions. On that day his laugh would be genuine.

His pleading look to Ern as he entered the main room of the tavern was greeted with another blank shrug.

'I thought you said they wouldn't be long.'

'Only been four days.' Ern stopped what he was doing and leaned against the wall to talk to Stigand. Stopping what he was doing seemed to be a favourite occupation.

'Really? It feels a lot longer.' Stigand took a seat by the door and waited for his normal plate of bread in wine to be brought over.

Mistress Angel complained at this luxury most vociferously with very many uses of the name "Stigand". No one else ate before the noon meal. Wasn't natural and wouldn't do him any good.

Stigand suggested that if everyone gave her as much money as he did, they could all have bread in wine in the morning.

She responded, as light-heartedly as she could manage, that if he was her husband she'd kill him.

He replied, a lot less light-heartedly, that if she was his wife he'd kill himself. Or her.

'How long you going to wait then?' Ern asked after his wife had slapped the dish in front of Stigand and stomped off, muttering.

'Long as it takes,' Stigand spoke through a mouthful. 'He'd be mad if he saw an opportunity like this go by.'

'Seems like you already got plenty of money. What you want more for?'

Stigand just gazed at Ern and shook his head slowly.

'Perhaps they ain't coming back this time? Could be the king has summoned them off to some other murder. Could be months.'

Stigand frowned and sucked at his bread. 'Anyone else around here have money then?'

'Not like Wat.' Ern rubbed his chin in thought. 'I suppose you'd have to try our lord.'

'What? Pray?'

'No, no, not the Lord, the lord. The lord of the land and estates hereabouts.'

'Ah, right. And who would that be?'

'Couple of years ago it would have been Edward, so I suppose it's his successor.'

'Edward eh? Edward who?'

'King Edward. You know. The king.'

'So his successor would have been Harold and now William?' Stigand suggested, with a weary sigh.

Ern thought about it. 'Ar, I suppose it would.'

'Don't think I'll bother.' He tucked into his bread for a few moments. 'I'll wait. The trade is coming to Derby just got to hope he doesn't miss it.'

Mistress Angel swept by, tutting at Stigand's meal.

'Then again, I could leave this afternoon and give it all up.' He glared at her back as she left.

He pushed the now-empty bowl away. 'Might as well wander up the workshop again. See if they've got any news.'

'I told you they always come by here. Got to start up my supply of food again. Mrs Grod is good enough for the rest of them, but once Wat's back, he wants a decent meal.'

'I know, but I can't just sit around here all day, waiting.'

'You mind you're not seen,' Ern warned. 'If they catch sight of you going up to the workshop in daylight we'll never hear the end of it.'

'I'll be careful. They haven't spotted me any of the other days.'

Stigand stood and went to the door. He'd take his usual aimless wander around the streets. Have a few words here and a few words there before he found himself, without any rhyme or reason, on the north road near the stream. From there it was easy.

The old boy, Hartle, who seemed to be in charge of the workshop while the weaver was away had naturally assumed Stigand was a customer and had shown him some pretty spectacular images before he managed to persuade the man that he just wanted to speak with Wat. Hartle said that would be fine, but warned that whatever he did, he was not to mention the tapestries to the monk, Brother Hermitage. There would only be one monk, so it shouldn't be a problem.

Stigand had agreed and nonchalantly asked about Cwen. In her case, he was told it was best not to speak unless he was spoken to.

On this morning though, the door of the tavern was opened from the outside while he was still holding it. He stepped back to accommodate the new arrival.

'Oh, sorry,' a head said, as it peered around the door. 'Didn't see you there.'

The head bore a mop of curly black hair and a youngish face full of ease and confidence. From what Stigand could see, the jerkin was very well made and the lone boot that strayed into the room was clean and close-fitting.

'Ern,' the head said, raising an arm.

Ern stopped what he was doing, again, and looked over. 'Oh, yes. Right you are then.'

And that was it. The head, the jerkin and the boot retreated, the door closed and Ern got back to what he was doing - which didn't look very constructive anyway.

Stigand mused for a moment about the new face at the door before shrugging his shoulders and reaching for the handle once more. As he made to leave he turned to Ern.

'Who was that then?'

'Who was what?'

'The man at the door?' Stigand's patience was wearing thin. 'The one who just called your name and you replied? That one? Remember? He looked quite well off.'

'Oh,' said Ern, with a smile of recognition. 'That was Wat the Weaver.'

Stigand contained himself to two very tightly clenched fists at this announcement. 'That's Wat the Weaver? The one I've been waiting four days for?'

'Oh, ar. You're in luck then. He's back.'

The door handle was grasped and the wood virtually thrown off its hinges as Stigand left. 'Don't touch my pack,' he called over his shoulder.

* * *

Seeing Wat emerge from the tavern, Brother Hermitage was reminded of the fascinating conversation he had had with his old abbot in a similar establishment. That had been all about the post-Exodus prophets, a very particular interest of his and one which he thought everyone else would find just as fascinating if they only gave it a chance.[1] He had tried to bring the topic into discussions with Wat and Cwen on several occasions, but they always had something else to do. Perhaps the presence of the tavern presented an opportunity to begin with a few preliminaries while they travelled the last miles back to the workshop.

'You know,' he began.

[1] This took place during The Case of The Cantankerous Carcass. We can all be grateful that the actual content of the conversation is not recorded.

'Wat? Wat the Weaver?' A voice called from the road behind them.

Hermitage grumbled his light and infinitely patient grumble.

The three of them turned and saw a rotund, bald fellow trying to run up the track towards them. The man was not built for running and the sight was worth the wait, even if the reason for the pursuit was not likely to be a good one.

'One of your old customers?' Hermitage sighed.

'Never seen him before.' Wat shrugged. 'Still, looks well enough off to spare a few pennies for a humble tapestry.'

'Just make sure it is humble.'

'Oh, Hermitage,' Cwen chided. 'You know we wouldn't do that sort of trade anymore.'

'Hm. I've been meaning to talk to you about that. I know that you two would no longer make any of the disreputable works that have cast a deep shadow on your past. I'm not so sure about Hartle though. I've seen him creeping about the place and I'm not sure he's up to any good.'

'If there are no tapestries being made, how can he be up to no good?'

'No new tapestries, perhaps, but what about old ones?'

'Why don't we just greet our visitor?' Wat spoke very quickly and stepped down the track. 'He seems very keen to meet us.'

Cwen and Hermitage followed and they met the new arrival halfway.

'Stigand,' the man panted, his hands on his knees and his breath wheezing in and out in complaint at being treated so harshly.

'Master Stigand,' Wat nodded acknowledgement. 'I better warn you that it doesn't usually pay to call my name out loud in these parts. Very sensitive people.'

'With good reason,' Hermitage commented.

Stigand held his hand up to indicate that words were available but the strength to deliver them was still on its way. Eventually, he managed two or three deeper breaths that induced some calm into his frame. 'I've been waiting for you at the tavern. The landlord's wife made her own views very clear.'

'Ah, Mistress Angel. She is particularly vocal on the subject. Goes a bit quieter when she's counting my money though.'

Stigand was able to stand upright now but still didn't look a very healthy colour.

'What makes you wait for me in the tavern then? Some trade perhaps?'

'Trade indeed. And if reports from the tavern are correct this must be Brother Hermitage, the King's Investigator?'

'Not just at the moment,' Hermitage didn't want any discussion of investigations disturbing the day. At least this Stigand was not a messenger from King William demanding attendance at yet another ghastly murder. He reproved himself for thinking that every encounter they had was about him and would lead to some awful business with dead bodies. The only problem was that it seemed most of their encounters were for him and did lead to a dead body or two. He had tried everything he could think of to avoid being King's Investigator and here were total strangers greeting him with the title on the road. There would be no going back at all at this rate.

'And Mistress Cwen?' Stigand bowed deeply. So deeply Hermitage worried that he might not get up again.

Cwen gave a short grunt in reply.

Stigand indicated that he was now capable of movement

once more and that they could continue the walk up the road.

'Trade with Master Wat?' Hermitage gave his disappointment free rein.

'But not tapestry.'

'Not tapestry?' Cwen gave Stigand a very well-aimed and very suspicious glare. One of her especially pointed ones.

'No.' Stigand gave her another small bow of the head and accompanied it with a genuine smile. 'Hawks.'

'Hawks?'

'Hawks.'

'What? The birds, hawks?'

'I've had this conversation before somewhere,' Stigand shook his head. 'Yes. The birds, hawks. And not trade with the hawks themselves. Not making tapestries of them and not even falconry. Well, not directly.'

'What would I want with hawks?' Wat asked. 'Never been interested really. Seems a lot of hard work just to get a pigeon or two.'

'And the Normans are very jealous of their hawks,' Hermitage said. 'I've heard the most awful things about what they do to people who interfere with their hawking. Mind you, I've heard the most awful things about what they do in a lot of circumstances; and have first-hand experience of some of it.'

'Yes, Hermitage,' Cwen interrupted and directed herself to Stigand. 'What trade can you have with hawks then? And why would we be interested?'

'It's an opportunity.'

'Oh,' Cwen was full of recognition now. 'Of course, it is. All you want us to do is give you a purse full of gold so you can do something or other with some hawks and then you'll be back in a month with two purses in return.'

'Not at all.'

'Makes a change, I suppose. These days all we get are Saxons saying that they're the prince of a distant kingdom and their fortune is being held hostage by the Normans. If we'll only give them five pounds to pay some bribes they'll give us fifty pounds in return.' She snorted her contempt for such people.

'I assure you that it is nothing like that at all. I have papers and everything. Papers from people I'd rather not discuss on the open road.' He looked around. 'Perhaps we could go to the workshop? I have been up there the last few days asking after you. Your man Hartle was most helpful.'

'Hartle, eh?' Hermitage snorted now.

'Hm,' Wat did not sound convinced. 'Not sure I'm looking for anything in hawks at the moment.'

'I will only take a moment of your time. And if you are not intrigued I will be on my way, no question.'

Wat looked thoughtful.

'And there is one other revelation I have to make, which really must be done in private.'

'Private revelations eh?' Hermitage had heard all about private revelations in the workshop of Wat the Weaver. He was not going to let any more take place.

'Of a very personal nature.' Stigand looked serious and sombre.

To Hermitage's ear that sounded even worse.

After a moment's pause, Wat reached a conclusion. 'Oh, come on then. It's been a long journey and a long time away from home. Time with all the usual complications.' He directed his look to Hermitage at this point. 'I want to get back and put my feet up. We'll hear you out and if it's a no, you're gone by noon.'

'Agreed.'

'And if you're not gone by noon we get young Gunnlaug to see you out.'

'Gunnlaug?' Stigand asked Hermitage as they walked on up the track.

'One of the apprentices. A unique fellow, must have ancestry from the north. He's just, what can I say, very big? Huge, in fact. Enormous. Giant, even. Nice boy, but very big. And strong. Did I mention strong? He can lift a loom on his own.'

'I see. Don't think we'll need to disturb Gunnlaug then.'

'Very wise.'

Turning left at the stream crossing, the party made its way up the final hill and the workshop revealed itself.

"The best building not in Derby", was how many described it. The emphasis being on the fact that the workshop of Wat the Weaver was not in Derby at all. It was outside the town and people should not just think "Wat the Weaver" whenever they heard the place mentioned.

The town moot was in constant conflict about the whole question. Strangers doubtless thought the worst of Derby simply because of the workshop and that was not good. Counting the taxes that Wat paid to the moot was very good indeed and usually helped soothe their troubled minds.

The place was big. It had to be to accommodate the apprentices and the workshops and to house supplies. It also had to be large to accommodate the extravagant spaces Wat insisted were completely necessary. The upstairs chamber for business and large tapestries, the downstairs for comfort, a separate kitchen of all things, and the individual sleeping chambers. All a complete waste of space that could easily be combined into a single large hall. A single large hall that Wat suggested would be “disgusting”. There was no way he was going to eat and sleep in the same room, let alone with a bunch of apprentices. He did have some very strange ideas.

Solid timbers formed the frame of the building, no wattle and daub with a few extra sticks for Wat. There was real glass in the windows and solid wood in the doors. It really did look like the manor house of a lord.

Hermitage knew that Wat's trade had been profitable. In the old days, with the old, disgusting, tapestries, very profitable indeed. Hermitage had managed to direct them to work of a more pious and proper nature but still, the money came in. There was no doubting that Wat was a skilful weaver and passed this skill to his apprentices. Cwen was perhaps the finest of them all with her delicate touch and fine eye. The works remained in demand and gave them all a very comfortable way of life.

When Wat suggested that he might solve the problem of the townsfolk of Derby by buying the whole place, Hermitage thought he was joking. When he looked on the workshop afresh, he began to wonder.

‘Ho, Hartle,’ Wat called out when they were within earshot.

The old man appeared at the main door and peered out to see who was coming. Wat raised an arm in greeting.

Hermitage was sure Hartle muttered something like ‘Oh, bloody hell,’ before scuttling very quickly back inside. His suspicions concerning the old man were growing. Perhaps it was the effect of too many experiences as King’s Investigator.

‘Very nice,’ Stigand commented at the sight of the workshop. ‘You’ve done well for yourself.’

'Serves its purpose. Lots of apprentices and jobs to accommodate. Wouldn't be so big if there wasn't so much work.'

'You now do tapestry for the church, Hartle tells me.'

'Yes,' Wat didn't sound too happy about this. 'Of course, we always did works for the church. It's just that they can talk about the ones we do now. And put them on display.'

'Wat and Cwen are doing a fine representation of Saint George and the Dragon just at the moment.' Hermitage was keen that discussion should not wander into the realm of the old works. A very different realm where most of the sins of this one seemed to go for their sport.

'The Normans have actually helped,' Wat said, to a growl from Cwen. 'Well, they have. They want their churchmen to be holy and to display devotion and all that.'

'Devotion and all that,' Hermitage muttered, in despair.

'So now they're all desperate for a good holy tapestry to hang on the wall in case a Norman wanders in. Can't turn them out quick enough.'

'Yes,' Stigand nodded slowly. 'Despite all their problems, the Normans have created a number of opportunities. If we go inside I can tell you about another one.'

As they reached the door, Hartle greeted them as if he thought they were dead. He had effusive hugs for them all, most particularly for Hermitage, whom he held at the door with a list of questions about how their journey had been and whether the investigation had gone well. None of these issues had concerned him in the slightest before, in fact, he'd been quite grumpy to see Hermitage on some occasions. He also kept looking over his shoulder, back into the workshop for some reason.

Eventually, satisfied that Hermitage was safely returned, and almost knocked aside as a couple of apprentices brushed past carrying bundles under their arms, Hartle released his grasp.

'You make sure those are stored safe,' he tutted at Hermitage. 'Apprentices eh? Don't know their warp from their weft, some of them.'

'Quite so.' Hermitage smiled without really knowing why.

He entered the workshop and looked around for the others. They had quickly settled into the downstairs room. As promised, Wat had his feet up and a tankard of wine had appeared from somewhere. Cwen was sitting on the hard wooden chair by the empty fireplace and Stigand stood by the window. It seemed they were waiting for him.

'Sorry. Hartle seemed very concerned about us for some reason.'

'Just wants to make sure the place is neat and tidy before we come in, probably.' Wat took a swig of wine. 'So. Master Stigand. This opportunity of yours.'

'Ah, yes,' Stigand signalled that Hermitage might want to sit as well and beckoned that he join Cwen by the fireplace.

'There are two very different matters,' Stigand began. 'And to be honest I'm not sure which one to broach first.' He thought for a moment. 'I think I will start with the trade. I wouldn't want you to think I am trying to influence you in an inappropriate manner.'

'Please yourself.' Wat swigged again.

'Hawks. As I said, the business is about hawks. But it's not for us to get involved with hawking or actually having to handle the birds. We, or rather I,' he nodded acknowledgement that Wat hadn't decided to get involved yet. 'I have been presented with a task. A fairly simple one, but a very profitable one.

'As you know, the Normans are very keen on hawking. If they're not actually hunting animals themselves, they're setting them on one another. Can't get them away from the hunt. Riding through the forest shooting deer or standing in a field watching their favourite hawk bring down a pigeon or two.

'And they use them to impress one another. Who's got the biggest hawk, that sort of thing. They have parties of all the best people, every one of them with a bird on their arm, showing that theirs is better than the next one.'

'Very nice,' Wat showed little interest.

'And of course, all this takes a lot of hawks. The whole Norman court has come over here and they've brought some of their own birds but they want new ones. Got to have the very latest thing in hawks or your neighbour will think you've lost your manhood. Or something.' Stigand shrugged. 'Don't ask me why they do all this, I don't get it either. They just do, and it's very important.

'So. There's a commission, direct from the king's court to supply them with hawks.'

'Good for the hawk owners,' Cwen said. 'Price of a good hawk has just gone up.'

Stigand held up his hand. There was more. 'One or two hawks would be easy. There's Saxons got hawks they don't need any more. Or rather hawks whose Saxons aren't in any condition to go hawking anymore. But that's not enough. How many hawks do you think the king's court wants?'

'Oh, I don't know,' Wat was showing signs of impatience. 'Why don't you tell us?'

'A hundred.'

'A hundred?' Wat's feet fell off his pack. 'A hundred hawks? What on earth are they going to do with a hundred hawks? As I understand it you're supposed to eat the prey, not the hawk.'

'Not a clue,' Stigand shrugged. 'If the Normans say they want a hundred hawks, someone has to get them a hundred hawks. They don't want to go to the trouble themselves so they commission someone to get the hawks for them.'

'Hawk suppliers?' Hermitage suggested, having no more idea about hawking than anyone else in the room.

'You might be able to get one or two, but a hundred? That's an awful lot of hawks.'

'I wouldn't even know where to get one,' Cwen expressed her own disinterest.

'Neither did I until all this came about. So I did some study. Apparently, you have to get a hawk chick to begin with before it's gone wild. Then you bring it up and feed it and whatnot and get it used to people. Then you train it and after a while, quite a long while by the sound of it, you've got yourself a hawk.'

'Lot of trouble,' Wat complained.

'It would be if you had to do all that. But the Normans have their own falconers. And they have special cages to keep them in. A mew, apparently. I tell you, it's big business.'

'Hawk chicks?'

'Correct. And do you know how much a Norman will pay for one hawk chick? Just the one?'

Wat was leaning forward now, the price of hawks being much more interesting than the birds themselves. 'Go on.'

Stigand left a silent pause and took a deep breath before he spoke. 'Half a pound of silver.'

Wat whistled. 'Bloody hell.'

'Quite. That's for a peregrine chick. They're the best, so I hear tell. Even a sparrow hawk will get a fifth of that. I'm sure you've already worked it out, but the Normans have about fifty pounds of silver ready to spend on their hawks. And guess who's got the commission to find them?'

Wat sat back again and looked at Stigand with a new expression. A not altogether healthy one. 'Good for you then? Going to make a lot of money.'

'There's the opportunity. Of course, the Normans aren't just going to hand over their silver on the promise of some hawks. They'll pay on delivery. I've got to go and get the hawks first.'

'And pay for them.'

'Exactly. Except I'm not going to pay fifty pounds for them.'

'How much?'

'Probably twenty pounds for the lot.'

'Leaving a profit of thirty pounds of silver.'

'This is all very well,' Hermitage spoke up, feeling the weight of avarice in the room starting to weigh him down. 'But where are you going to get a hundred hawks in the first place?'

'Denmark.'

'Denmark?' Now Hermitage almost fell off his chair. 'Where the Vikings come from?'

'That's it. The centre of the hawking world, they say. Go to Denmark, buy a load of hawks with twenty pounds of silver, bring them back and sell them for fifty.'

'But go to Denmark?' Hermitage quaked. At least he was clear in his mind that if Wat did decide to go into this trade, he would be staying in Derby. He never got on terribly well with Vikings.

'Why aren't you on the way to Denmark then?' Cwen asked. 'Not got twenty pounds of silver?'

'No, I haven't. I mean, I'm comfortable enough.' Stigand held his hands out to show that his own clothes were well made and expensive. 'But I don't have twenty pounds of silver lying about doing nothing.'

'How much have you got?' Wat asked.

'I could probably get five pounds together.'

'Enough to buy a few hawks, bring them back, sell them and then back to Denmark to buy some more.'

'It is, but the Normans want at least thirty in the first delivery.'

Wat rubbed his chin.

'And then there's the white hawks.'

'White hawks?'

'Exactly. The Normans want ten of the hawks to be white. For the king himself, I expect.'

'And white hawks fetch a premium?'

'They do. Double.'

Hermitage thought that Wat was starting to dribble.

'A pound of silver, for one hawk?' If wasn't dribble it was certainly drool.

'You can see my problem. I've got the chance to turn over a lot of money very quickly, but I've got to buy the hawks first.'

'Why on earth would the Normans ask you to supply their hawks? You don't seem to know the first thing about them.'

Stigand stood proud. 'I am a leading Saxon hawk trader. Even advised King Harold.'

'The dead King Harold who isn't in a position to actually vouch for you?'

'Regrettably so. And it seems that all my other customers got killed at Hastings as well.'

'Ha ha,' Wat clapped his admiration. 'And you can prove this order, can you?' He was back to his business-like self.

'Of course. I've got the parchment from the king's man. Can't read most of it, but I took it from his hand.'

'Hermitage can tell us what it says.'

Oh, thought Hermitage, I can, can I?

'He can read anything. He's very clever like that.'

Hermitage would be pleased to help.

'Why me?' Wat's eyes narrowed. 'With a certain method of making money, why come to me? Why wait in the tavern for days and come just to me? There's plenty of merchants would lend you the money on a job like this.'

'They would, but they'd want a massive share of the takings.'

'And I wouldn't?'

'From what I've heard, you're fair in trade. Expensive, but fair. If you put up fifteen pounds of silver and got your fifteen back plus another five you'd think it was a good deal. And there's a meeting here. Derby's a nice central point between the Danes and the Normans. I can meet the Danes here and get the trade underway.'

'I thought Harold defeated the Danes?' Hermitage asked.

'The ones trying to invade he did, but there's still a whole country of them in the north-west. As well as the ones left over the sea in Daneland.'

Hermitage didn't take much comfort from this.

Wat was thinking hard and looking through narrowed eyes at Stigand. 'Thirty-eight pounds.' he said. 'With me putting three-quarters of the silver in, I'd get three-quarters back.'

'Twenty.'

'Thirty-five.'

'Twenty-five.'

'Thirty.'

'Done.'

'Always assuming Hermitage tells us that the documents

are genuine and that one of us comes with you to collect the little birdies. And these Danes are coming here?'

'The ones from the north are. Already made contact. They're just waiting for the money. Show of good faith and all. Then it's over the sea. Goodness knows where they get these hawk chicks from but they say they've got plenty.'

'Hm, you'll need someone who knows about hawks. God knows what the Vikings would give you otherwise.' Wat noticed that Hermitage had his hand up. 'Yes, Hermitage?'

'Can I just make it clear at this point that I will read whatever you want but I am not going to Denmark?'

Wat laughed again. 'Didn't for a moment think you would. I'm sure there's someone in town who can tell a hawk chick from a kitten. They can go.'

Although the deal seemed to have been done, Wat was still watching Stigand with caution. 'I still don't see why me. I can understand you don't want to go to merchants but there's still a lot of people who could come in on this.'

'Ah,' Stigand dropped his eyes. 'That's the other thing I have to tell you.' He looked at Cwen, for some reason. 'And I hope you will understand why I dealt with the hawk business first.'

'Go on.'

Stigand now ignored the others in the room and turned to face Cwen directly. She looked her normal, defiant self, ready to ask him what the devil he thought he was staring at.

'Mistress Cwen,' he bowed again. 'Mistress Leofcwen.'

Cwen started to look very suspicious now. The next step would be to jump across the room and punch him in the face if he said something inappropriate.

'Mistress Leofcwen of Arundel.'

Hermitage thought that odd. Even he didn't know where

Cwen came from, she never told anyone about her past.

'What?' She growled like a dog about to bite.

Stigand took another of his deep breaths. 'I am Stigand of Arundel. And I am your father.'

Caput III

When Cwen's Not Happy

Hermitage and Wat had to escort Stigand from the premises, very quickly, and call upon Hartle and Gunnlaug to restrain Cwen. Even then, the oaths she swore and the threats she made would not be out of place coming from a foul-mouthed Viking being pecked to pieces by hawks.

Wat managed to persuade Stigand to go back to the tavern where they would come to find him once things had settled. He made no promises about how long things would take to settle. Hermitage hoped the man had come prepared for a long stay.

Returning to the workshop, making sure that Wat went first, Hermitage could fully understand why Cwen was as angry as she was. His comprehension was less good when it came to speculating what she might do. He had seen her angry of course. She seemed to spend a lot of her time cross about something or other. But there was cross and then there was angry and then there was the state she was in now.

His mind wandered back to the monastery at De'Ath's Dingle and the appalling Prior Athan.[2] There was a man who could do angry. Of all the angry monks and priors and abbots that Hermitage had had to deal with, Athan stood out. He was probably standing out shouting at people. But somehow his anger had direction and control, which made it even worse. He knew who he was being angry at, why and what he was going to do to them. And he went to quite a lot

---

[2] Read all about it! The Heretics of De'Ath

of effort to explain it all at the time.

Cwen's anger on this occasion was more natural somehow. It was the natural anger of a bear with his leg in a trap. Or a bull being taunted by children on the other side of a wall. Or being taunted by having a bear with his leg in a trap, biting him on the head.

He could hear the commotion from the front door and his natural sympathy welled up; sympathy for Hartle and Gunnlaug.

As they approached the door to the room it was flung open and Hartle appeared. His clothes were dishevelled and he was panting for breath. It was unfair to expect a man of Hartle's age to deal with something like this. He frequently said he was fifty, although few believed such an extravagant claim.

Next out of the door came Gunnlaug. He had to duck to get through and made Hartle look like a doll as he stood next to him. His physical condition was better, but the look on his face said that this was an experience he would carry with him to his grave.

'I only came here to do weaving,' he whispered, his ashen lips barely moving to make the words.

Wat looked at Hermitage and Hermitage looked at Wat. They both took deep breaths. Then they looked at the door and at Hartle and Gunnlaug. Then they looked at one another again.

'After you,' Wat beckoned towards the door. 'She's less likely to do damage to a monk.'

'No, no, I insist. After all, it sounds like it's your furniture being broken.'

Wat took a very deep breath. 'Cwen?' he sang gently; far too quietly to be heard over the din coming from the room.

'Can I come in?'

After one almighty crash, which sounded very expensive, Cwen replied. 'Do what you like.'

Wat winced, even with an inch of solid oak between him and the voice. He reached for the wooden latch and gently lifted it as if it would bite his finger off if he moved too quickly. After that he slowly pushed at the door, expecting to feel some resistance, at which point he could give up and come back in a day or two.

'Cwen?' he called again.

'It's all right, you can come in,' Cwen's voice was being controlled with great effort. An effort that sounded like it could fail at any moment.

Wat entered the chamber and Hermitage followed. Cwen was standing still amongst the wreckage of the room. Chairs and tables were overturned and even one of the windows was broken. She was breathing heavily and looked prepared to break some more things if they were brought in.

To Hermitage's eye, it seemed impossible that this slight, young woman had anything to do with the state of the furniture. Surely, she had survived some whirlwind or catastrophe that had left the place in ruin, not actually been the whirlwind and catastrophe rolled into one.

Wat held his hands out in front of him, perhaps urging Cwen to calm down, perhaps preparing to defend himself.

'Are you all right Cwen?' Hermitage asked quietly, not able to think of anything else. He certainly didn't want Wat asking about who was going to pay for his window.

'I'll kill him.'

'Kill who?'

'Who do you think? The landlord's cat? Him. Stigand. I'll kill him.'

'Now then.' Hermitage knew she was upset and that everyone said things when they were upset that they didn't really mean. 'You don't mean that.'

'Don't tell me what I mean, Hermitage.' Cwen pointed, vigorously. 'I am going to kill him. That'll be good, won't it?'

'No, it won't be good at all.'

'At least you'll have a nice tidy investigation. One dead Stigand and me who did it.'

Hermitage tried a different approach. 'I know you want to kill him and I dare say that you could. Without any trouble at all. But last week you wanted to kill the blacksmith and you didn't do that.'

'The blacksmith didn't come up here claiming to be my father.'

'No. You still haven't told us what he did do, but you still said you wanted to kill him.'

'Apparently, he asked if he could make Cwen a personal set of needles.' Wat said.

'That sounds nice,' Hermitage suggested.

'Not the way he said it,' Cwen snapped.

Hermitage left a moment's thoughtful silence. He suspected that it was only him doing the thoughtful bit. 'I can understand that this is a great insult. But threatening people with death is not the answer.'

'Really?' Cwen replied, clearly not believing that at all, but starting to wither in the face of Hermitage's calm and reasonable demeanour.

He could see the anger rising in her again and prepared to run.

'How dare he?'

'Quite.'

'I mean, really, how dare he?'

Cwen was directing her comments to Hermitage so Wat used the opportunity to draw close to her. She seemed to be two people just at this moment. One was talking to Hermitage, well, saying things anyway, while the other was watching Wat. There was really no telling what either of them was going to do.

After a short pause for reflection, one of them spoke. 'I'm going for a walk.'

'A walk?' It seemed an odd thing to do in the circumstances.

'Yes,' Cwen's eyes warned Hermitage that this was not to be challenged. 'I will be back in a while and I don't want anyone nearby. There's no telling what I may do.'

Hermitage spotted Wat about to speak and gestured him to silence. It would doubtless be some very unhelpful remark about the damage she had already done.

She stomped from the room, scaring the loitering Hartle and Gunnlaug back to their tapestry. Once out of the workshop and striding across the field, her screams of anger and frustration were incoherent but sincerely alarming.

Hermitage breathed deeply. 'Perhaps it's for the best. Let her calm a little and get her thoughts in order before we discuss what to do next.'

'Calm a little?' Wat gestured at his broken room. 'Perhaps she could have gone for the walk before she discussed the situation with my furniture.'

'This is a very difficult time for her.'

'It's not marvellous for me.'

'Wat, you really must have some sympathy for the poor girl. What would you do if someone turned up claiming to be your father.'

'I'd make a tapestry of him and sell it for a fortune. He's

been dead for twenty years.'

'Will you take nothing seriously?'

'Fifty pounds of silver, maybe.'

'We must help our friend.' Hermitage's scowl was of the disappointed type. It was the one he used when discussing tapestry and it generally had an effect on Wat.

'All right. I suppose. But I shall add the furniture to Stigand's bill.'

Hermitage was grateful that they waited in relative silence for Cwen's return. Perhaps his words had their effect on Wat. Although the grumbles and muttered complaints that accompanied the tidying up of the room didn't give him that much hope.

Eventually, after Wat had managed to find enough pieces of one chair to put it back together again and sit on it, he folded his arms and waited quietly.

'This is ridiculous,' he said after a few more minutes. 'I'm going back to work. She can come and find us when she gets back.'

The front door slammed loudly just as he stood. 'Oh good. She's feeling much better then.'

The door to the room opened again and Cwen stood on the threshold. She looked rather breathless as if her walk had been taken at a very fast pace.

Good to get the anger out of her, Hermitage thought. He then thought that there looked to be quite a bit of it still left.

Wat stepped over to her. Hermitage hoped it was to offer some comfort but he suspected it was to protect his furnishings.

The weaver risked putting a hand on her shoulder. When she didn't shrug it off, or reach for the remains of a chair to smash it to bits, he took her elbow with his other hand and gently turned her back towards the door. Hermitage could see the sense of this, there was only the one chair left to sit on and that looked ready to collapse again at any moment.

'Just who the hell does he think he is?' Cwen demanded as she was ushered out.

Hermitage expected Wat to take her to the kitchen where they could find her something to drink. Quite why anyone would want something to drink in these circumstances he couldn't immediately think, it was just the sort of thing you did.

Instead, Wat turned towards the front door and the outside. Perhaps that was best. If she did revert to outright anger once more, the wide-open spaces might be safest for all. Unless she'd already broken them on her walk.

Once outside, Wat turned to the left and led the still complaining Cwen round to the side of the workshop. Hermitage couldn't think what there was around here that would be any use. The only thing was the log store. Certainly, she could do no damage but that hardly seemed sympathetic.

They stopped at the large wooden shed with lattice walls and a solid roof of planks that contained the workshop's store of winter fuel. Much of it was ready to burn, but a larger pile was still waiting to be chopped; usually by the worst-performing apprentice of the week. Still, in her distracted condition, Cwen didn't move from where she was placed but continued to mutter and grumble about Stigand.

Wat stepped away for a moment and then came back and placed something in Cwen's hand.

Hermitage took several paces backwards and wondered about the wisdom of this at any time, let alone now.

Cwen looked down at her hands and smiled a very unhealthy smile at the large axe she now held.

Wat cautiously placed a log in front of her on the chopping block and quickly got out of the way.

The slight young weaver, only a foot or so taller than the axe she wielded, swung the thing in a blur and brought it down on the log.

As Hermitage would later report, the log didn't split so much as get out of the way, in two halves. It was a good job the chopping block had been there for years and was as hard as rock. It was a surprise she didn't simply bury the thing three feet into the ground at the first blow.

Wat hurriedly put a new log in place of the old one, careful to match the movement of the axehead to the movement of his hands.

The axe swung again and another log faced the inevitability of disintegration.

As she got into a rhythm, Cwen managed to express her outrage at Stigand in time with the death of each log. 'The deceitful (bang), dishonest (thump), disreputable (crash), dog (whack).'

'Absolutely,' Wat agreed.

'Who does he think he is?' Cwen asked as the axe rose and fell.

He thought he was Cwen's father, wasn't that the point? Hermitage knew far better than to mention anything along these lines to a Cwen with an axe in her hands.

'At least there's no question of doing any trade with a stinking pox breath like him.'

Wat didn't reply to this one.

'How dare he claim to be my father?' Cwen destroyed a particularly large log at this and, in that instant, her energy seemed to fade. She rested the axe on the floor and looked at the fine load of firewood she had made. Hermitage thought that perhaps facing this claim directly would be for the best. Facing it outside was probably a good idea and it would help if the axe was somewhere else altogether.

'Quite outrageous,' Hermitage agreed.

'Awful,' Wat nodded.

'Saying he's my father just to get a bit of trade?' At least she was now waving her hands about without an axe in them. She even started to pace around the space. Hermitage and Wat found logs to sit on. It still seemed best to leave her to it.

'Have you ever heard of anything so disgraceful?'

'Absolutely not,' Wat nodded. When Cwen was at the furthest distance in her perambulations he went on, slowly and very carefully. 'Of course…'

She stopped and looked in shock at Wat. She pointed a very clear and explicit finger. 'He is not my father.'

'Right. Got it. Not the father. That's clear then.'

'Let there be absolutely no question in either of your minds that that man,' her finger moved to the direction of the town and shook a bit with its barely controlled rage. 'That man is not my father. Clear?'

'Clear.'

Cwen seemed to contain some internal battle with no clear victor. 'And if he was my father,' she burst out and walked away, 'that would be even worse.' She turned back up to them and rested her hands on the shaft of the axe once more, perhaps taking some comfort that it, at least, was reliable.

'Worse?' Hermitage asked. Had he heard a confession that this Stigand might be her father, or at least that it was possible? If she didn't know who her father was, why couldn't it be Stigand? After all, he did seem to know where Cwen came from, Arundel, wherever that was.

'Of course.' Cwen's anger now encompassed Hermitage for

not realising this immediately. 'Where's he been for the last seventeen years to suddenly turn up here, asking for Wat's gold?'

'Silver,' Wat corrected, which was not a wise thing to say, judging from the look he got.

'No sign of a father all my life and then one turns up wanting money? That's no father at all. A real father stays with their family until they're grown up at least. What if the mother dies in childbirth? The father has to stay then, doesn't he? He has to work the fields and do his tithe to put bread on the table. That's his duty. Wherever you go.'

'I don't know this Arundel place,' Hermitage tried, thinking that approaching the subject from the side might be a bit safer. 'I imagine it's the same as everywhere.'

It did seem to distract Cwen from her immediate plans for death and destruction. 'Hole of a place in the south. Barely anyone there, couldn't wait to get away.'

'I see.'

'Nearest big place was Lyminster.'

'Ah,' Hermitage smiled broadly. 'Saint Cuthflaed.'

'If you say so.'

'I do. It is reported that the body of the Blessed Cuthflaed is buried in the church there.'

'I never looked.'

'And you thought the place was dull.' Wat reprimanded her and risked a small smile. This did get some sort of grimace in return.

'Or it might have been Leominster.'

'What?'

'It's not terribly clear. You see there was a saint Cuthfleda at Leominster and a Saint Cuthflaed at Lyminster. Well, you can see the potential for confusion.'

'Of course,' Wat nodded, very seriously. 'Goodness knows what the consequences would be of having the wrong saint in the wrong grave.'

'Oh, I'm sure they're in the right graves, it's just that we don't really know which is which.'

'Must be a worry.'

'Not particularly.' Hermitage was glad to see Wat taking an interest but this was a fairly minor matter. Probably not if you were the Abbot of Lyminster or Leominster. But then he wasn't either of them.

'And what did they do?'

'Who?'

'Cuthflaed and Cuthfleda. Sound like a couple of mummers to me.'

'Wat, really. Cuthfleda was a virgin saint who was abbess of the nunnery at Leominster endowed by Leofric, Earl of Mercia.'

'Oho.'

'Pardon.'

'Leofric eh? That Leofric.' Wat nodded and grinned.

'What Leofric?'

'The Leofric husband of Lady Godiva. The Lady Godiva.'

'We were talking about Saint Cuthfleda.'

'Now we're onto Lady Godiva. I tell you, I've made a good few coins out of that good lady. Everyone wants a tapestry.'

'Yes, I don't doubt that they do. But they should not. And it is hardly for you to be peddling such things and encouraging bad behaviour.'

'Well, she should have put some clothes on.'

'Excuse me,' Cwen interrupted, quite loudly.

Wat and Hermitage turned back to her.

'We were actually talking about my father,' she reminded

them. 'How on earth did we get on to saints and Lady Godiva?'

'Ah, well,' Hermitage began to explain. 'It was when you mentioned Lyminster.'

'I know, Hermitage. I was suggesting that this is not the time to be discussing dead saints.'

'Ah, right. Yes.' Hermitage realised that he had got a bit carried away, but at least Cwen seemed calm now. You could always rely on a saint or two to bring order. 'Arundel. Yes. So you're from Arundel. I didn't know that.'

'You do now. Yes, I'm from Arundel.'

'And this Stigand?'

'Claims to be from Arundel but I don't know him from Adam. Never seen him before, never heard of him. Didn't even know there was a Stigand of Arundel. Believe me, when there are only four houses in the village, you tend to know who people are.'

Wat asked the next question with exaggerated nonchalance as if they'd just come back from a long walk and he was enquiring after her feet. 'And your, erm, mother?'

Cwen's mouth, already narrow, seemed to disappear between her own lips. 'Never mentioned anyone called Stigand.'

Hermitage's concern bubbled as this reply was tense and harsh.

'Who, erm?' He didn't like to come out with, "so who is your father?" It sounded terribly rude.

'She never said. Never would say. All she ever told me was that he was dead and that I didn't need to worry.'

'At least you didn't do it then,' Wat smirked.

Cwen simply walked over and punched him on the shoulder. For many people, this is a playful and harmless gesture. When Cwen punched people on the shoulder they tended to have a wait a day or two to get the feeling back in their arm. 'Shut up,' she instructed.

'How old were you when you left?' Hermitage got back to safer ground.

'Fourteen,' Cwen replied.

Well, thought Hermitage, fourteen eh? What on earth was she doing loitering around at home at such an advanced age. It was certainly very late to be leaving home if she had a trade. Obviously, if she'd been an ordinary peasant she'd have stayed with her parents until she married. Or died. What had been going on? Youngsters needed to be out making their way in the world by eight at the latest.

'I'd always been good with sewing and tapestry and general needlework, so I did jobs around the village.'

'For four houses?' Wat expressed surprise.

'And further afield,' Cwen retorted. 'Word spread and people would bring me all sorts to do. Mother would bring work in and take it back again, mostly too much of it, but I was the skilful one. She knew that.' A strange, misty look came into Cwen's eye. It was seldom seen at all, never mind in a situation like this. Her mother must have meant a lot to her.

'So, when weaver Briston came along and offered to teach me the tapestry business, it was an opportunity I had to take.'

'I wondered when he was going to appear,' Wat grunted.[3]

'So your mother let you go to seek your fortune,' Hermitage sounded wistful now. He'd known the monastic life was for him from a very early age. He'd love to have left at eight. It had taken him years to persuade his father.

[3] The tale of The Tapestry of Death goes on at great length about Briston and Cwen and weaving and so forth.

'Hardly,' Cwen bit the word off. 'I was making a good living for her. I only got to leave because she sold me.'

'Sold you?'

'And I don't think Briston wanted to pay at all.'

'He wouldn't,' Wat said.

'I said she couldn't make me stay. I was fourteen and old enough to make my own decisions. She said she'd put the Shire Reeve on me and have me dragged back.'

'How awful.' Hermitage shook his head in sympathy.

'So Briston had to pay.'

'I bet that hurt.' Wat grunted.

'Well, actually he lent me the money, which I gave to him to give to my mother.'

'Sounds like Briston.'

'And I had to pay it all back; and more. Which I did with the first couple of tapestries. You know, the sort Hermitage doesn't approve of.'

'It's not just me. The whole world disapproves.'

'Not quite the whole world, I think you'll find.'

'Well, they should.'

'And there you have it.' Cwen held out her hands to indicate that there was no more. 'Born and raised in Arundel. Left at fourteen to learn tapestry with Briston and three years later you two find me.'

'And you wind up investigating murders for the king.' Wat shook his head at this last, unbelievable step.

'And in all that time, no mention of your father?' Hermitage checked. 'No name, no indication of what he did? No mention of hawks at all?'

'Nothing. She wouldn't talk about him. She only said that he left her as soon as he knew I was on the way. You know men.'

Wat and Hermitage looked at one another. One a weaver of rude tapestry and the other a monk did not feel they had sufficient insight into the behaviour of the entire male half of the world to offer a useful comment. Silence seemed best.

'So why would he mention it now?' Wat pondered.

'Obvious,' Cwen's anger was rumbling around again. 'Get Wat's silver.'

'But he'd virtually got that already. If the parchments checked out it was a very good deal. Buy a few hawk chicks…,'

'From Vikings,' Hermitage pointed out.

'If they're the ones with the birds, that's where you go. Bring them back and sell them to the Normans. Simple business. I'd have gone for it. Yet after all of that he goes and claims he's your father. Doesn't make sense.'

'Maybe he thought you weren't persuaded?' Hermitage offered.

'He's a merchant, it's obvious. He's got some money, he knows how trade works, he looks right and talks right. He knew I was hooked.'

'So you trust him.'

'Good God no. Like I say, he's a merchant. I wouldn't trust him with a bucket of swill.'

'Then?' Hermitage was lost. Again.

'That's trade, Hermitage. You try to rob me, I try to rob you and if neither of us succeeds we call it trade.'

'Oh, Wat.'

'Don't look at me like that. It's not my fault that that's how the world works.'

'You're right,' Cwen was thoughtful. 'Why on earth would he claim to be my father? What did he gain out of it? In fact, he's made the whole deal collapse.'

Hermitage noted that Wat remained silent at this and in fact gazed at the workshop, apparently looking at the holes where his window used to be.

'We can ask him?' Hermitage suggested, innocently.

'We'll do no such thing. We are never seeing that man again.' Cwen's instruction was very clear indeed. 'You can go and tell him to clear off. Not you.' She pointed her finger at Wat. 'If you think it's a good deal you'll go and do it regardless of me.'

Wat held his hands out in innocent and humble supplication. It didn't look very innocent or humble.

'Hermitage can go on his own. He can tell this Stigand that the hawks are off and he can go back to wherever he came from.'

'Of course, I can. And, of course, I will, if that's what you want. But there is one thing that puzzles me.'

'Only the one? What is it?'

'If this Stigand had no need to say he was your father. If, as you two tell me, the trade with the hawks was as good as done. Perhaps there was another reason?'

'What reason?'

Hermitage knew this was going to cause trouble, but he had to say it. 'He really is your father?' Cwen looked ready to explode once more. 'Or, at least, he thinks he is?'

Hermitage knew that if Wat had said that, more damage would have been done. Cwen would never hit a monk. Well, not seriously, anyway.

She did do a lot of pointing and grinding of her teeth, but Hermitage could see that the possibility that he was right was creeping into her mind.

After a long wait for a response, she said, 'Then he's wrong.'

'Of course, of course. But perhaps we could find out why he thinks he's right? And put him on the straight path? That way he won't claim to be your father anymore. Or mention it to anyone else.'

'Why would he tell anyone else?' Cwen seemed angry and horrified at this suggestion.

'It's just the sort of thing that comes up in conversation. You know, "got any children? Oh, yes, two boys. You? Just the one, Cwen the tapestrier, do you know her?"' Hermitage noticed that Cwen was reaching for the axe again.

'After all, anyone would be proud to be your father. A fine, talented, successful young woman such as you?'

The hand paused before the axe. 'That's it.'

'That's what?'

'That's why he wants to be my father. It's not just this hawk nonsense, it's the future. Years to come. Here I am, successful and talented as you say.'

Wat cleared his throat.

'What better daughter for an old man to have? He comes along here thinking I'm going to look after him.'

'Lot of trouble to go to, I'd have thought. And surely he'd be found out?' Hermitage couldn't imagine most levels of deceit, which always got in the way when he was investigating murders, but pretending to be someone's father just to get them to look after you? Surely that was a bit extreme.

'Maybe he really did go through Arundel once and heard all about me. I'm probably the most well-known person who ever lived there. And let's face it, no one else from Arundel is ever likely to go to Derby, are they?'

Wat and Hermitage both nodded that this would be a ridiculous coincidence. Cwen hadn't said exactly how far south Arundel was, but if it was the other side of

Northampton say, who on earth would travel such a distance? Apart from a merchant, of course.

Wat now seemed content that Cwen could be let inside once more, the risk to his household goods being sufficiently diminished. 'Come on, let's go indoors and think what we really need to do next.' He took the full force of a glare from Cwen. 'Obviously killing Stigand still being available for discussion.' He rolled his eyes at Hermitage, who at last understood why Wat and Cwen kept doing the same thing when he started on about the post-Exodus prophets.

As they rounded the corner of the workshop, heading back to the main entrance, Hermitage's heart stopped. Either that or it had decided to get out of his chest by the shortest route possible and had simply dropped to his feet. As if they didn't have enough problems to deal with at the moment, this was piled on top.

Coming up the path were two Normans. Big Normans. Armed Normans. Although they weren't actually brandishing any weapons at the moment, Hermitage knew that the brandishing could be only a moment away and he knew why they had come. An investigation.

Caput IV

And Now There's Normans

He had only just got back from helping out his old abbot, he was in the middle of dealing with Cwen's crisis, and King William sends two of his largest to drag him away.[4] And it would really only take one of them to achieve some very effective dragging. Probably with one hand tied behind his back. Perhaps the other was going to drag Wat and Cwen as well. He'd have a hard time with Cwen just at the moment but it was hardly Hermitage's job to warn him.

He kept telling the king that he only had to send a request; he didn't need to dispatch armed men to fetch one humble monk every time he had a question about a murder. What was it going to be this time? Perhaps someone had killed the king and he was going to have to investigate that? He put such uncharitable thoughts from his head and waited for the inevitable.

Wat and Cwen stood at his side. 'Not again,' Wat mumbled.

'For God's sake,' Cwen hissed like a viper being trampled by a bull with a bear biting its head. 'Can't they see we're busy?'

The two Normans drew near and at least didn't start their brandishing immediately.

Up close they were even bigger if that were possible. They were clearly soldiers, or just wore mail and helmets and

---

[4] The helping out of his old abbot being reported at great length in The Case of the Cantankerous Carcass

carried swords naturally. In the prime of life, they looked ready to tackle anything thrown at them. Not that Hermitage would dream of throwing anything at anyone. He had actually been to Normandy and so knew that the ordinary folk did not dress like this. Definitely soldiers then.

'Weaver?' one of them asked, in a rough accent which clearly liked getting straight to the point. He took a slight step forward. A threatening step.

Hermitage breathed again, despite the antagonism. Perhaps these two were not from the king at all. There were a lot of Normans in the country; they couldn't all be wanting investigation. They did all seem to be soldiers though. It could be these two just wanted Wat for his weaving. That was bad enough.

'Possibly.' Wat was as cautious as any Saxon would be when questioned by large Normans.

'Hm,' a Norman grunt came from the second man who took his own step forward, getting closer than his companion. He did do a bit of brandishing but at least it was only a finger from his mailed glove. 'Wat weaver?'

'Yes,' Wat nodded reluctantly. 'Me weaver.'

Hermitage thought that antagonising these men was not at all wise.

'Stigand?'

'Stigand?' Wat didn't have to fake his confusion. 'No, Wat. Wat the Weaver.'

'Yes.' The first Norman now put an arm out and guided his companion back a step. This first one was clearly in charge; perhaps the second was just there in case physical intimidation was necessary. Hermitage hoped they realised that the intimidation had already been done.

'I am Roland.' This one clearly had a better command of

the language. 'You are Wat and we want Stigand. The people at the tavern said he was here.'

'Ah,' Wat smiled and nodded his relief that they didn't want him. 'How nice of them. No, he's gone, I'm afraid.' The Normans frowned at one another. 'He was here. Now he's gone.' Wat waved his arms to indicate someone being here and then going away.

Roland the Norman didn't seem so happy about this. 'You then.' That didn't sound so good.

'Me?'

'Yes.' Roland muttered a few words of Norman to his companion. He pointed at Wat. 'You clearly know Stigand, the man at the tavern said Stigand was looking to you for his trade. You can give us the hawks.'

'Hawks?' Wat sounded that he had never heard of anything called a hawk and was trying to bring the word to mind.

'Yes, hawks.' Roland wasn't taken in by this. He pointed to the workshop. 'Are they in there?'

'In there? No, no hawks in there.'

'Where is your mew then?'

'Beg pardon?'

'Mew. Where is your mew?'

'Look around,' Wat held his arms out to encompass their surroundings. 'No new.'

'Mew.'

'Yes. Not one of those either.'

Roland and his companion were starting to look frustrated. Frustrated Normans were bad. Always.

'Perhaps our visitors would like wine,' Hermitage suggested.

Wat looked at him askance, but then saw the sense of it.

Better two Normans full of wine outside your home than one angry one indoors.

Roland frowned at Hermitage. 'What's a monk doing here?'

'Oh,' Wat said. 'You know monks, they get everywhere. This is Brother Hermitage.'

Brother Hermitage thought that it was entirely unnecessary to bring his name into the discussion. He was hugely relieved that these Normans showed no sign of it meaning anything to them. It was looking very hopeful that this was absolutely nothing to do with the king or investigation.

Wat gestured that they should sit outside the workshop while Hermitage fetched wine. Letting anyone this size inside would be trouble in any event. The rooms simply weren't built for it. Any expression of Norman anger would make Cwen's furniture destruction look like the attentions of a weak-willed woodworm.

Hermitage was happy to scurry inside and find wine and cups. He still worried that any moment these Normans would recognise the King's Investigator and ask him to find their hawks. And what was it about hawks? Was everyone hawk-mad at the moment? He would be intrigued to hear what the Normans actually wanted with Stigand. Perhaps they were the ones who had given him the job of getting the birds in the first place? And now they wanted delivery. That seemed a little unfair as Stigand hadn't even got to Denmark yet, let alone gathered the silver to buy the chicks from the Vikings. There was a thought. These two Normans might be big, but at least they weren't Vikings asking for their silver.

Outside, the Normans were happy to accept the wine and even seemed to be of slightly better cheer as they quaffed deeply. Relative for a Norman, that is. They raised cups and drank. They then dropped their cups and frowned at the contents. Noses were turned up and lips smacked in the manner of people who've just found out their milk went off last week.

'Where is the wine?' Roland asked.

'That's it,' Wat nodded at the cups.

Both Normans sighed heavily and shook their heads, probably at the disgusting conditions they had to put up with. It didn't stop them holding out for refills though. Which they got.

Eventually, after much belching, Roland got back to his question. 'So. Stigand. Hawks.'

'Stigand, yes,' Wat nodded extravagantly but added a shrug that said he had no more to add to the name. 'If it's the same Stigand, of course.'

Hermitage thought that unlikely. How many Stigands were there wandering the country trading in hawks? He then thought that Wat might be trying to deceive the Normans. A very risky strategy. As well as a dishonest one.

'Where are the hawks?' Roland asked, amiably enough.

Wat looked around the sky. 'No hawks here. No Stigand. No hawks.'

'Where is Stigand?'

'Gone, as I say. Gone away. Was here. Not here. Gone. If it's your Stigand.'

'Gone where?' There was more of the Norman and less of the amiable about this question.

'I couldn't say,' Wat shrugged again.

Roland stood now and looked down at Wat, his hand resting on the pommel of his sword. He held his hand out to indicate that his companion could remain seated for now. He would be called upon when reinforcements were required. The man did very well at getting a goodly quantity of threat into his words. 'So Stigand was here. Why? To trade for hawks?'

'Just passing through. He's a merchant, I'm a weaver, it pays to keep in touch.'

'Good,' Roland smiled. Which did not seem good. 'Back where we were then. You're a friend of Stigand. You give us the hawks.'

'There are no hawks.' Wat smiled back.

'Wrong,' Roland's smile became a grin now. Which seemed very bad. He gestured to his fellow who stood as well and the two of them looked very prepared to tear the place apart, looking for hawks.

'We have no hawks,' Wat now pleaded.

'Then give us Stigand.'

'We have no Stigand either.'

'We look.' The Normans strode off towards the door now, Wat hard on their heels. No one with any sense was going to try and stop them.

Hermitage and Cwen walked along behind.

'I knew it,' Cwen muttered as the Normans entered the workshop in front of them.

'Knew what?'

'That Stigand is a lying, cheating, dung-chewing, scab-faced arse.'

'Cwen!' Hermitage stopped at the threshold. He didn't want her anger expressed all over two large Normans. It wasn't the damage they might do to her, it was the friends they would come back with after Cwen had damaged them.

'Well, he is.' In fact, the arrival of armed men searching for Stigand seemed to have calmed her considerably. She even gave rein to a small smile. Not a very nice one, but a smile nonetheless. It was as if her rage and hatred of the man had just been vindicated. She was at liberty to think the worst of him if other people did as well. 'The Normans obviously think he's already got the hawks when he hasn't even got the silver yet. Ha.'

'Which seems a bit presumptuous. After all, the poor fellow only just got here seeking the money to buy the birds in the first place.'

'Poor fellow! Hermitage, you do make me laugh.'

Hermitage hadn't noted that as one of his effects.

'All we know is what the wretch told us. That he needed the money to go and buy the hawks that he was getting for the Normans.'

'Well, what else is there?'

'He lied?'

'Lied?' Hermitage knew people lied. They did it right in front of him sometimes. After these few short years of investigating murder, he ought to be able to spot it by now. 'About what?'

'Oh, I don't know. Everything, perhaps?' Cwen sounded quite nonchalant about it. 'I grant that the Normans do seem to be expecting some hawks from him. Well, these two do. Are they for the king? Who knows. Is he being paid fifty pounds of silver? I doubt it. Has he spoken to the Vikings? Probably not. Does he have the first clue about getting hawks anyway? Wouldn't think so. Have the Normans in fact already paid him for some hawks that he hasn't delivered? That sounds more like it.'

'Paid him?' Hermitage was getting lost in all this deceit. He understood that people did sometimes stretch the truth, he had been forced to do it himself on occasion. Naturally, he spent hours in repentance afterwards. He also accepted that people lied even if he couldn't spot it. After all, he had plenty of evidence for that. To put so many lies into one simple piece of business just seemed unnecessarily complicated.

'If he'd already got money from the Normans for their birds, but had, in fact, spent it without getting a single hawk, he'd want some more silver. Who better than a rich weaver to get him out of a hole? A hole with big, angry Normans at the bottom.'

'It's, it's,' Hermitage couldn't immediately think of the word.

'Stupid?'

'Exactly. What sort of person would spend money the Normans have given you for hawks, and not get any hawks?'

'Lying, cheating, dung-chewing, scab-faced arse?'

Hermitage tried very hard to put himself in a merchant's place. He heard so much about them from Wat and observed some of their practices first-hand. He just had to think in the right manner; disreputable and probably dishonest with standards of behaviour that would be unacceptable in a baby. And all the while supremely confident that they were right and that everything would work out fine in the end.

'It could well be that he has promised the Normans that he can get their hawks and that he will be paid when he delivers. If I understand trade correctly it doesn't matter that he hasn't actually got any hawks, or the money to buy them in the first place if it's profitable enough. Or even that he knows anything at all about hawks or birds of any sort, as long as he sounds confident. He first makes the promise, then he works out how to meet the expectations. He comes to someone like Wat to get the silver for the hawks and then he sells them and they split the proceeds.'

Cwen was looking at him with exaggerated surprise. 'Hermitage, we'll make a merchant out of you yet.'

'No thank you.'

Their conversation was disturbed by some banging noises from inside. It seemed the Normans were moving things to see if there were any hawks behind the furniture.

Hermitage stepped quickly to the door. 'Maybe he said he'd deliver the hawks a bit too quickly, not knowing much about the business?'

'Oh dear,' Cwen sounded not a bit sorry. 'Looks like the Normans are going to get him before Wat can hand over any silver.'

Inside the workshop, the Normans were standing amidst the wreckage of the room Cwen had largely destroyed.

'Just rebuilding,' Wat was explaining to Roland who was holding up a broken chair.

'Fight with Stigand, eh?'

'Not at all. Just a little local difficulty.' Wat's eyes tried to pierce Cwen but she looked not in the least concerned.

Roland grunted and set off for the rest of the building. In a rapid series of entrances and exits, disturbing work and frightening the apprentices, the men quickly concluded that Stigand was not to be seen. They looked carefully into the rafters of each chamber and seemed satisfied that the hawks weren't roosting up there.

Back at the main door they turned and examined the workshop as if weighing it up to see if they could knock it down on their own. Eventually, Roland reached out and grabbed Wat by the scruff of his neck.'Where is Stigand?'

'I don't know.' Wat bleated and sounded a lot more scared than he looked. He pointed down the path. 'He went that way. Probably back to town.'

Roland stared down the path, perhaps expecting Stigand to still be there, or at least be hiding in the bushes. He frowned and was clearly debating what to do. In the end, he decided that pointing a large finger at Wat was required. 'We will go into the town to look and if we do not find him we will come back. You will stay here.'

'Not going away,' Wat smiled and nodded and indicated with a look over his shoulder that his workshop would not be moving anywhere in the near future.

'If we do come back I will let Ralf ask you questions.' He nodded to indicate that his companion was called Ralf and that if Ralf asked you questions you would remember the experience for years to come.

Roland put Wat down again and with further glares and pointing fingers the Normans left.

The three Saxons stood at the door of the workshop as if waving away welcome visitors who were leaving too soon. The moment the Normans vanished from sight Wat breathed heavily. 'Roland and Ralf eh? What a pair.' He then called back into the building 'Hartle! We're going to the tavern. Quick,' he gestured to Hermitage and Cwen. 'Let's get there before they do.'

'Why?' Cwen asked, not moving an inch.

'Because they look like they want to pull some bits of Stigand off.'

She shrugged. 'They'll probably do a better job of it than I can.'

'Oh, come on,' Wat tried to make it sound as if Cwen was not serious. 'We don't leave any Saxons to be manhandled by big Normans with swords.'

'Some we do. Ones who claim to be someone else's father to get a bit of business or to just plain rob a girl.'

'We don't know what's true. Like Hermitage said. And we'll never find out if the Normans pull his head off.'

'Won't be a problem for either of us then, will he? Apart from what to do with the head.'

Wat looked to Hermitage for some support.

'Wat and I can go on our own.' Hermitage understood that Cwen did not want to aid Stigand in any way. He also thought that she might come to regret it in the days to come, but she was a grown woman, she had to make her own decisions.

'Please yourself. I still say leave him to it. Two big Normans with swords are all he deserves.' With that, she turned and stomped back into the workshop. Hermitage got the clear impression that she was not going to tidy up.

'Come on then.' Wat set off down the path for a short distance before diverting on to what was a shortcut into town. 'They won't know he's at the tavern but they still might try there first.'

'And what do we do then?' Hermitage was following blindly. He assumed that they were just going to warn Stigand that the Normans were coming and then leave the man to his own devices. The main device being running away. If they were expected to hold off large Normans with weapons, Hermitage was tempted to go back and see how Cwen was getting on.

'Warn him about the Normans, of course. But also try to find out what's going on.'

'Really?' Hermitage was panting a bit now as Wat's pace was a quick one.

'Of course. Is there really a deal with the king for hawks? Does he have this parchment and does it say the right thing? If so, why are these two Normans after him now?'

'And Cwen?'

'Pardon?'

'And his claim to be Cwen's father.'

'Oh, that. Yes, that too.'

'Wat, I despair of you sometimes.'

'I know you do. Quite often, I think.'

'Our own Cwen is in a terrible state and all you can think of is silver.'

'If the man with fifty pounds of silver turns out to be her father I imagine she'll be quite pleased.'

'I don't think so.'

They had to push through some dense undergrowth to get onto the path into the town. This route was used by some who wanted to get to Wat's workshop without being seen to get to Wat's workshop, but they covered their tracks well.

Once onto the main road, Wat looked left and right to see if there was any sign of large Normans. 'Perhaps they've gone the wrong way,' he suggested, optimistically.

Hermitage half ran and skipped and shuffled to keep up with Wat. 'We really must tackle Stigand about his claim to be Cwen's father. All this business about the hawks may be just that, business, but Cwen's well-being is our major concern. Just as we would think of you, or you two would think of me.'

Wat just grunted something.

'If you go back to the workshop and all you can report is that the business with the hawks is going well, what do you think Cwen will say? What will she ask? She will ask you what he had to say for himself about being her father. And what will you say? "Oh, I didn't ask"? How do you think that is going to end? You've already lost the contents of one room.'

Wat stopped his progress and turned to Hermitage. He

studied the monk's face as if the answer to his dilemma were tattooed on his forehead. 'I suppose,' he reluctantly accepted. 'But she doesn't need to know that we asked about the silver first.'

Hermitage shook his head. He thought that he had achieved so much with Wat. The rude tapestries were a thing of the past, well, making new ones was, and he did seem to regret the lifestyle that had led him to this place and time. And he had shown signs of caring for Cwen. He had even caught them holding hands for goodness sake. Put fifty pounds of silver in front of him and he went completely to pieces. Having only seen an ounce or two of silver in his life, he could imagine that fifty pounds was quite a lot.

He knew that old King Aethelred was reported to have paid the Vikings 10,000 pounds to get them to stop what they were doing. How anyone got 10,000 pounds of silver into a boat without it sinking was a mystery he would ignore for now.

The only comparison he had was the strange and hopefully useless knowledge that removing a nun from a nunnery without permission led to a fine of two pounds. He didn't know whether the nun concerned got the money or if it went somewhere else. Presumably, nuns, taking vows of poverty, wouldn't need it. By this calculation, if Wat got thirty pounds he would be able to remove fifteen nuns from nunneries against their will. If Hermitage had just the two pounds necessary he certainly wouldn't spend it on a nun.

He accepted that removed nuns were not a very sensible unit of currency but at least it put things in perspective. Thirty pounds got you a lot of nuns. And all of the nuns Hermitage had come across were best left exactly where they were. Getting any of them to do anything against their will was a challenge well beyond his capabilities.

This idle and unhelpful speculation had brought them to the edge of the town, where people appeared to be going about their daily business. If two large Normans were prowling around looking for anyone the streets would be empty.

Wat spotted one fellow he knew coming down the street with a chicken under his arm.

'Ho, Botwulf, seen any Normans about?' he asked quietly.

'Who are you?' Botwulf with chicken replied.

'Who am I?' Wat looked very confused. 'It's me, Wat.'

'Wat who?'

'Wat the Weaver, you ungrateful wretch.'

Botwulf appraised the both of them. 'Never heard of you.'

'Never heard of me eh? Perhaps I'll go and ask Mistress Botwulf if she's seen any Normans. I can say that you might have bumped into them when you were at my workshop a week ago.'

Botwulf almost dropped his chicken and looked quickly up and down the street. 'Quiet, for God's sake.'

'Never heard of me!'

'Shut up. There were a couple of Normans earlier but they've gone. I haven't seen them since and as far as Mistress Botwulf is concerned I've never seen you at all.'

'And these Normans didn't get sent up to my workshop by Mistress Angel perhaps?' Wat glared.

'Why would she do a thing like that?'

'Probably been talking to Mistress Botwulf.'

'I'm sure she wouldn't. And anyway, the Normans only spoke to a couple of people and went in the tavern.'

'That's where we're headed.'

'There you are then. And if Mistress Botwulf ever asks

you..,' Botwulf left the question hanging.

'Mistress who?' Wat winked.

Leaving Botwulf to scurry away, and probably swear his chicken to silence, Wat led on to the tavern.

'Why would Botwulf have been at your workshop?' Hermitage asked, very pointedly.

Wat shrugged. 'You know what people are like. Even though I don't make works of that sort anymore they still come looking.'

'And why would they come looking if there's nothing to see?'

'You'd have to ask them.'

'Hm. I think I will.' Hermitage had tried talking to one or two of the local men to see if his suspicions about Hartle were justified. They all gave perfectly harmless and innocent answers but he was beginning to suspect they might be lying. Now that he knew Botwulf had been up there he would be able to question him more intensely.

They arrived at the tavern and Wat lifted the latch to push the door open. Ducking inside, they saw Ern still spitting and polishing the same mug that he had been the night before. And would probably still be doing tonight. Mistress Angel was nowhere to be seen but the sounds of furious work and loud complaint could be heard drifting through the walls.

'Morning Ern,' Wat gave the landlord a serious nod. 'I need a word with you.'

Ern smiled at Wat and frowned at Hermitage. 'That was quick.'

'What was?'

'Getting here like that.'

'Was it?' Wat looked to Hermitage with a very puzzled expression.

'Very impressive.'

'The Normans been back already then?'

'Normans?' Ern twitched and put his mug down. 'What Normans?'

'The ones looking for Stigand. The ones who were seen coming here. Roland and Ralf, Saxons beaten to order.'

'Oh,' Ern had a sudden recollection. 'Those Normans.'

'That's them. Straight after being here they fly like crows to my workshop. Someone tell them that Stigand was there? How is your dear wife?'

'Not me. I didn't tell them anything and Angel's cleaning up. They only spoke to Stigand himself.'

Wat couldn't disguise the surprise in his voice. 'They spoke to Stigand?'

'They did. He came back from chasing after you. Looked very pale he did like something horrible had happened. Did he find you by the way?'

'Yes. Yes, he did. And nothing horrible happened. Well, not to him, anyway.'

'Right. Well. He settles down in here and then the Normans come in asking for Stigand and his hawks. Before I could say a word he jumps up and takes them off to one side. With him going on about hawks all the time, I thought that was what they were going to talk about.'

Wat folded his arms. 'And what did he say to them?'

Ern looked mightily offended at the suggestion that he would eavesdrop on his customer's conversations. 'I didn't listen.'

'You mean you couldn't hear.'

Ern grunted. 'He took them off in a corner. I couldn't catch a word.'

Wat shook his head and looked to Hermitage. 'They must

never have actually met him before. Must be errand boys just sent to collect from our Stigand. You know, I begin to wonder if Cwen isn't right.'

'About what?'

'Stigand probably-not-the-father-of-Cwen. He obviously told the Normans to come up to my workshop. Doubtless said that's where they'd find the Stigand they were looking for and their hawks.'

'Why would he do that?'

'The alternative being to tell two large Normans with swords that he was Stigand and that no, he didn't have their hawks.'

'Ah,' Hermitage got it. 'That's very deceitful.'

'Isn't it.'

'It's no wonder that you expected me quickly, once you knew the Normans were on their way to the workshop.' Wat nodded sympathetically to Ern.

'But I didn't know. Like I said, I couldn't hear what they were saying. All I know is that Stigand spoke to them and off they went. He hurried to his room straight after, looking even worse. I didn't know where they were going. At least they weren't in my tavern anymore.'

'So,' Wat looked confused. 'Why were you surprised we got here so quickly?'

'It's him really,' Ern nodded towards Hermitage.

'Me? Why were you expecting me?'

'King's Investigator,' Ern announced solemnly.

'Yes?' Hermitage was none the wiser.

Ern nodded to where the noises from his wife were still rattling around. 'Come to find out why Stigand's dead.'

Caput V

A Death in the Family

Hermitage had to sit down. Then he had to have some wine, which he drank with very little caution. Even then he had to hold his hand up to stop any further explanation until he had taken his breath and got his mind into a state to accept the information.

'Dead?' He didn't really want the word repeated too often.

'Ar,' Ern nodded confirmation, showing little concern that his one paying guest was dead.

'You're sure?' Hermitage was reluctantly confident that the landlord would not think a person dead if he wasn't. Sleeping deeply was completely different.

'The way Mistress Angel shouted at him would be enough to wake the dead, and he didn't move a muscle.'

Hermitage didn't have the strength for detailed discussion at the moment. 'How?'

'She's just very loud, really.'

'No, I mean how did he die?'

'How do people do it generally?'

'All sorts of ways.' Hermitage sighed.

Ern rubbed his chin. 'Doesn't the King's Investigator find that sort of thing out?'

'Yes. Yes, he does.' Wat was sitting at Hermitage's side and had said nothing while the dumbfounded investigator gathered his wits about him. 'Dead eh? That's a bit suspicious.'

Hermitage looked at him as if only now recalling that he was there. He was about to say that of course, it was suspicious. Perhaps this set of circumstances could inform a new definition of suspicious. Stigand, Cwen, hawks, Normans and now death. What else did anyone need before calling an event suspicious? But then again..., 'Maybe it isn't,' he tried, rather hopelessly.

'Not suspicious? Really?'

'Could be entirely natural. Not suspicious, just bad timing. A coincidence. Stigand's time had come and it arrived while he was here.'

'Just as he happened to be asking for pounds of silver to buy hawks for large Normans who turn up asking where they are?'

Hermitage took another breath and looked at the ceiling. 'It is suspicious, isn't it?'

'It certainly is, my friend. And you right here at the time. How helpful is that?'

'Yes, I am aren't I.' Something nagged at the back of Hermitage's mind, but he was used to that. It would sit there, minding its own business until it jumped out on him in its own good time. 'I suppose we'd better look?' He hoped that someone would say that there was no need for this at all. Perhaps Wat would offer to go in his place and report back.

'Good idea,' Wat stood and made it quite clear he was waiting for Hermitage to do likewise.

'I've never seen an investigation,' Ern was enthusiastic for some magnificent display.

'There you are.' Mistress Angel burst upon the scene from the door at the back of the room. 'About time too. What are you going to do about this dead hawk man?'

'He's going to investigate,' Ern said, proudly, as if privy to the mysterious art of the investigator.

'I don't care what he does, but I want him out of my tavern.' She nodded her head backwards, making it quite clear that it was Stigand who needed to leave.

'Why don't you hang on to him for now?' Wat offered.

'You!' Mistress Angel spat, only just now noticing that Wat the Weaver was in the room with them. 'I won't have the likes of you in my house.'

'What if I was dead?' Wat taunted.

Mistress Angel replied immediately as if she'd had the thought on many occasions. 'That would be fine.'

'We really better see Stigand. The sooner we do that, the sooner we can sort things out.' Hermitage didn't believe a word of this himself, but it was better than getting caught in the middle of a fight between Wat and Angel. He also had no idea what they were supposed to do with the body. Or why anyone would think it was his responsibility.

'When did you notice he was dead, mistress?'

Angel gave her least angelic look to Wat but spoke with some civility to Hermitage. 'I went to tell him the noon meal would be ready soon. Not that he needed it as he'd already had bread and wine when he got up.'

'Really?' Hermitage thought that peculiar.

'I know. Bread and wine in the morning. Whoever heard the like? And I told him so. Behaving like some lord in my inn. I won't have it, see.'

'She won't,' Ern confirmed.

Hermitage held his arm out, indicating that Angel had better lead the way to the deceased. He still held out a hope that the mistress was mistaken. Perhaps Stigand had simply had too much wine with his bread and was sleeping heavily.

It really was unfair that every time someone died, he had to deal with it. Being King's Investigator was bad enough, being everyone else's as well was just taking liberties.

He had to conclude that there were lots of deaths he didn't get involved in at all. People died regularly and he wasn't called upon. Suspicion, that was the key. If ever there were a suspicious death, he got dragged into it. And he always seemed to be in the vicinity when one of these suspicious deaths occurred. Surely that was suspicious in its own right?

It was unreasonable to think that suspicious deaths only occurred when he was passing by but, as far as he knew, he was the only investigator. This must mean that there were suspicious deaths that didn't get investigated at all? His mind followed a fascinating path of reason. If and only if there existed a single suspicious death that was not investigated, then no suspicious death needed investigation. He could go home.

He returned to his senses from this flight of fancy and saw dead Stigand lying in front of him. But it didn't look suspicious.

The man was on his cot as if he had dropped off for a sleep. His hands were folded across his large stomach and his eyes were closed. He didn't actually look very well, but then he was dead.

'Is this how you found him?'

'What do you think?' Mistress Angel was now content to snap at Hermitage as well as Wat. 'I don't go mucking about with dead bodies. This is a respectable house, this is.' She glanced at Wat. 'Or at least, it was.'

Everything about the scene was unremarkable. The room was small but had space for several people to sleep if need be. There was only one cot and Stigand was occupying it. There was no other way in or out, it was just a simple space divided from the rest of the tavern by a wall of wattle and daub.

Hermitage risked going a little closer. From the pale look and complete lack of breathing, it seemed unlikely that Stigand was going to jump up and surprise him.

There was no knife sticking out of the body, which, despite its deeply unpleasant nature he always found to be quite a valuable clue. There was no blood at all, no sign of injury or even disturbance. It was as if Stigand had gone to bed, got comfortable and then died. Where was he to find suspicion in this? And where on earth would any investigation begin?

'There doesn't seem to be anything out of place,' he informed the room in general.

'Apart from the dead body,' Wat pointed out.

'There are dead bodies everywhere.'

'Not in my house.' Mistress Angel was clear about this, although the looks she continued to throw at Wat said that if a second one was required she had a list with one name on it.

'It could be as I said. Nothing suspicious at all. The man looks as if he simply died. As people do.'

'It's a bit odd dying just now though, isn't it?' Wat asked. 'Surely that's enough suspicion to be going on with.'

'Oh Lord,' Hermitage felt a swell of despair at this. 'If we have to include "when" as well as "how" in calling a death suspicious, where will it end? It'll get to the point that if anyone dies without a physick standing over them, we'll have to have an investigation. I haven't got the time to do all that. We'd need an army of investigators.'

Wat put a calming hand on Hermitage's shoulder. 'Perhaps just one at a time?'

Hermitage took a breath and considered the body before them. He held his hands out to make sure everyone knew which death he was talking about. 'We can't tell how he died. There are no marks, no sign of struggle, nothing.'

'We haven't turned him over yet,' Ern put in, sounding quite keen on the idea.

'Turned him over?'

'Yes, you know. Maybe someone stabbed him in the back.'

They all looked at the two-inch gap between the cot and the floor and dismissed the idea of an extremely thin man with a knife crawling in to do the deed.

The suggestion had set off some more worrying thoughts in Hermitage's head though. 'Or someone put him here?'

'Like this?' Mistress Angel now had a new target for her anger. The person who went around leaving dead bodies in her beds.

'We know he's dead and that there are no signs of injury. We have assumed that he died here but that may not be the case. He does look remarkably comfortable. If he died in his sleep I could imagine him making no movement but it was the middle of the day.'

'Wouldn't stop him sleeping,' Mistress Angel complained. 'Lazy lump.'

'What if someone killed him elsewhere and then laid him out here, like this. Perhaps to make us think that his death was natural?'

'It's a lot of trouble to go to,' Ern said, who never liked going to a lot of trouble over anything. 'And I think I'd have noticed them pass by.'

'I have unfortunately found that the people who go to the trouble of killing someone in the first place, also put a bit of effort into not getting caught.'

'Ar?' Ern sounded very impressed with this piece of information.

'There wasn't no one dragging dead people through my parlour,' Mistress Angel explained.

'I think we'd better take a closer look at him.' Wat nodded Hermitage towards the body.

Not being able to come up with a credible reason to avoid this step, Hermitage was at least grateful that there were four of them. Stigand was a large fellow and moving him was not going to be easy. He did think that Mistress Angel might not be much help but Ern was probably keen. He nodded reluctantly and moved towards Stigand's feet. Wat went to the head and Ern stood back and watched.

'We'll probably need you to help?'

'Oh, right.' Ern grinned at the prospect of hauling a dead body around.

'Don't you drop him on my floor. I've only just swept,' Angel warned them.

'What? You swept around the dead body?' Wat asked, in considerable surprise.

'I didn't know he was dead, did I?'

'He must have been pretty quiet.'

'Like I said, lazy lump, that's all. Bread and wine in the morning, sleeping when he felt like it. Disgusting.'

'How long ago was this?' Considering the fuss she was making, Hermitage did think it a bit odd that Angel would do the housework while a corpse was lounging on her cot.

'Soon after he came back in here. He spoke to the Normans while I was doing the fireplace. I had the back to do and then I came round here.'

'That's very quick,' Hermitage noted. 'Maybe he wasn't dead when you swept, maybe he really was asleep and then he died.' He risked putting a hand out and laying the back of his palm on Stigand's forehead. 'Cold, but not very. And how long ago was it that you swept?'

'I don't know, I haven't been counting.'

'About an hour,' Ern offered. 'And he walked to his room of his own accord. Didn't seem very dead then.'

'What on earth could have made him die in such a short space of time?'

'I don't think it takes long to do it,' Wat said. 'It's usually all the preliminaries that take up the time.'

'Preliminaries?'

'Yes, you know. Being chased, stabbed, fighting back, all of that.'

'None of which he did.'

'Ah. No.'

'I don't think we're going to find anything but let's turn him anyway.' Hermitage took the feet and gave them a half-hearted twist that had absolutely no effect at all.

They managed to coordinate their efforts and Stigand began to roll. It was hard to control the body as the cot was narrow and Ern had to lean over Stigand's stomach to pull. It seemed almost inevitable that the deceased was going to end up on Angel's clean floor.

When they got the body onto its side Wat leaned forward from the head. Digging one elbow into Stigand's neck to stop him from rolling backwards, he ran his other hand across the man's back. 'No knife. In fact nothing at all.' He nodded to the others and they let the hawk merchant resume his resting position.

'Nothing?' Hermitage needed something if he was going to investigate this. If it needed investigation at all. 'So it could be a natural death, nothing to worry about.'

'I still think it's a bit odd,' Wat rubbed his chin. 'Dying right now? In the middle of all this?'

'Ah, well,' Hermitage nodded knowingly, without being knowing. 'Odd deaths are probably someone else's business. Investigation might only be for obvious murder, you know, knives, swords, missing heads, that sort of thing. Could be the king has someone else entirely to look into odd deaths.'

Wat was looking at him with the clear understanding that Hermitage was grasping at straws like the last flea in the bed.

'How did he die then? Tell me that? If it was suspicious.' Hermitage folded his arms.

Wat shrugged. 'Could be anything. Poison?'

'In my house?' Mistress Angel shrieked. 'I'll give you poison,' and it looked as if she would like to. 'It's bad enough having you in here at all, never mind accusing people of poisoning.'

'I'm not accusing anyone. If I'm doing anything I'm accusing Stigand here of being poisoned.'

'That's right, blame him who can't speak for himself.'

'Perhaps we'd better discuss things outside,' Hermitage nodded extravagantly to Wat, indicating that being away from the landlord and his wife was preferable to anything just at the moment. 'Now that we know there's no knife or missing head or anything, we need to think about it.'

'Missing head?' Mistress Angel was having a bad day.

'That was another business altogether.' Hermitage reassured her.[5]

'If his head is going to come off you can take him away now.'

'His head is not going to come off. He'll be perfectly fine here.'

'You can take him with you. I'm not having the likes of him cluttering the place up. It was bad enough when he was alive,

[5] Intrigued? Try Hermitage, Wat and Some Murder or Other.

all his odd habits and bad company.'

'Bad company?' Wat asked. 'Who, exactly.'

'You.'

'Ah.'

'And them Normans. And people banging around the back, shouting and carrying on.'

Hermitage latched on to this fresh piece of information. 'People shouting and carrying on? Who was that?'

'They was round the back wasn't they? I can't see around the back. All I know is that there was others, as well as the Normans and you lot. I tell you, he's probably better off dead. Get a bit of peace and quiet.' She glared at everyone in the room, Ern included. 'Now you lot can shift him. It's me does all the work around here. Make yourself useful for once. Throwing out the drunks is your job, dead bodies is just like drunks.' She brushed from the room, leaving the men all looking at one another, doubtless wondering if they could just sneak out.

'We'll have to move him,' Ern whined. 'I'll never hear the end of it.'

'Where to?' Wat asked. 'He's not going to fit under the bed.'

'Out of here completely.' Ern looked at Hermitage. 'You're the investigator. You must know what to do with the bodies.'

'There's usually someone else around to deal with all of that.'

'The church then,' Erm concluded. 'That's where the dead go. They can have him.'

'I'm not sure that the priest will be keen on that.' Hermitage knew that the local priest was never very keen on anything, most particularly engaging with his flock. Even the ones who were still alive. Hermitage had only seen him once and even though they shared clerical garb and would clearly have a lot to talk about, the man ignored him completely.

'Go and talk to the moot,' Wat advised. 'They deal with trouble in town. That must include dead strangers.'

Ern gave a disinterested grunt. 'I suppose they did manage that horse that dropped dead a year back.'

'Horses, people, all the same.' Wat waved him to leave.

Obviously thinking that wandering about the town looking for the moot and the headman was better than lumping dead bodies out of bed, Ern shambled away.

'Come on then,' Wat urged, once Ern had gone. 'Don't want to loiter anywhere near Mistress Angel when she's got high expectations.'

'Shouldn't we stay? As a mark of respect until Stigand is dealt with properly.'

'We didn't even know he was dead until we came in here. Not going to make much difference now.' Wat actually manhandled Hermitage away from the bed and out into the main room of the tavern. 'You know what happens when we get too close to dead people. The king or one of his men turns up demanding that we do something about it, or rather you do.'

Hermitage found himself back in the street before he had a chance to protest the point. Not that there was much protest he could make. Wat was right. Deaths, especially those of other people, tended to cause him a whole world of trouble. As he considered it though, he realised that most of the trouble, in this case, had already arrived. 'I can't really see this one just going away. The Normans have already been round once asking for Stigand and his hawks. When they get back here and find he's dead, they're not going to take it well.'

'Unless they did it and are now on their merry way.' Wat

stepped back up the street towards the workshop, Hermitage was forced to walk alongside, despite his reservations about leaving the deceased to the ministrations of Mistress Angel. Mistress Angel who might just minister him onto the rubbish heap if he wasn't taken away quickly.

Hermitage pondered Wat's suggestion but it was full of holes. 'If they wanted to kill him, why would they be asking for his hawks? Not going to get their birds if he's dead.'

'True, but then they didn't know who he was. They spoke to him in the tavern and he sent them up to us. We sent them back again. Perhaps they really wanted to kill him all along. You know. Norman doesn't get what he wants. Norman kills the person who should have given it to him. Then kills people who tell him how stupid it was to kill the person who was going to give him the thing in the first place.'

Hermitage shook his head at this nonsense. 'They would have simply said, "where's Stigand, we want to kill him." They're not usually reticent about that sort of thing. Or scheming or deceitful. Just out with it. And then we've got these people around the back. The ones making noise and disturbing Mistress Angel.'

'Doesn't take much to disturb her.'

'But if there was someone else, maybe they did for Stigand.'

'Why?'

Hermitage didn't know. 'Could be any reason. He does seem to behave in a rather dangerous manner. Promising Normans that he'll get them some hawks when he doesn't know much about them and hasn't got the money anyway.'

Wat dismissed this with a wave. 'That's just business. Perfectly normal.'

'That's what I told Cwen,' Hermitage said. And then he went very cold indeed. He stopped in his tracks and after a few paces, Wat noticed the fact and turned back.

'Thought of something already?'

'Cwen,' Hermitage breathed.

Wat looked to Hermitage and then up the road. 'Oh, God, yes. There's no telling what damage she's done while we've been away. Us going to see Stigand could have set her off all over again.'

'No, no. Not your workshop for goodness sake. Cwen and Stigand.'

'What about them?'

'Think about it. I'm sure I'm wrong and I feel awful just contemplating the fact that I've contemplated the question.'

'What are you going on about?'

Hermitage swallowed. 'What did Cwen say she wanted to do to Stigand?'

'Eh?' Wat sounded disinterested and distracted. 'I don't know.'

'Yes, you do.'

'Well. Yes, I suppose she said she wanted to…,' Wat stopped as well now. He looked at Hermitage much more intently and did look genuinely disturbed. Not the sort of disturbed that revolved around money. This was something much more sincere.

'She wouldn't.' Hermitage told himself out loud and with confidence.

Wat gave a low whistle. 'She did say she wanted to kill him.'

'And she did disappear from the workshop while she went for her walk.'

'And Mistress Angel did hear noises around the back.'

Hermitage left a long pause. 'She wouldn't.' He tried to convince himself.

'She broke a lot of my furniture.'

'She couldn't.'

'Well,' Wat didn't sound so sure about this. 'I'm sure she could, actually.'

'How?'

'I don't know. Hands, feet, something blunt and heavy.'

'No, no, I don't mean how physically. I mean how could she? How could she kill anyone, in a moral sense?'

'Oh, right.'

'And how can we even think it of her?' Hermitage felt his own personal despair.

'I suppose we have to be, what's the word you keep using? Rational?'

'That's the one.'

'We have someone who said that they wanted to kill the person who is now dead. Someone who had the opportunity to do it.'

'But she's one of us. She simply wouldn't.'

The two of them stood in the middle of the street and weighed up the situation. 'You're right, of course.' Wat spoke clearly and decisively. 'Of course, she wouldn't. We're talking nonsense. What are we thinking? She goes on about killing people quite a lot, particularly Normans, but she's never done it. She smashed up my furniture but she never attacked us.'

'Hartle and Gunnlaug looked a bit the worse for wear.'

'That was just terror, not physical damage.'

'And we still don't know that Stigand didn't simply die. There's no injury. It could be poison, as you say, but I don't think Cwen would have the time or the knowledge to poison someone just like that.'

'And if she really did kill him I think she'd have made a meal of it.' Wat left the thought and Hermitage trembled at the image.

'We've got to tell her that he's dead though.' Wat looked nervous.

'Which may upset her again.'

'Or make her very happy?'

Hermitage drew a deep breath. First, a dead body to deal with, now a living Cwen. The day was not getting any better.

'There's one thing we've got to be absolutely clear about though.' Wat looked Hermitage in the eye and was his most serious. 'Under no circumstance whatsoever, from this day forward and for the rest of our lives do we even breathe the idea that we thought for a moment that she might have done it.'

'Oh God, no,' Hermitage quaked.

Caput VI

She's Not Going to Like This

The walk back to the workshop got progressively slower as the place drew near. A monk of deep piety and integrity and a weaver of the world, capable of dealing with the most trying circumstances. Neither of them was in a rush to return to the slight young woman and give her the news that the person she wished was dead was, in fact, dead. There was just no telling what was going to happen.

Their trepidations became almost physical when they caught sight of the building and spotted Cwen sitting on a stool outside.

'Aha, she's waiting for us then?' Hermitage tried his best to sound bright and positive.

'Yes, she is. Isn't she.'

'But at least she's sitting.'

'And the stool is in one piece.'

Hermitage tried clapping his hands together in the manner of a woodsman about to tackle the largest tree in the forest. 'Come now. There's nothing for it. On we go.'

Wat took a breath and held it. 'Right,' he released it. 'Let's go.'

'Yes, indeed.'

Wat was now finding the stones of the path quite fascinating and was examining the trees nearby to see if any would be suitable for coppicing this year.

'You took your time,' Cwen's voice called across the space and got their feet working once more.

'This is ridiculous.' Wat muttered. 'We just tell her for

goodness sake.' He strode on with Hermitage happily scuttling a couple of paces behind.

'Have you been waiting here for us all this time?' Wat asked when they got to the door.

Cwen grunted. 'Hartle said I had to go outside. I was frightening the apprentices.'

'Not broken anything else though?'

'No, I haven't. I have calmed down quite a bit.' She breathed deeply to demonstrate her calm. 'Although whatever that dung basket has to say for himself will doubtless be more cause for annoyance.'

'Stigand,' Hermitage thought putting the name in would make the subsequent conversation a lot easier.

'Of course Stigand. Who else would we be talking about? Well?' She gave them consecutive glares. 'What did he come up with this time?'

'It was very interesting, actually.' Wat made it sound positive. 'An interesting experience, at least.'

'Oh yes?'

'Yes. Absolutely.' Wat nodded.

'Well?' Cwen's anger was rising again. This time it was heading in their direction.

'Hermitage probably has the best explanation.'

'What?' Hermitage had thought that standing at the back would be safest. Wat's behaviour at times could be really quite trying. This was one of those times.

'Hermitage?' Cwen asked.

'Yes?'

'What is this explanation you have?'

'Well, I don't know that it would be me in particular.'

'Ern was waiting for Hermitage specifically,' Wat explained.

Hermitage would be waiting for Wat specifically after this.

'One of you is going to tell me what's happened, very quickly,' Cwen explained the situation.

Hermitage tutted at Wat's avoidance of a simple statement. A simple statement he could clearly no longer avoid. 'You see Ern was waiting for me in my official capacity.'

'Official capacity? What on earth does that mean?'

'You know, the proper title I have. The appointment I was given.'

Cwen frowned hard at him as if he was speaking gibberish. 'What? King's Investigator?'

'Aha, yes, well done. That's the one.'

'Why did he want the King's Investigator?'

'Why does anyone?' Hermitage asked, lightly.

Cwen looked to Wat and then back to Hermitage. 'Usually, because someone's dead.'

'There you have it.' Hermitage was glad that this was all explained at last. It hadn't turned out so bad after all. He didn't know why they'd made so much fuss now.

'Who's dead then?'

'Who? Ah, who eh? Good question, who. Isn't it a good question, Wat?'

'Eh?' Wat was started to life, obviously thinking he had escaped this tricky task.

'Yes, Wat,' Cwen demanded. 'Who?'

He took a breath.

'Not Stigand?' Cwen's voice was hard to interpret at this point. It sounded as if she was more disappointed than anything. And most of the disappointment was for the people who had brought her the news.

'Stigand,' Wat repeated slowly as if trying to recall the name of the corpse they'd just examined.

'He's dead?' She looked at them both, eyes wide.

'He is.' Hermitage said it gently. At least she had got to the nub of the problem herself. Giving confirmation was a lot easier than breaking the news in the first place. At least her reaction seemed to finally close the ludicrous idea that she might have had something to do with it.

'Dead?'

'Just so.'

'In bed.' Wat added, unhelpfully.

'I don't care where he's dead.' She contained herself for a moment, but only a moment. 'How dare he?' she shouted as she rose from the stool. 'How dare he die when I wanted to kill him? I'll kill him.' She gazed in the direction of the town, perhaps thinking that she could pop down there and kill him for a second time.

'He is definitely dead,' Hermitage confirmed. 'We saw him. At the tavern.'

'What was he doing being dead?' she demanded.

'Just sort of lying there. You know. Dead.'

'Has someone else killed him?' She cast a very specific accusation at the pair of them. It was clear that if she found out that they had killed Stigand they were going to be in serious trouble.

'We don't know. He was just dead. As Wat says, he was lying there. Ern thought we'd come to sort out the death, not just to speak to the deceased.'

'And Mistress Angel simply wanted him out of the place.'

'Because if someone else has killed him, I'll kill them. Where is he now?'

'Still there. Where we left him.' Hermitage shrugged. 'Ern went off to find the moot and see what to do about him. Being a stranger and all.'

Cwen was having trouble taking all of this in and she walked up and down in front of the workshop, the various thoughts pushing her eyes from side to side. At one point she even went and took hold of the axe again, which made Hermitage and Wat look for the best route of escape. All she wanted to do was hold it though, probably for comfort.

'Was he murdered?' she asked after she'd stared at the axe head for a worryingly long time.

'We couldn't tell,' Hermitage reported. 'There were no signs of injury, no disturbance, nothing suspicious of any sort.' He directed this at Wat. 'It is quite possible that he simply died.'

'Or he could have been poisoned.' Wat got a frown from Hermitage for this. 'Well, he could. It is a bit suspicious him dying now. Just when he's come here looking for silver, there are Normans asking where him and his hawks are and he claims to be your, erm, that it is he, erm, made certain claims. You know.'

'He claimed to be my father, you mean?'

'That's it.'

'That's all just circumstance.' Hermitage protested. He thought about it for a moment. 'You might say it was just circumstantial evidence.' He liked the sound of that.

'What?' Cwen and Wat asked together.

'The only evidence for the crime is that the circumstances point to it. We found no knife or injury or anything. No what you might call hard evidence. Only circumstantial.'

'If you say so.'

'It could come in very handy. You never know. There might be all sorts of cases where circumstantial evidence is key.'

'But he's definitely dead?' Cwen asked Wat, ignoring

Hermitage and his nonsense altogether.

‘Certainly is. Mistress Angel wouldn’t let him lie around in bed all day if he wasn’t.’

Cwen scowled at the air around her. ‘Someone did it.’

‘As Hermitage says, we couldn’t see anything.’

‘Doesn’t mean it wasn’t done. Sounds like first of all we need to find out how it was done and then who by.’

‘But if it was just a natural death?’ Hermitage continued to press his case.

'I wanted to kill him, now I'm not going to get the chance. I want to know who did. I don't believe he went and died all on his own. What a coward. Well, I tell you,' she pointed her finger at them both. 'He's not getting away with it.'

'Getting away with it,' Hermitage repeated, starting to lose understanding of what was going on here. 'But Cwen,' he made a point of not looking at Wat when he made this statement. He had to say it though. This might be the only opportunity he would get to bring the topic up in normal conversation. Not that this conversation was even remotely related to normal. 'You wouldn't have killed him really.' He sounded sympathetic and understanding. 'Not actually killed him.' He hurried on. 'Naturally, you are very angry and, if the fellow is a complete, you know,'

‘Arse scab.’

'Quite. If he is an erm, one of those, I'm sure your anger would be justified and that he would have to feel the full force of it. But not murder. We've seen what murder's like. It's sticking a knife in someone, or a sword, or doing something very physical that stops them being alive anymore. Would you really do that? Could you?'

Cwen did glare at him for a moment but then looked away. ‘Well, I suppose not. Not actual murder. ’

Hermitage smiled and Wat sighed.

'But it would have been close,' she made this very clear. 'If I got hold of him he'd have wished he was dead. That's for sure.'

'Absolutely.' Hermitage and Wat nodded that this was entirely reasonable.

'There's a thought though.'

'What thought?' Hermitage asked, pleased that he had moved Cwen on from murderous ideas.

'I could have got someone else to do it for me.'

'I beg your pardon?' Was Cwen trying to prove that she was a killer after all?

'You know, a big knight or someone. On a horse. I'm sure they kill people if you pay them. Probably do it for nothing, they seem to like it so much.'

'Cwen, that's awful.'

'Tell that to the knights. And I'd let Stigand have some armour as well. Just to be fair.'

'He doesn't need any armour and we don't need to tell any knights anything. Stigand is dead already. And I think paying someone to kill someone else is as bad as doing it yourself.'

Cwen snorted at this unreasonable conclusion. There was clear disappointment that she was missing the opportunity for a very one-sided tourney. 'Still, serve him right.'

'This could be the end of it.' Hermitage was very hopeful that now they had got Cwen over the news without any more damage to person or possession, this might all go away. 'He has died and we can see no evidence of a killer. He may have been a deceitful fellow who has got his just reward, but that is that. He is dead. What more can we do? If it really was a natural death and no one is to blame?'

'We can do a lot more,' Cwen was firm on this. 'We're not

just going to stand here and assume the man dropped dead just to avoid his responsibilities. We need to make absolutely sure that no one else was involved in this before we let it go. If we ever let it go.' She finished with a less than charming smile.

'Still could have been poison.' Wat said.

'There you are,' Cwen grinned. 'And if there was poison, there's a poisoner. Unless he took it himself?'

Hermitage tried to pretend that Cwen had accepted the possibility of natural death. Perhaps if he believed it she would too. 'Oh, Wat. I know your circumstances point to something but we have nothing else to go on. Yes, there are Normans about but they seem to want Stigand, not his body. Once they know he's dead they'll probably be on their way.'

'I wouldn't count on that,' Wat didn't sound hopeful. 'And in any case, there's this.' He reached into his jerkin and pulled out a neatly folded piece of parchment.

From what Hermitage could see it looked to be a piece of quality and of a good size. His natural reaction to the sight of parchment, any parchment, was to reach out and try to touch it. Then he would smell it, gaze upon it, make it comfortable and finally when he was fully settled, read it.

His arm rose and his fingers prepared themselves without conscious intervention.

'What's that?' Cwen asked, breaking the reverie.

'This,' Wat held it up in a rough manner and even waved it about a bit, which gave Hermitage the shivers. 'This is Stigand's parchment.'

'What? What do you mean, it's Stigand's parchment?' Hermitage was disturbed from his adoration of parchment in general.

'It's the one that was in his jerkin, anyway.'

'Where did you get it?' Hermitage hadn't noticed any parchment.

'From his jerkin.'

'When?'

'When we rolled him over and I propped him up on the bed. I saw it sticking out a bit and thought it might be useful.'

'The parchment from a dead man's jerkin?' Hermitage was appalled.

'Not going to be able to read it now, is he?'

Hermitage looked at Cwen to confirm that she shared his horror at stealing from the dead. She didn't seem to.

'What does it say? she asked, full of enthusiasm.

Wat held an arm out towards Hermitage. 'Our resident reader and writer will tell us.' He looked around. 'Perhaps we'd better go indoors. You never know who might be listening.'

Hermitage sincerely hoped that no one was listening to this revolting tale. He loved parchment but even he drew the line somewhere.

Wat led the way back into the workshop, waving the parchment behind him, right in Hermitage's face.

Still, it was parchment after all. And they needed to know what it said. He would just have to go along with this for now and then complain about it later. It was an approach he used quite regularly. He followed the parchment with his eyes and his nose and found that he was on a leash.

Wat chose the damaged room for their conference, perhaps thinking that they were less likely to be disturbed in a place where there was nothing to sit on. It was also possible he wanted to remind Cwen of the havoc she had wreaked. If that were the case it had little effect as she simply swept the wreckage aside, cleared a space on the floor and sat cross-legged.

Rather than a good, traditional dirt floor, or even the extravagance of flagstones, Wat had used wood of all things. Carefully cut lengths of timber had been produced at enormous expenses and then simply laid on the floor and held in place with long wooden nails. It was quite ridiculous and one of the things a lot of people pointed at and laughed when they came in. He said he liked it as it kept his feet warm. He may be good at tapestry but he was an idiot when it came to house building.

When he asked how dirt or flagstones would work upstairs, they simply noted that he shouldn't have floors upstairs in the first place.

He can't have been envisaging a time when they would have to sit on the floor because all the furniture was broken, but this layer of wood was actually quite comfortable. He said it would catch on, but then he thought rude tapestry would catch on.

As they entered the room Wat reached for the chair he had repaired, only to find that it fell apart in his hands. With a pointed tut toward his bits of furniture, he sat cross-legged as well and placed the parchment between them. He opened it, smoothed it out and looked up to Hermitage who was still standing.

Hermitage gasped. The sight before him was a wonder. The quality, the colours, the writing, the words. So many of them. Every one called to him to come and join them. He slowly lowered himself to his hands and knees and gazed with rapture at the article before him. He dared to reach out a hand and turn the magnificent piece so he could see it the right way up.

'It's a good one then?' Cwen asked with a smirk at Wat.

Hermitage's mouth was open and he had to be careful not to dribble on the parchment.

'The best,' he breathed.

'Best eh? Stigand had good quality stuff then?'

'No, no,' Hermitage had to explain but his mind was trying to do too many things at once. 'Not the best as in highest quality or really very good. This is best. Simply the best. The very best piece of parchment I have ever seen.'

Wat and Cwen exchanged looks of good-humoured patience. Bless Hermitage and his obsession with parchment.

'You haven't been around much. What with being a monk and all. There's probably lots like this.' Cwen waved a vaguely interested hand towards the piece, which did seem to be reflecting a myriad of colours into the grey room. There was no denying it was the centre of attention.

At the top of the page, there was a massive, multicoloured mess of some sort or another, which, upon closer examination, revealed itself to be just one letter. It looked like an awful lot of trouble to go to for one letter and an awful lot of ink to use up. There were bright blues and reds and yellows, many of which put Wat's tapestries to shame. Of course, there weren't any naked people on the parchment, which put Wat to shame. But then shame had been his business anyway.

And you had to look hard to make out the letter at all. It was covered with swirls and bands and tiny images of animals and plants and people. It could be an A, in which case why not just write A? It must have taken months to produce this.

Hermitage was breathing heavily. 'There are none like this. None at all. Yes, I've been a monk and that means I have seen documents locked away from prying eyes; treasures in parchment that would astound you.'

Cwen looked like it would take a lot more than some coloured parchment to astound her.

Hermitage waved his arms around to try and get their understanding. 'I have been in the presence of Saint Augustine's own Gospels. The ones that brought Christianity to the country in the first place. The ones written by Saint Jerome himself only a few years after our Lord's death and resurrection.'

'That must have been better than this, surely?' Wat looked worried that Hermitage was losing his senses.

'Don't be ridiculous, I wasn't allowed to see it. It was in a locked chamber behind the altar and I was at the back, minding the door. I just imagined that it must be like this. This is incredible. The amount of time and effort that must have gone into producing this is simply unthinkable. It could only have come from the king. No one else could afford it.'

'Really?' Wat was intrigued. 'So that bit is true.'

'Or it's true that he stole it from the king,' Cwen snorted.

Hermitage shook his head slowly. 'I can't imagine anyone being able to steal this from anywhere. It would be too closely guarded. I imagine that the Scriptorium master in charge of it didn't even want to let it go at all. He probably only let the king look at it if he asked nicely. How it got out of court at all is a mystery, never mind what it's doing with a man who wants to buy hawks.'

'A dead man, who used to want to buy hawks.' Cwen corrected.

'So,' Wat ignored all this and got down to practicalities. 'Mystery aside, what does it say?'

'Pardon?'

'What does it say? The parchment. All the words. What are they?'

'Oh,' Hermitage emerged from his reverie, but only slightly. The very sight of this masterpiece was surely enough for anyone. He would be happy to simply gaze upon it and study its construction for a year or two. He would save the unbearable pleasure of actually reading it, perhaps forever. He could go through the rest of his life happy that any moment now he would read the parchment. And if he never read it at all? Well, he would have all the pleasure of anticipation without the risk of disappointment.

He looked down upon this marvel once more, the horror that the poor thing had been folded and stuffed in Wat's jerkin only a distant worry. Having his mind directed to the words themselves his first concern was that this really would be all about hawks. That would be such a waste. Something of this nature ought to reveal the truth of the human spirit or be a king's divine expression of his duty to his God and his country. Not a lot of nonsense about hawks and how many should be white.

Before moving on to even read a word he concluded that it wouldn't be about hawks at all. No one, not even a hawk-mad Norman would go to the expense of a parchment like this for some birds. He had no idea how many hawks you could buy for the price of this one document, but he knew it would be quite a flock.

The makers of this would never hand it over to someone like Stigand for him to brandish around the country trying to get money out of rich weavers. They wouldn't let it out of their sight at all.

If this was a message, it was not the sort that got sent to people. It was the sort they got invited to come and look at. Probably forming an orderly queue.

'Yes, Hermitage,' Wat pressed. 'What does it say?'

He took a deep breath. He was going to have to read it. Still, mayhap he could just skim the words to get their meaning before returning at his leisure to consider the content in detail. Followed by a more prolonged period of study and interpretation, after which he might even consider making the most modest copy of the smallest part. By the time that was done he should be about fifty.

'Read,' Wat instructed, quite rudely.

Hermitage read. 'A.'

There was a pause, not a long one. 'A what?'

'Just A. That's the first letter. A.' Hermitage pointed out the first letter which was the most marvellous of them all. It could take days just to read that A. With any luck.

'If you're going to read this slowly I'll have a go myself.'

'No,' Hermitage almost screamed as Wat reached out to touch his precious.

'Ad Gratiam Dei,' Hermitage went on, a slight smile broached his face.

'By the Grace of God,' Cwen said. 'We've come across that before.'

'Odd though, isn't it?' Hermitage asked. 'Not the sort of thing you start a document about hawks with.' His confidence was high.

He read on, trying to take the meaning from the words without letting them touch the sides on their way through. They demanded much better attention than this and he was the one to let them have it.

'By the Grace of God, William king, etcetera etcetera.'

'Why does it say that?' Cwen asked.

'It doesn't, I'm just getting to the important bits.'

'About time,' Wat huffed.

'Erm, be it known that. We hereby grant. Let or hindrance.

Ah, here we are. All the preliminaries out of the way. Mind you there are a lot of preliminaries and they're very good ones.'

'Hermitage!'

'Sorry. Yes.' He read on. 'Oh,' his disappointment was clear.

'What is it?' Wat leant forward to read the upside-down words. 'Not about hawks at all, eh?'

'No. Quite the opposite. It is all about hawks. That's all it's about. It really does say King William will give fifty pounds of silver for one hundred hawks. It even mentions the white ones.'

Hermitage looked up to see Wat rubbing his hands.

'It can't be right.' Hermitage was tempted to lift the parchment and see if the real material was written on the back. No, this had to be it. This great work, one of the greatest, really was all about buying some hawks. The king must really love hawks.

'Sounds right to me,' Wat smiled. 'The king has fifty pounds of silver and he wants some hawks. Lot of money, fifty pounds of silver.'

'But even then he wouldn't go to this trouble. He'd just send word of mouth. Or a hurriedly scribbled note.' He nodded obsequiously toward the parchment. 'This hasn't been hurriedly anything. There's a life's work here for one scribe. There must have been several working day and night to get this done. Surely his hawks aren't that important. This is the sort of thing that's too good to send to the pope!' Hermitage breathed deeply, he was starting to get carried away. That such a thing of beauty could be mired in simple trade was too much. Were the Normans really such heathens? Yes, of course, they were.

'So why did Stigand come to you asking for silver?' Hermitage still saw no reason behind this. 'He had a parchment in his jerkin worth pounds of silver on its own. One straight from the king promising even more money.'

Wat leant back on his hands, looking very content for some reason. 'The king wouldn't give him the fifty pounds, he gave him this instead.' He waved in a very disrespectful manner towards the parchment. 'Stigand obviously has to go and get the hawks and then the money changes hands. Except no sensible Viking is going to hand over one hundred good hawks without being paid. Stigand pays the Vikings, gets the hawks, delivers to the king and takes the silver. Nothing mysterious at all. Your nice bit of parchment just proves the deal is a good one and persuades the Vikings to do business.'

'Nice bit of parchment,' Hermitage sighed and shook his head. 'Please don't talk about this masterpiece like that. And you don't understand. This is too much. It's too much for anyone. It's certainly too much for some hawks, even if they do weigh fifty pounds in silver. It's too much for me, and you know how excited I get over a nice bit of parchment.'

He hadn't impressed Wat or Cwen with his argument. 'I tell you, there is more to this than just fifty pounds of silver.'

'Hermitage,' Wat chided. 'Please don't talk about fifty pounds of silver like that.'

Cwen folded her arms and looked hard at Wat. 'And fifty pounds of silver is a very good whatnot for murder.'

'Whatnot? Hermitage asked.

'Yes, you know, that word you use when someone has a very good reason to kill someone else'

Hermitage thought about it for a moment. 'Motive?'

'That's the one. Good motive for murder, fifty pounds of

silver.'

'I suppose it might be. Unless the man wasn't murdered at all.'

Wat was looking thoughtful, which Hermitage was now starting to take as a very bad sign. 'So following the trail might lead to a killer. If there is one.'

'Following the trail?' Hermitage asked with suspicion. 'Like tracking you mean. Vestigare in Latin, Investigate?'

'What a good idea,' Wat tried to make it sound as if Hermitage had suggested it.

'If it was a natural death then there is nothing to investigate,' he reminded them.

'Of course, of course. But if it wasn't? Seems the best way would be to follow the trail of the silver.'

Hermitage just shook his head at the unnecessary confusion Wat was causing.

Cwen was looking at the weaver with more cunning in her eye. 'Don't tell me. You're now thinking of going into the hawk trade.'

Wat gave a what-can-I-do-about-it shrug. 'The king wants his business done. He will have his hawks, one way or another.'

'And one of the ways would involve you getting his fifty pounds of silver.'

'I can afford a few hawks.'

'From Vikings?' Hermitage sounded as worried as he was.

'It won't be a problem. It's all official business.' Wat nodded towards the parchment. 'And the king knows me from your investigations.'

'I'm not sure that's a good thing,' Hermitage muttered.

'I think we go and find the two big Normans, explain Stigand's little setback and see what we can do.'

'You're mad.' Hermitage said.

'And greedy,' Cwen added. 'Although I suppose Hermitage can give them a thorough going over and see if they look like killers who might have done for Stigand.'

Hermitage just gaped at that.

'Share and share about,' Wat went on. 'After all, Stigand did bring us the parchment and he did claim to be your father. That could be why he came to Derby. He was probably going to look after you if this all came good, not the other way round.'

Cwen bridled at this. She pointed the finger at Wat. 'You be very careful.' She narrowed her eyes in a gaze that would have got her into most snakes' nests. 'How much?' she asked.

'Oh, really,' Hermitage interrupted this bout of competitive avarice. 'I tell you, this parchment is a pool of deep, dark trouble. It may be a marvel of the modern age but it is dangerous.' He hated to say this but knew it was right. 'We should simply get it back to the Normans somehow. Preferably without them knowing it came from us. In fact, we had better get it back into Stigand's jerkin so that they find it themselves. I'm not sure putting parchment into a dead man's jerkin is any better than taking it out but if the Normans find us with it there could be no end of trouble.'

'Oh, Hermitage,' Wat shook his head in disappointment. 'If you want to get ahead in life you have to take some risks.'

'But I don't want to get ahead in life.'

Wat waved such nonsense away. 'Come to think of it, if this parchment is as good and important as you say it is I think the big Normans will come and find us. Far better to have them ask us to get their hawks and take their silver than we go and offer.'

'Is it sensible, baiting Normans? Particularly big ones.'

'Big ones who want some very important hawks it seems.' Then he did something that broke Hermitage's resolve completely. He leant forward, put one finger on the parchment and pushed it across the floor. 'And if we are just going to wait, why don't you look after this.'

Brother Hermitage did start dribbling now.

Caput VII

The Dead Are Never Popular

The street of Derby was once more alive with movement closely connected to Stigand of Arundel. Obviously, it wasn't Stigand doing the moving this time, although Mistress Angel was impatient for something to happen in that regard. She stood at the door of the tavern looking up and down for the return of Ern, hopefully with a cart and some help to get the deceased out of her home.

She had stood there so long that people were starting to look and her impatience with Ern was reaching new heights. A few of the other wives of the town gave her respectful nods as they walked by. The sort of nods that said they were going to start talking about her as soon as they were out of sight.

She was on the verge of going in again when Cnut wandered by very slowly, even for him. His proud parents had named him after the old king but there was no one in Derby less king-like than Cnut. Not unless old King Cnut did some really rather nasty things when he was on his own.

'What do you want Cnut?'

'Oh, nothing, nothing.' Cnut smiled at Mistress Angel. He'd never done that before.

'Really?'

'I hear you've had a bit of bother.'

'Not at all. No trouble here.'

'No dead strangers then?'

She gave him a stern frown. Ern had obviously spent more time blathering to the rest of the town than getting on with the job he was given. At least some things didn't change.

'All being sorted out,' she assured him.

'Ah, yes, yes.' Cnut nodded and surreptitiously glanced up and down the street. 'Can I, erm, can I have a look then?'

Mistress Angel almost fell back into her own tavern. 'Can you what?"

Cnut beckoned her to be quiet. 'Just a quick look. At the stranger. Don't get dead strangers around very often. Especially well to do ones.'

Mistress Angel appraised him with the utmost horror. She thought that her opinion of the man was the very lowest there could be and here it was sinking further. 'You want to have a look at the dead stranger?' She made it clear that such a request was disgusting, disgraceful and beyond belief.

'There's a quarter penny in it.' He held out a grubby hand containing a rough triangle of thin metal.'

'You're not supposed to cut the coins,' she scolded as she took the offering and stepped aside. She too looked cautiously up and down the street to make sure that this transaction had not been spotted. And to see if there was anyone as disreputable as Cnut who might have spare coin. Perhaps this Stigand might continue to pay his way even after he died.

Once Cnut had had his fill he scuttled back into the street, doubtless to spread word further. There was a risk that the reputation of her tavern would suffer as a result of this but as it was the only tavern in town, the damage would be slight.

She took up position out of sight of the street but able to see passers-by and do what she did best; cast judgement upon them. If her opinion was poor enough she would appear in the door and offer a knowing nod. If they had bumped into Cnut or Ern there was a good chance they would approach as well.

Her capacity for the instant appraisal and dismissal of the people of Derby was well-honed but Normans were another barrel of herring altogether. The two large men walking down the street with clear purpose would need careful handling. All Normans needed careful handling but she worried that having a corpse in her house probably meant even more trouble; even though it was the Normans who put most of the corpses in the houses in the first place.

She slid back into the tavern but it was no good. The Normans were heading straight for her.

'Good morrow gentlemen,' she called loudly as she stepped to her door to bar the way. She could only hope that the call had alerted old Ealdred who was still indoors. One of Cnut's closest companions he had already spent more time with dead Stigand than was probably healthy.

The one called Roland simply grunted. 'Stigand?' he asked.

'Aha, Stigand,' Mistress Angel nodded knowingly. 'Been talking to my Ern eh?' She was aware that Normans were strange people with strange ways. No reason they shouldn't be strange in the same way as Cnut and his friends. 'It's a penny.' She held out her hand.

'Penny?' The Norman looked troubled and slightly angry at this. The way his hand rested on his sword made her withdraw hers sharpish.

'But no charge to our Norman friends.' Angel knew which side her bread was not burning to the ground.

The two men brushed her aside and she followed them into the room. 'This way,' she beckoned, her obsequious bow scraping so low she could have cleaned the floor while she was down there.

As they stepped across to the room Ealdred appeared, gave a little squeak and ran for the door. All three of them watched him go with varying levels of surprise.

Taking the Normans to the bedside she held her hand out as if revealing the hobby-horse in a mummer's play.

The Normans looked at the body and then looked at Angel with puzzled expressions. They seemed to be wondering why this strange woman was presenting them with a dead body.

'That not Stigand,' Ralf looked particularly confused and shook his head.

Perhaps they didn't speak the language very well. 'That's right. Not Stigand anymore. Dead now.'

The larger Norman growled and sighed at the same time. 'This is not Stigand. This is the man who sent us to Stigand. We have wandered your town for hours and we end up back where we started. Everyone we ask says Stigand is not here, try somewhere else.' He rested his hand on his sword again, which always did wonders to promote conversation. 'We have now run out of somewhere else and want Stigand.'

'But this is Stigand.' Mistress Angel even looked herself, just to check. She didn't like to contradict Normans but a dead body was a dead body after all. What else was she supposed to say? 'It always has been Stigand. He was staying here, at the tavern. Well, he still is I suppose, but he'll be gone soon.'

'You say this is Stigand?' The Norman was looking very cross indeed now and Angel took half a step back towards the door.

'Of course, my Lord. Stigand of Arundel. That's what he said.'

'He sent us to the weaver. He said Stigand was there.'

'I'm sure I don't know why he'd have done that.' Angel knew perfectly well why he'd have done that if two large

Normans with large Norman swords were looking for him.

'He lied.'

'No! How awful.'

The second Norman, at least the one who spoke less, could contain himself no longer and let out a loud shout. He stepped up to Stigand and took him by the scruff of his neck. He shook the corpse up and down with a vigour that a simple tavern cot was not built to stand. Mistress Angel listened to the cracking noises and then watched in mute horror at the expense as her best cot collapsed into a pile of firewood.

Many words of Norman were thrown at dead Stigand, none of which Angel could understand but none of which sounded very nice. There seemed to be no mention of repair to her broken cot.

Roland grabbed Ralf by the shoulder and half-heartedly tried to pull him away. He spoke some words of his own and eventually, the body was left alone.

The attacker stood back and simply glared while his companion took a much more rational approach. He looked Stigand over and proceeded to search him. Patting up and down and looking inside the jerkin, the man seemed disappointed that he could not find what he was looking for. He reported this fact to his companion who had to be restrained from leaping forward to remonstrate with the deceased once more.

Exchanging looks that were questioning and concerned, the larger of the two eventually reached a conclusion. 'We return to the weaver. Again.' He was grinding his words rather than saying them now.

'Good idea,' Mistress Angel nodded, hoping it would be quickly.

With one last look at Stigand from the more thoughtful of

the Normans, and a swift kick from the other, the two men stomped from the room Mistress Angel bobbing in their wake.

Once at the door she waved them goodbye with a broad smile, partly because they were gone from her tavern but mainly because Wat the Weaver was going to be on the receiving end now. And it was no more than he deserved.

Just as she turned to go back in she felt a tug at her sleeve. Behind her, a woman stood watching the backs of the departing Normans.

'Yes?'

'Stigand?'

Angel frowned. This woman was a stranger, and a rather doubtful one if Angel's powers of instantaneous appraisal were anything to go by. There was nothing of note about her appearance. She looked neither pauper nor princess, but a strange woman in town asking about Stigand was enough to raise doubts on her own. She must be about Stigand's age so was perhaps a companion or relative of some sort. She certainly said the name as if she knew him well.

She had the looks of a working woman about her and those of someone who had travelled far. Her dark grey mottled hair was pulled back into a tight tail and brown eyes were clear and forthright. They did not look well-stocked with patience nor were they prepared to tolerate any nonsense.

'There's no Stigand here.' Angel saw a business-like and down to earth woman of a practical and sensible nature, completely lacking in good humour. There wasn't room for two of them in Derby.

'That's not what I've been told.' The woman's accent was so peculiar as to be almost foreign. It rang a bell somewhere in Angel's mind but she'd already made that up about this new arrival.

'You've been listening to the wrong people then. I told you. There is no one called Stigand living at this house.' Angel didn't like to lie outright, not unless it was absolutely necessary.

The woman moved not an inch.

'You could try at the weaver's workshop. That's where most end up sooner or later.' She nodded in the direction of the departing Normans.

The woman's mouth and eyes pinched as tight as her hair as she considered the suggestion. 'I'll do that. And if I don't find him I'll come back.'

'Please yourself.'

'That I will.' The woman turned and strode off after the Normans, but not fast enough to catch up.

'I'll be here,' Angel muttered. She certainly wasn't going to put up with any in Derby getting the last word over her.

And now a new voice called from down the street. 'Mistress.'

Good heavens above was there to be no rest this morning? Still, it might be another customer for Stigand. She supposed it didn't matter that the body wasn't lying on a bed anymore. And she had to pay for a new one somehow.

She turned a smiling face to the newcomers. When she saw who it was her face made no movement but the smile tried to leave as quickly as possible. 'Oh, God preserve us,' Mistress Angel whimpered.

...

The weavers' workshop was enjoying a moment of relative

calm for a change. Wat had placated Cwen that he would send an apprentice to get word from the moot when they'd decided what to do with Stigand. And no, they wouldn't let anyone put him in the ground until they'd given the body a proper look and Hermitage had had a chance to consider any possible investigation.

She was still determined that Stigand was not going to escape her wrath by dying of his own accord. If someone had done it to him that was fine. She would be angry with them instead. Anyway, two large Normans seemed a good place to start for anyone looking for possible killers.

There was no question of even considering that he might actually have been her father. That was disproved by the fact the man had died. She argued that it was completely ridiculous for anyone to turn up claiming to be someone's father only to die hours later. That sort of thing didn't even happen in made-up stories.

Wat bit his lip on any possible connection between telling Cwen you were her father and being found dead straight afterwards.

Hermitage had simply agreed to anything anyone asked of him in his rush to get to his studies. He was now alone in his small chamber with his parchment. Obviously, it wasn't his parchment, that would be most improper. Rather he was tending it while the rightful owner was located. That he wasn't actually doing anything at all to locate the rightful owner was irrelevant. Here was a parchment and who best to look after it? It was extremely fortunate that this weavers' workshop happened to have a monk on hand for exactly this situation.

Just now the parchment was on the bed and Hermitage was on the floor. Not only did this make examination more comfortable but it seemed right, somehow. Hermitage knew his place and it was at the feet of this marvel.

With peace and quiet to consider the piece, he gazed at it with a look that took in all of it and nothing at the same time. There was too much to accommodate. The overall shape and size and appearance and quality and age. And then the presence; the smell, the touch, the weight, the very fabric. And then there were the words. And words weren't as simple as that. There were letters. And the lines that made up the letters. And the shapes that made up the lines. And the ink that made up the shapes. And the quill that had made them. And where had the goose come from?

He simply sat on the floor and looked. At the back of his mind, he knew that this moment would not last and that he had to make the most of it. Detailed study was ideal of course, but detailed study didn't take in the overall impression. And the overall impression was one of wonder. Once just looking at it was over he would be able to consider it in more depth. Perhaps just another week or so.

The only blot on his horizon, not that there were any blots on the perfect parchment, was that the whole thing was about hawks. Hawks, for goodness sake. No one cared about hawks. Well, a lot of people did, clearly, and most of them seemed to be wandering around Derby at the moment, but surely they weren't the sort of people who also cared about producing great manuscripts. The poor head scribe who was asked to create this treasure must have been horrified when he was given the text. All of his life's training and preparation for some birds.

He considered the work once more, looking for some scintilla of evidence that there was more to this than just hawks. Perhaps the hawks were a symbol of some sort. An image of the soul in flight to paradise perhaps? No, here was a passage about how excellent the hawks would be at slaughtering pigeons.

And money? Surely money should not sully a work such as this. No, this section went on at some length about the silver and how it was promised by the king.

A small thought slithered across the back of his mind like a worm. If this parchment was about something so unimportant as a few hawks, perhaps no one would miss it? Maybe Stigand really had been given proper possession? And he was dead. And who knew who it belonged to now? Cwen? She certainly wouldn't want it as Stigand wasn't her father. Hermitage had better look after it until someone came along and claimed ownership. And if he never told anyone he had it, and swore the others to secrecy, and hid it somewhere devious, and only got it out at night when no one was watching, it might never leave.

He found himself smiling in the closed-off gloom of his chamber and looked with surprise to see his own hand gently stroking the edge of the material.

. . .

Wat was talking to Hartle in the apprentice workshop when Hermitage burst upon him. Their conversation had been quiet and almost secretive as the apprentices busied themselves at their various tasks. The main activity in the large room being the creation of Saint George killing the Dragon and rescuing the maiden.

Two of the apprentices were working on the dye for the various colours that were required while another was sorting through the wool for the appropriate quality of thread. Two more, including Gunnlaug who had the strength for it, were attending to the frame of the work, altering the tension so that the final piece would lay properly. Only the most skilled and advanced were actually putting wool to the work and even then were supervised by Cwen, who was not backwards in offering criticism. There would be much discussion in the dormitory that night about what had put the woman in such a foul mood.

She had been seen chopping wood and the assumption was that Wat was punishing her for something. After all, wood chopping was a punishment for all sorts of things. An alternative assumption was that Cwen was simply demonstrating what she was going to do to Wat if he ever said/did/thought whatever it was that he had done.

A huddle of three boys, the most troublesome, if Hermitage had paid any attention to who they were, sat in one quiet corner considering some alternative designs they had come up with for the maiden. These boys had been with Wat far too long and should really have made their own way in the world by now. If Hermitage could see their suggestions he would throw them out there and then.

'Take it, take it,' Hermitage wailed, thrusting the parchment in a very rough manner into the weaver's hands. 'It is temptation itself.'

'Eh? What?'

'I told you that this thing would be trouble, well it is. I should never have touched it. You hold it until its owner comes.'

'I thought you liked parchment?' Wat looked to Hartle who was no help at all, not having a clue what the monk was talking about most of the time anyway.

'Of course, I like parchment, but not this one.'

Wat looked at the piece as it hung from his hands. He had very little interest 'What's wrong with it?'

'What's wrong with it?' Hermitage saw the question as a revelation. 'That's it. That's it exactly.'

Wat frowned at him. 'I assume you know that you're not making any sense.'

'There's nothing wrong with it.'

'Well, good.'

'No, not good.'

'You're saying there should be something wrong with it.' Wat looked for Hartle once more only to find the old man had slid off to examine some wood shavings in the corner.

'Exactly.'

'There should be something wrong with the parchment? You want a parchment that's faulty.'

'Yes. No. I mean I don't want a faulty parchment, but this should be one. It's only about a bunch of hawks for goodness sake.'

'Lease.'

'What?' Hermitage was thrown off his train of thought.

'Apparently, it's a lease of hawks. If you've got a few of them. Hartle told me, he knows quite a bit about hawks as it happens. It's not a flock, it's a lease.'

'Never mind what their names are. Who goes to this much trouble about hawks? I said the parchment was good enough for the pope and it is. And no one, not even a hawk-mad Norman king would spend this much money on a parchment.'

'But…,'

'Just keep it away from me.'

'Please yourself,' Wat shrugged, which was a bit of a disappointment. 'I wish you'd make your mind up.' He put the parchment back in his jerkin and Hermitage felt a weight lift from his shoulders as it disappeared from sight. 'We'll find out more if and when the Normans turn up.' That didn't make Hermitage feel any better at all.

At that moment the hubbub of the workshop fell to an eerie silence. It was as if all the joy and pleasure of their chosen trade had been sucked from the room. A door onto darkness had opened and light-heartedness had been swamped. Even the apprentices on the receiving end of Cwen's instruction felt their meagre portion of happiness dwindle and die.

One of the younger apprentices, still a child really, let a pitiful whimper into the room as he gazed upon the awful shape of Mrs Grod as she darkened the door. 'It's not time to eat is it?' he pleaded.

Even Wat gave an involuntary start as he was closest to the door and the sight of his cook was the last thing he'd expected.

Mrs Grod surveyed the place as if trying to understand whether she'd come to the wrong room or if the stock in the meat store had started moving about.

'Men,' she grunted and it wasn't at all clear if this was a request, a piece of information or a list of ingredients. 'Big ones,' she added, which didn't make it any clearer.

'Normans?' Wat suggested when he'd regained his composure. One of these days he really must do something about Mrs Grod, but she was such an indomitable force. Perhaps he'd get Cwen to do it.

Mrs Grod just shrugged and shambled from the room. The apprentices sighed.

'Come on then,' Wat rubbed his hands and beckoned to Cwen and Hermitage. 'Let's see what's on offer.'

Hermitage followed with a heavy heart. At least he had resisted the temptation of the parchment and voiced his concerns, not that he ever really expected Wat to take any notice. He had managed to persuade the weaver away from his shocking works. Getting his mind to move on from money was going to be a much harder task.

Caput VIII

Hawks and Weavers

It was indeed the Normans. Roland and Ralf were still big and they still had swords. And they weren't happy. Hermitage had frequently noted that none of the Normans he met were particularly happy, or even moderately so. The king and his direct associates always seemed to be in a terrible frame of mind and he wondered why they didn't do something about it. The answer seemed obvious to him but he felt it wasn't really his place to suggest that if they found their current circumstances such a trial they might like to go home.

Somehow he couldn't imagine them being happy anywhere. Their Norman home and hearth, presumably back in Normandy somewhere, was doubtless a dour place full of misery and complaint. He had visited Normandy once, at the king's behest of course, and actually found the ordinary people quite a jolly bunch.[6]

Perhaps it was just the ones who went abroad that fell to melancholy and despair. And perhaps that was because they kept killing people. It could be that their misery was their curse; the one they got for murdering most of the people they came across. He was positive that killing yet more people wasn't going to cheer them up, but you couldn't tell a Norman anything. And these two looked ready to plunge themselves deeper into their miserable state.

---

[6] He did. It's in Hermitage, Wat and Some Murder or Other. It's quite good.

Roland even proved the point by drawing his sword and pointing it at Wat, who was still smiling at them as he stood in the frame of his front door.

'Stigand is dead.' It sounded like an accusation.

'Really?' Wat did surprise very well. 'Gosh. Dead eh? Well, I never. He was all right when he left here.'

'And it turns out it was Stigand who told us to come here looking for Stigand.'

'That seems a strange thing to do,' Wat looked thoroughly confused.

Roland put a halt to further discussion as he barged forward, pushed Wat ahead of him and walked into the workshop as if he owned it. Which he could, of course, if he went and got some miserable Norman friends to help.

'And you, and you.' The Norman waved at Hermitage and Cwen who were trying to keep out of the way. 'You're always together, you come too.'

Hermitage's sinking feeling, which he always kept close at hand should it be called upon, was now called upon. And it performed admirably. His knees made gyrations of their own as he tried to follow the Normans.

Cwen's piercing gaze was firmly attached to the big men. It was clear that if she got any inkling that they had killed Stigand, they were very quickly going to regret being Norman.

Roland drove Wat backwards into the kitchen area. The kitchen area occupied by Mrs Grod.

The woman turned at this disturbance to her preparations and gave the Normans such a look of frank disbelief that anyone would even think of coming into her kitchen when she was cooking, that they stopped.

'Not here,' Roland concluded. He was confident about this

although something in his face said that he didn't know why he wanted to leave the room, just that he did.

'We can take wine in the chamber upstairs,' Wat offered, his smile never wavering. 'I might have some better stuff somewhere.'

A Norman grunt signalled acquiescence and the weaver led the merry troop up to the main business chamber. Asking Mrs Grod to bring wine was an entirely hopeless task so Hermitage offered to fetch it.

A few moments later he joined the group in the upper room and found a picture of grim silence. It looked as if they were waiting for the wine to join them before the conversation could start. Wine often had the effect of starting conversations but a lot of them ended quite badly. The greater the wine, the worse the conclusion.

Hermitage handed the mugs around and the Normans drank deeply. Roland still had his sword out and used it to make quite a dent in Wat's wooden floor.

Taking the empty flagon from his mouth, he wiped his lips on the back of his sleeve and belched. 'Not much better,' he summarised the drink. 'Where is it?'

Wat looked around the room as if the man was speaking to someone else. It was obvious that he didn't have anything at all so the question can't have been directed at him.

'Come. Where is it?'

'Where's what?' Wat really did sound completely confused. It was a very good act.

'The parchment.'

'Parchment?'

'Weaver,' Roland leaned forward on his sword and made "weaver" sound like the sort of detritus you got on your sword after doing something particularly gruesome. 'Stigand had a parchment. He saw you, now he does not have a parchment. The parchment is here.'

Hermitage thought that this was a very good argument but it missed the point that Stigand may have been to lots of places and any of them could have the parchment. Except, of course, Wat did have the parchment.

Hermitage could see that Wat was very rapidly assessing his options. It took less than a moment, a moment that the Normans had probably missed completely.

'Oh, the parchment,' Wat sounded hugely relieved that he now knew what they were talking about. And of course, the parchment was not a problem at all. 'Yes, he left me a parchment. Safe-keeping he said. And if he's dead like you say, seems like it was for the best.' He fished into his jerkin and produced the parchment which he happily handed over.

Both Normans looked hugely relieved at this. They even gabbled away to one another with quite some animation as they opened and appraised the document.

After a suitable pause, Wat spoke again. 'Brother Hermitage here says it's quite a good one.'

Hermitage tried a smile as the Normans turned in his direction. They frowned, obviously wondering why the idiot monk was grinning at them.

'Of course,' Roland confirmed, 'King William's charter would be the best.'

Wat nodded, deeply impressed. 'For the hawks, I gather.'

Roland looked very suspicious now, as if Wat were a hawk-eating weaver.

'Yes, for the hawks. Why do you ask?'

'No reason. No reason at all. Just idle curiosity. I expect you will want to take your charter back to King William. Do give him our best, won't you? Brother Hermitage, Wat the

Weaver.'

'And Cwen,' Cwen added.

Hermitage wished Wat hadn't done that.

'You know the king?'

'Oh, yes,' Wat leant back in his chair as if discussing his oldest drinking companion from Ern and Angel's tavern. 'We have regular contact with his majesty and my lord Le Pedvin.'

Hermitage really wished he hadn't mentioned that awful man. Hermitage might be King William's investigator but it seemed to be Le Pedvin who gave out all the really awful jobs.

The Normans had another low exchange in their own language.

'And of course, he is very keen on hawks,' Wat nodded. 'But then, who isn't?'

Roland gave him a very deep frown now. 'Last time we were here you behaved like you didn't know what a hawk was. Now we find you with this parchment and talking about hawks.' Roland started turning his sword from side to side, drilling a nice hole in Wat's floor.

'Ah, well,' Wat held his hand out in surrender. 'Not all Normans who come visiting are as reasonable as you. You might have got the wrong idea.'

'Oh, I've got lots of ideas,' Roland said with a grim smile.

'Of course, Hartle is the real hawk-man,' Wat said, brightly.

'Hawk-man?'

'Falconer,' Hermitage corrected.

'That's the one. I don't have the time for all the details myself but there's nothing quite like being out there in the field with a hawk on your erm,'

'Arm.' Hermitage said.

'I know. Arm.'

'I see.' Roland looked thoughtful, which was an improvement on deadly. 'And you have read the whole parchment?'

'I have. We have,' Wat nodded his thanks to Hermitage, who didn't want them.

'So you know that King William wants to trade for hawks.'

'We do. And quite a lot of them.'

'And Stigand had promised to get them for him.'

'But now he's dead,' Wat sounded very sorry about this.

'He is.'

'We, erm, thought that perhaps you might have erm, you know?' Wat nodded towards the sword.

Roland looked at it himself as if seeing it for the first time. 'What? Killed Stigand? Why would we do that?'

'Oh, you know, Normans, swords, dead bodies. Just seems to happen quite a lot.'

'He was getting the hawks. Why would we kill him?'

'Why indeed?' Cwen asked.

Hermitage had a question. He should keep it to himself, really he should. There had been a lot of questions in his young life that he should have kept to himself. He no longer had any of them. They'd all escaped. Just like this one. 'Are the hawks overdue then?'

The Normans looked confused. Perhaps by the question, perhaps by a monk.

'Are they late?' he spelt out very clearly. 'Is that why you're here? Stigand is late with the hawks?'

Yet another short conversation in Norman French. 'Exactly. The hawks are late. Stigand is late. They both are late. Arrangements for these hawks were made weeks ago and should have been completed by now. We've been sent to find Stigand to see what is going on.'

'But you didn't know what he looked like?' Wat asked, clearly thinking that looking for someone when you didn't know what they look like was a pretty stupid thing to try and do.

'How many people called Stigand are there looking for hawks?'

'Good point.'

'And now Stigand's dead,' Cwen pointed out. 'Not going to get any hawks, being dead.' She looked at everyone in the room, slowly and carefully. 'What if someone didn't want the king to get his hawks eh? What about that?'

'What about it?'

'Someone else might have killed him just to stop the king getting the hawks.'

The Normans gave one another blank looks. 'They're only birds.'

'Exactly,' Wat said, brightly. 'And birds that must be got eh? Can't have the king not getting the hawks he wants.'

Roland now considered Wat as if he ate Normans once he'd finished off the hawks. He held his sword a little closer as if worried that Wat was going to steal it. 'So now you say you can get hawks?' He even stood to give his suspicion more weight. And height.

'Me?' Wat sounded very surprised. 'Me, get hawks? Good heavens what a thought. Me get hawks eh?' He smiled broadly at Cwen and Hermitage to get them to join in this marvellous joke. Neither of them smiled. Now he sounded as if he had been brow-beaten for hours and reluctantly agreed to help an old lady with her pile of kindling. 'I suppose I could. If I had to.'

Roland smiled horribly. 'You have to. You know Stigand, you know about hawks, you can get them now.'

'Hartle's your man, as I say. Well, he's my man, but he knows all there is to know about hawks.'

Hermitage seriously doubted that this was the case and scowled at Wat.

'Where will you get these hawks?' Roland was testing Wat's knowledge.

'Me? Ah, well, if it was me getting hawks for the king obviously I'd want chicks.' He nodded without looking at anyone, assuming that so much was blindingly obvious. He went on to talk to himself as if he was the world's foremost expert on hawk chicks. 'Let's think now, hawk chicks, some white, that sort of numbers, who'd be best? Normally I might think of old Bleddyn the hawk merchant up Chester way but I'm not sure he could handle an order of that size. Might be good for a dozen or so.' He pondered on, much to Cwen's contemptuous impatience and Hermitage's horrified disappointment at such blatant lies.

'Only one place for it,' Wat announced after much brow-furrowing. 'It's risky though. Not easy people to deal with.'

'Who?'

'The Danes,' Wat announced, quickly. 'There. I've said it. If you want to go elsewhere that's absolutely fine and I won't shed a tear. But if you wanted me to get that many hawks for the king, I'd have to go to Denmark. Take it or leave it.' He folded his arms.

Hermitage was absolutely horrified. Wat's behaviour had gone from bad to worse and now it was residing wherever things went when worse wasn't bad enough. He knew what Wat was going to say, "It's only business". If lying, deceiving and cheating was business then he was going to have to sort that out as well as weaving.

'The Danes, eh?' Roland said "Danes" as if it were what fell from the sky when a hawk with a bad stomach flew over. He did look impressed with Wat's clear and expert reasoning concerning the supply of hawks and smiled at Ralf.

'And you have the silver?'

'Ooh,' Wat sucked breath through his teeth. 'That is a bit more difficult.'

No, it isn't, thought Hermitage, that's the easy bit.

'If you are to get the king's hawks you must have the silver.' Roland sounded a bit cross about this and perhaps ready to walk away.

'Don't worry about the silver. I know where I can put my hands on it.'

The Normans seemed content with this complete fabrication and Hermitage could only hang his head. At least his urge to warn them loudly that they were being duped was only slight. Wat was his friend after all. A friend who was going to get a very long talking to. Honestly. The traders in the temple weren't as bad as this.

'Excellent.' Wat stood and raised his mug to drink to hawk chicks, about which he knew nothing yesterday. The Normans had their drinks refilled and barked some sort of Norman cheer. Either that or they were choking on the wine. 'Still take a few days to sort out though. What with the silver and the Danes and the hawks and so forth.'

The Normans nodded that they were content with this. 'We stay,' Ralf smiled happily.

'Stay?' Wat wasn't so happy.

'Of course. We let Stigand out of our sight and he took weeks to do nothing, now he's dead. This time we stay.' Roland explained.

'Aha, stay, yes of course. Not a problem.'

'If I might ask?' Hermitage had to go again. Wat was giving him some very fierce looks.

'Yes?'

'Why don't you get the hawks yourself? If the king wants them and Stigand was going to get them why were you following Stigand? Why don't you simply go and get the hawks yourself?' He thought it was a very reasonable question and one that absolutely needed to be answered. From the look on Wat's face, he did not share this opinion.

The Normans seemed to find the suggestion very funny indeed. 'Us?' they laughed heartily.

'Yes.'

'We don't do business with Danes,' Roland guffawed at such a ridiculous idea. 'We kill Danes. They do not sell hawks if you kill them.' There was much back-slapping and happy reminiscence at this, probably at the death of some Danes.

'Aha,' Hermitage gave his best pretence of understanding any of this. He did cast a look at Wat that he hoped hit home. 'But we all know Danes don't kill Saxons, do they?'

. . .

'What are you doing?' Hermitage demanded after the Normans had been found accommodation at the back of the workshop - as far away from everyone as possible so as not to scare the apprentices or alert Mrs Grod. He felt positively testy at Wat's behaviour. The weaver seemed to be in thrall to the thought of the silver. It was as if his senses had left him and Hermitage was going to have to find them again.

'What?' Wat asked as if nothing in the world were amiss. They had returned to the upper chamber and the weaver drank from a fresh mug of wine as he looked at some drawings one of the apprentices had brought him. Cwen was peering over his shoulder, her familiar scowl resting lightly on her face.

'Deceiving Normans is what. All that nonsense about hawks and Hartle and Bleddyn of Chester.'

'It's not nonsense. I do know a lot about hawks. All I learnt from Stigand and Hartle.'

'Which was only a few hours ago and was from a man who didn't know anything about them himself.'

'Hartle does though. He's a bit keen on hawks. And I never knew that. Amazing what you find out, isn't it? He'll be just the man to go to Denmark and get the birds. Perfect. I don't have to go and find anyone. And there is a merchant called Bleddyn in Chester.'

'Really?'

'Yes. Wool.'

'A wool merchant.'

'That's right. But he's Welsh. Hardly likely to bump into the Normans and mention me I'd have thought.'

'And you'll really send old Hartle on his own to Denmark, the home of the Vikings to get some birds?'

'Not on his own. I'll send Gunnlaug with him, they'll be fine.'

'The same Gunnlaug who turned white when Cwen shouted at him?'

Cwen gave a hollow laugh at the giant apprentice's feebleness.

'Don't worry about this, Hermitage. It's all just business.'

'Ha!'

'Ha, what?'

'I knew you'd say that. As if calling it business makes

everything all right.'

'Well, it is. And it does. This is how business works. You trade. You buy and you sell and you travel. After all, if I hadn't been travelling in my trade I wouldn't have found you being beaten to death by some robbers, would I?'[7]

Hermitage did look at the floor thinking that although Wat was right, there was bound to be some withering response that would put him in his place. He would think of it in an hour or so.

'And the further you travel the more you tend to make. If the Danes have lots of hawks that's where we get them from. Chicks will go cheap in Denmark and then we can sell them here for much more. There's bound to be someone else doing it already. It's probably a well-trodden trade route. Where do you think hawks usually come from?'

'But you lied. You lied that you knew about hawks. You made them believe you thought of Denmark on your own when you only heard about it from Stigand and you lied that Hartle is your hawk man.'

'He is now. And when he sees the big bag of silver he'll be off for Denmark before you can say "Viking."'

'You talk to him,' Hermitage instructed Cwen. Even his excessive supply of patience was running low.

'It could lead to our killer,' she thought out loud. 'If someone did do for Stigand to get at the silver.' She raised a finger as the idea took hold. 'If his hawk supplier knows that there are fifty pounds of silver in it why take less? Why sell to Stigand for twenty when you could get all fifty? An extra thirty pieces of silver is enough motive for murder.'

'It certainly is,' Hermitage said loud and clear. Neither

---

[7] The Heretics of De'Ath, where all this nonsense began. Who was to know, eh?

Wat nor Cwen got the reference. They were too busy in their own worlds.

'So, if we take over and go to get the hawks..,' Wat sounded as if he were already counting the silver.

"This supposed killer may kill us as well?' Cwen suggested.

'No. There's three of us, there was only one of Stigand. I'll admit these Normans don't seem to want Stigand dead so perhaps it's the next person up the line.'

Hermitage saw that their passions were getting in the way of common sense. 'You just said you were going to send Hartle. How's he going to cope with a murdering poisoner?'

'Hm,' Wat did give some pause at this. 'Could be that we all need to go after all. Don't know how Hartle's going to carry a hundred hawks anyway. How big are hawk chicks?'

'You tell me,' Hermitage did have his riposte ready this time. 'You're the hawk expert.' He knew very well what things getting out of hand felt like. And it felt like this. Cwen seemed obsessed with the murderer and Wat with money. They were both happy arguing that there was a killer involved in this somewhere and then happy to go chasing after him. 'And we have to take the Normans with us. Not much chance of finding anything out with them around. People will run a mile.'

'Doesn't sound like they want to go to Denmark though,' Wat noted. 'Which is a bit odd considering that they're all Norsemen anyway.'

'I really can't see that either of you is thinking this through. Wat, you don't actually need another thirty pounds of silver, do you?'

Wat looked at Hermitage as if the monk had just taken his immortal soul out of his body, laid it on a table and insulted it.

'In fact, nobody needs thirty pounds of silver at all.'

Wat found his voice. 'Hermitage, if you are going to talk nonsense there's no point talking at all.'

'And Cwen. It could well be that Stigand simply died. It is a coincidence and a strange circumstance but these things happen. Our lives would be far calmer, less troublesome and dangerous and just more manageable if we gave all this up.'

Wat shook his head this time. 'Who wants a life like that? A monk might do. And we've got the Normans expecting their hawks now. We have to see it through.'

Hermitage dropped himself into a chair and just looked at them both with his best disappointed face.

'And you never know,' Wat sounded cheery. 'We might get a big bucket of silver and find a killer. That'll be good, won't it?'

Hermitage was running out of the strength to argue his case. He would just have to wait until the next disaster befell them and start again. He had a very strong suspicion that such a disaster was not far away at all.

'Hello?' a voice called from below, a female voice and a strange one.

Hermitage raised an eyebrow. Female visitors to the workshop were few and far between.

Wat wiped a hand over his face. 'Who have I upset now?'

Cwen seemed frozen to the spot at the sound of the voice. Her eyes had widened and her fists had clenched. Perhaps some woman coming to complain about the workshop was the last thing she could deal with just at the moment. Hermitage was about to ask her if she was all right when Wat called down in a disinterested manner. 'Up here.' He stood to greet the arrival. 'No point letting Mrs Grod deal with her,' he shrugged to the others. 'That really can cause trouble.'

A face appeared at the top of the steps, the hair still pulled tight back as it had been at the tavern. The woman had obviously followed Mistress Angel's directions very promptly.

'Ah,' she said, as she appraised the three of them, focussing most intently on Cwen. 'I wondered if I might find you here.'

Hermitage looked to Cwen who was still stiff and unresponsive.

'What can I do for you, mistress?' Wat sounded rather bored.

Cwen did now step forward and put an arm across Wat's chest, pushing him out of the way. She squared up to the woman and looked her firmly in the eye.

'What are you doing here, mother?'

Caput IX

Family!

Hermitage looked from one woman to the other and could see some similarities. He supposed that it was possible that this new arrival was Cwen's mother. Of course, the fact that Cwen had called her mother was a helpful clue. He felt a tug on his sleeve as Wat gently guided him away from the encounter.

'Just think,' he whispered in Hermitage's ear. 'Cwen and Cwen senior.'

Hermitage saw the point and took an extra step back.

'Quite the family reunion.' Wat fell silent at Cwen's glance.

'I've come looking.' Cwen the elder replied, with a stare that matched her daughter's.

'Looking for what?' Cwen demanded.

'Your father.'

That did break Cwen's trance. 'My father?'

'Your father.'

'What do you want him for? You never bothered the rest of my life. Why now all of a sudden?'

'Quite simple really. I'm going to kill him.'

Hermitage's urge to step forward and offer the very latest pertinent information on this topic was controlled by the natural reluctance to step between their Cwen and an older, more experienced version.

'Kill him?' Cwen scoffed. 'What, put a knife in him, or a sword or beat him to death. Really? Actual murder?'

Hermitage was pleased that some of his teaching was working.

'Well,' mother Cwen dropped her eyes. 'Perhaps not actually kill him but he'll wish he was dead.'

Definitely Cwen's mother then.

'And why after all these years do you want to kill him now? And why here?'

'Because this is where I heard he'd come.'

'And you followed? We must be a hundred miles from Arundel. You told me there were devils in the next the valley and I'd be captured and burned in hell if I so much as went five miles.'

'You were only a baby.'

Hermitage was starting to see where Cwen got it from. Quite a lot of it, anyway.

'And you expect me to believe you have just tramped half the length of the country because you've suddenly got a bit annoyed with him? Why the interest? You never even told me who he was. Now you turn up in my house asking for him?'

'Your house?'

'Yes. The place I live.'

'With Wat the Weaver?'

'At least I chose to be here. I didn't get sold to Briston, who was twice as bad if you're at all interested.'

The woman now looked to Hermitage and Wat. 'I gave her a chance no other women get and this is all my thanks?'

Hermitage and Wat both looked back trying to make it very clear that they wanted absolutely nothing to do with this.

'Gratitude?' Cwen shrieked a bit. 'You want gratitude. From me? It's you should be thankful. All those years of work I did for you and what did I get? Sold off to the first passing weaver who offered you a week's wage. What sort of mother does that?' Cwen threw the question at the two men who did their level best to avoid it. A few non-committal shrugs and sympathetic yet hopeless looks seemed to do the trick.

'And you turn up here asking where my father is. How would I know? He could walk right by me and I wouldn't recognise him. Any stranger could turn up claiming to be my father and I'd have to say, "sorry, I don't think we've been introduced". Call yourself a mother.'

'Typical. It's all about you, isn't it.'

Hermitage did step forward now. He had the strong feeling that this conversation, if conversation it was, could get very heated and go on for a very long time. And the two women were between him and the stairs. If he didn't make a move for escape now he could be here for hours.

'Ladies,' he said, instantly realising that it was entirely the wrong word but not being able to think what the right one would be.

They both turned to him and he felt the full force of the glare of two Cwens. 'What?' they both snapped.

'Perhaps we should get comfortable. Some wine? While we sort out what's what?'

'She's not staying,' Cwen instructed.

'I wouldn't stay here. Not if you paid me.'

'Yes you would,' Cwen bit back. 'There's lots you'd do if you were paid.'

His awful foreboding came to pass as Hermitage found himself between the two women, literally between them. He wasn't sure if Cwen had gone for her mother first or vice versa. It didn't matter really, they were both reaching around and somehow through him to get at one another.

Thankfully, Wat stepped up at this moment and put his

arms around Cwen lifting her back from the fray. Hermitage had to rely on the fact that he was a monk, and women shouldn't hit monks, for his protection from the mother.

'I really think,' Wat got out between kicks on his shins from the struggling Cwen, 'that we need to answer some questions and then get on with our lives. I'd rather I didn't lose mine up here in the next five minutes.'

'Quite so,' Hermitage agreed, loudly. 'Mistress? What shall I call you?'

'I'll tell you what you can call her,' Cwen called out from her captivity.

'Eadgyth,' the woman replied, ignoring the fact that her daughter was squirming to get at her and inflict something pretty personal.

'Mistress Eadgyth. Shall we just deal with the matter in hand and then we can go our separate ways?'

'Suits me.'

'Cwen?'

Cwen growled back.

'It does seem to me that you can both gain from this. Cwen, you have a chance to find out about your father.' This got an incoherent noise from Cwen. 'Regardless of the rights and wrongs of the situation,' he added, hurriedly. 'And Mistress Eadgyth, you may have your questions addressed, even if the answer is not to your liking.'

Eadgyth gave a bored shrug.

Wat had a further proposal 'And if you try to kill one another we'll throw you down the stairs and let you get on with it.'

Hermitage fetched a chair and put it at the top of the stairs indicating that Eadgyth should take this.

Wat carried Cwen to the other end of the room and

deposited her in a seat, pointing a finger to indicate that she should stay there. Remarkably, she did so.

Wat stood between the protagonists as if about to start a cockfight. 'Now then. Mistress Eadgyth, you say you're looking for Cwen's father.'

'Ask her why.' It seemed that Cwen was not going to speak directly to her mother, which Hermitage thought was good progress.

'It is a reasonable question. Why are you looking for him?'

'Tell her that's my business.'

Without coming to any agreement it seemed that Eadgyth would talk to Hermitage who would relay messages to Wat who could then pass them to Cwen. Any replies would take the reverse route. And all of them sitting in the same small room anyway.

'She says that's her business,' Wat reported.

'Not going to find anything out then, is she?'

Eadgyth gave a heavy sigh as if generously helping out despite having no cooperation. 'I've heard that he's got some business with the king. Well rewarded business.'

'Aha,' Cwen crowed. 'So suddenly, after years of complete silence, why does she dearly want to find my father? Because he might have some money. Doing profitable trade without her getting her grubby hands on it.' She did speak to Eadgyth directly now. 'Maybe if I'd paid you all those years ago you'd have told me his name?'

'If he has money he needs to look after his family. He didn't have any before. Now he does.'

'Look after you, you mean. If I hadn't happened to be here I wouldn't have heard a word about this.' At least they were both talking to one another now. Not that it would be safe for Wat or Hermitage to leave the chamber. He had seen what damage one Cwen could do to a room. Two didn't bear thinking about.

'I just followed his trail to Derby. The innkeeper's cleaning woman told me to come up here and so I did. I knew she was with weavers.' Eadgyth nodded her head towards her daughter. 'So I thought she could be here.'

'She knew I was with Briston because that's who she sold me to. And who would be next after Briston? Wat the Weaver, who else? And still, you had the effrontery to come up here.'

'Only going where I was told.'

'And who is this father of mine?' Cwen asked. 'Are you going to tell me now? Now that there might be some money in it for you. Perhaps now I can afford it I can pay you.'

Eadgyth's eyes narrowed at this.

'Yes,' Cwen hammered home her advantage. 'I have money. From my weaving. If I throw you a shilling or two you'll tell me who my father is.'

Hermitage could tell that Cwen was upset now. Not just angry, that wasn't unusual, but upset that she had already worked out Stigand really was her father. His claim had been true and now he was dead. How would she manage when she heard it from her mother's lips?

'Of course, I'll tell you. I don't want your silver.'

Hermitage could also tell that Eadgyth did want Cwen's silver. He was quite pleased that he was picking up what was going on here.

'His name's Stigand.'

'Stigand,' Cwen managed to get out, without her voice breaking. 'Big help.'

'Stigand of Worthing.'

'Worthing?' Cwen managed to contain the surprise in her

voice. 'Not Stigand of Arundel then? I haven't even got a father from my own town?'

'Of course not Stigand of Arundel. I don't know any Stigand of Arundel. My Stigand was a fine merchant from far off Worthing.'

'So fine he cleared off completely. Unless you drove him out of course.' Cwen now calmed considerably and sat back with a very knowing smile. 'That's it, isn't it?'

'Don't know what you're talking about.'

'Yes, you do. You sent this Stigand on his way all those years ago and now he's rich you want him back. Did he even know I existed?'

'How can I know what he knew? I'm not a witch.'

'I wouldn't be so sure. And if you do find him and kill him he's not going to be able to give you anything, is he? Stupid woman.'

'Don't you call me stupid, you impudent brat.'

'Mistress Eadgyth,' Hermitage reprimanded. 'Cwen. Please. Let's just conclude the discussion, shall we?' He wasn't going to say anything about Stigand or hawks or silver. He was usually a trusting fellow but something about Mistress Eadgyth gave him pause. He glanced at Wat to make sure he would leave Cwen to decide what information should be revealed.

Wat was regarding Mistress Eadgyth as he did the tricksters in the town who tried to sell you genuine dragon eggs.

'Well, you are stupid. Traipsing all the way across the country on the off chance that someone you knew years ago might have some money. And that that person might even dream for a moment of giving you any.'

'Just tell me where he is.'

'Even more stupid. I don't know, do I? Knowing where my father is could be quite handy you know. I could meet him. Talk to him. Do all the things that children usually do with their fathers. Except in my case, it's too late. Until a moment ago I didn't even know his name.

'I have never met Stigand of Worthing, I have never seen Stigand of Worthing and no one of that name has even been talked about in Derby. Perhaps you've just wasted weeks of your life. At least you've wasted less than an hour of mine.'

'Why did the washerwoman send me up here then?' Eadgyth did look a bit frustrated at this news.

'First of all, she's not a washerwoman; that's Mistress Angel and she owns the tavern. Typical of you to get that wrong. Second, she sends everyone up here because she hates Wat. Anyone who looks like trouble of any sort gets sent straight to the weavers' workshop. And you must admit,' Cwen cast a very disparaging look at Eadgyth's appearance. 'You do look a state.'

Eadgyth stood. 'I did not come here to be insulted.'

'Your usual place couldn't fit you in?'

'Is this true?' Eadgyth turned her attention to Wat and Hermitage.

'What's that then?' Wat asked as if he'd been in another room all this time.

'There's no Stigand?'

Wat shook his head. 'Mistress, I can honestly tell you that Stigand of Worthing is a complete stranger and we hadn't even heard the name until you mentioned it.'

'Why did all the talk on the road say that he was coming to Derby then?' she demanded.

'It's a big place. He could be anywhere. Have you looked?'

'Have I...?' Mistress Eadgyth's anger focussed itself on her finger which she raised and pointed at Wat. It was exactly the same mannerism as Cwen. 'I shall go back to the town and if I find I've been led astray.'

'Oh, wouldn't that be shocking,' Cwen mocked. 'Just imagine, being led astray. Almost like someone not knowing their father's name!'

Eadgyth stood and headed for the stairs, which Hermitage found to be a huge relief. He had no idea where things were going to go from here but was sure it wouldn't be long before Eadgyth discovered that there was a Stigand in Derby and that he was already dead. Yes, he was now calling himself Stigand of Arundel but that was surely yet another deceit in this sorry saga.

He could only imagine that it would lead to more trouble. What he couldn't imagine was what even more trouble than this would look like.

'I hope you find him,' Cwen shouted. 'And I hope he's got no money at all or is already dead.'

'You always did have a wicked tongue, my girl.'

'Your girl?' Cwen followed Eadgyth as the older woman took to the stairs. Wat made sure he stayed between the two of them. 'If I ever do find my father my dearest hope is that he'll tell me one thing.'

'And what's that?'

'That you're not my mother.'

Mistress Eadgyth had made it to the door now and the gathering seeing her off was standing at the foot of the stairs.

Ranged down the corridor to the kitchen was the rest of the workshop. Hartle and the apprentices, obviously disturbed or intrigued by the noise, had left their work to come and see what on earth was going on.

'I knew you'd come to a sorry end,' Mistress Eadgyth threw

back from the door, aiming a lot of it at Wat and his workshop.

'A sorry end? In my seventeen years I've made more of my life than you have in, what would it be, fifty, by the look of you.'

This insult brought an appreciative "oooh" from the massed apprentices.

'Seventeen?' Mistress Eadgyth sounded surprised and mocking at the same time. 'And the rest.'

'Rest?' Cwen's livid and pulsing anger suddenly went very quiet, which really scared Hermitage.

'Who told you you're seventeen? You're twenty if you're a day. Never could count.' with that Mistress Eadgyth stepped smartly down the path.

The apprentices looked on in stunned silence.

'I'll kill her,' Cwen absolutely screamed as Wat held her once again and took the brunt of her thrashing. Despite the obvious discomfort Hermitage was sure he could see a faint smile on Wat's face.

Once Eadgyth was out of sight Wat felt safe enough to release Cwen. She glared at each of them and turned to go back up the stairs, her face a picture of something not very nice at all. She looked at the apprentices. 'Get back to work,' she said, rather like a wolf growling at a flock of lame ducklings.

They went.

. . .

There was nothing for Cwen now but containment. Giving her an axe to vent her fury would have been asking for the entire workshop to be reduced to kindling.

At times they let her wander the upper chamber, like some

dangerous animal that has got into the house and you hope will eventually jump out of the window. At other times Wat fended her away from the more fragile pieces of furniture, like a sheepdog with a crazed and dangerous fox. Occasionally he jumped to sit in a seat that she looked like she was about to punish.

Eventually, she calmed to some sort of exhausted goat that has stunned itself by butting its head against too many trees. She breathed very deeply and very loudly and was biting her lip most cruelly. After a while, odd words emerged. They didn't make any sense on their own but sounded like escapees from some internal monologue that wasn't going well for Mistress Eadgyth.

"That woman. How. And I never," were finally joined by a prolonged "arrgh" which seemed to be a release of some sort.

Cwen now turned to Wat and Hermitage with a relatively calm and resolute look on her face. The resolution did not look like a good one.

'Well. At least we now know who killed Stigand.'

'Er, We do?' If they did, Hermitage hadn't got it.

'She did, of course.'

'Eadgyth?'

'Of course Eadgyth. She came to kill him and now he's dead.'

'If it's the same person.'

Cwen was not taking questions well. 'Of course, it's the same person. How many Stigands would be wandering the country with that dung slopper's bed wife after them? Arundel, Worthing? They aren't that far apart. Perhaps he's changed his name? I would if I was married to her. Anyway, who cares! She's killed my father, Hermitage. The father I had only just met has now been killed by my own mother.'

Hermitage thought about reminding Cwen of her confidence that Stigand was not, in fact, her father. He thought that something completely different might be best. 'But she seems to want him for his money. As you said, she can't get any if he's dead.'

Cwen sighed her impatience at such stupidity. 'It's all a ruse, obviously. She came asking for money, found Stigand, he said no and so she killed him. Simple.'

'Surely she would just run back to Arundel if she had committed murder?'

'Not if she was on the verge of getting a share of fifty pounds of silver. She'd stay and pretend she knew nothing about any death. She's devious like that, you've seen.' Cwen's eyes widened indicating the arrival of some great idea. She held up a finger and used it to emphasise every word of her great new concept. 'And she's throwing us off the track.'

'What track?' Wat asked.

'Hermitage's track.'

'My track?'

'You're always saying how you come from a vestigarhay.'

'Erm,' Hermitage had to follow this train of thought slowly and carefully to try and see where Cwen was taking it. He came from a small village but it certainly was called A Vestigharhay. That really would be a coincidence, him being investigator and all. Aha. 'The Latin vestigare? Hence investigate?'

'That's it. Except what do you say vestigare means?'

'To track.' Now he got it. 'Except I don't say that's what it means, that is what it means.'

'And that's what she's doing.' Cwen actually hopped slightly at her next idea. 'She probably knows you're the King's Investigator. She realises that the King's Investigator is here and is going to get her for killing Stigand. Not only does she try to keep one hand on the silver by staying here instead of running, she's probably covering her tracks as well.'

'She's covering them now?'

'Of course. That's what people do isn't it, cover their tracks? Hunters and the like.'

'I suppose so.' Hermitage had not a clue what hunters and the like did.

'She says she asked Mistress Angel but how do we know it's not all lies. Covering her tracks, see? And she needs to wait so that when Stigand's silver turns up she can claim it as his loving wife. She's very good at lying. She's had years of practice.'

Hermitage thought he heard Wat mutter "at least twenty of them" but he could have been mistaken.

'What do you suggest then?' Wat asked. 'What do you want us to do with your mother? Report her straight to the moot? Chase her out of town?'

Cwen considered them both with a very calculating look. A look that made Hermitage's skin tingle.

'We investigate and don't get thrown off any tracks. We do what we do best. We investigate thoroughly.' She frowned as she brought the necessary steps to mind. 'We uncover evidence, we consider facts and possibilities and then we carefully analyse all the information before reaching our conclusion. Isn't that right, Hermitage?'

'Absolutely.' Hermitage was very pleased that she had really taken all this in.

Cwen nodded. 'The conclusion that she did it.'

'Ah, now,' Hermitage had to speak up. 'What if she didn't?' He still thought it unlikely that a killer would wait around and then go asking after their victim.

'She did. It's just the sort of thing she'd do.'

'But when you asked her, quite properly, if she would really go so far as actually killing someone with knife or sword or blow, she said no.'

'She would, wouldn't she? Particularly if she'd already poisoned him anyway. No need for a blade of any sort.'

Hermitage frowned quite deeply. He wanted to do the best for his friend but could see that it was simply Cwen's wishful thinking that her mother was a killer. Obviously, such a finding would cheer her enormously and Eadgyth did not seem the most charming of people. Her motivations were fundamentally suspect but there was no evidence of any murder at all.

'I can see what you're thinking,' Cwen accused him. 'It's too much of a coincidence though, isn't it? Man turns up with parchment and the promise of silver and says he's my father. My mother turns up saying she wants the silver and that she's going to kill him and lo and behold, he's dead. How many of your circumstances do you want?'

'There could be many but it still wouldn't mean murder. We saw no evidence of murder on Stigand's body.'

'So it's definitely poison like Wat said. I know my mother's a nasty piece of work but she's probably not strong enough to take on Stigand in a fair fight. She's bound to have done something sneaky and underhand.'

Hermitage sighed.

'She killed my father, Hermitage. I'd only just met him and she killed him.'

Hermitage didn't like to point out that Cwen had wanted to kill him herself a few short hours ago. And had denied that he could be her father at all. Still, he supposed that her mother confirming the fact was pretty persuasive.

'Naturally, we can investigate,' he said with a nod and a genuine smile. 'It is the very least we can do. But we shall do it as we have with all the other investigations.'

'How's that?' Wat asked. 'Wait until someone accuses us and then hope something occurs to you at the last moment?'

'Not at all.' Hermitage scowled at his levity. 'There is no king or Le Pedvin demanding that we find a killer in this instance. It is for Cwen. But we will see what facts we can find and draw a proper conclusion. If we find that Mistress Eadgyth has anything to do with it then that is that.'

Cwen smiled and nodded.

'But if we find that she did not, then that is that as well.'

'Hardly likely,' Cwen snorted.

With this promise of investigation made, the atmosphere of impending doom or violence or both dissipated somewhat. Perhaps Cwen now had some activity to focus upon and so would not brood upon her father, or mother or whether the latter had killed the former.

'I imagine we need to see the body,' she said, in a business-like manner as they went down the stairs. She was half facing backwards as she went and so didn't see the new arrival at the door until she was in front of him. 'Oh,' she started.

'Ah,' Hermitage bleated when he saw the visitor.

'Oh, bloody hell, what now?' Wat sighed and tried to smile.

The large man facing them spoke. 'We are looking for Stigand and the woman at the inn said to come here.'

'I bet she did,' Wat muttered. 'Why don't you come in?'

Hermitage stood back and hoped that the man would duck when he entered and not do any more damage to the workshop, or hurt his head. His mind was so shocked at the sight before him that it went straight for a completely pointless question. Why were Vikings so tall?

Caput X

How Many More?

'Don't tell me,' Wat said when they had settled the two Vikings in the upper chamber with yet more wine. 'You're looking for Stigand because he bought some hawks from you and hasn't paid. And Mistress Angel at the tavern told you to come up here and join everyone else.'

If the Normans were big, the Vikings were bigger. Fortunately, the Normans were in the farthest back room of the workshop while the Vikings were in the front.

As they'd walked up the stairs Wat had whispered in Hermitage's ear. 'All we need now is some Celts and we can have our very own war.'

'What happens if the Normans meet the Vikings?' Hermitage trembled.

'They probably don't talk to one another.'

'That'd be good, I think.'

The Vikings did not look particularly threatening, apart from the natural way most Vikings looked, which was threatening. They did have weapons strapped to waist and back and looked young and well trained and ready to use them. At the moment though, they seemed happy just to talk. They were obviously English Vikings if there could be such a thing, doubtless coming from the Danelaw part of the land rather than from over the sea.

Hermitage dreaded to think that the ones from Denmark could be any more Viking-like than these two.

'Ragnar and Ulrik,' the Vikings even introduced themselves, not something most Vikings bothered with if the tales were to be believed.

'Pleased to meet you,' Wat replied. Which was also something seldom heard when Vikings turned up uninvited.

They didn't seem surprised to hear that Wat knew about the hawks. 'Stigand has not taken any hawks yet, but the trade is promised.' Ragnar, or was it Ulrik, explained.

'And he's late,' Wat stated a fact.

'He seems to be dead,' Ulrik or Ragnar noted with nothing more than a raised eyebrow. 'And we're not exactly sure what a weaver has to do with it.'

'Me neither,' Wat sighed.

Hermitage gave him a sharp glance at this as it had only been a few moments ago that Wat was promising the Normans that he could get hawks. If this was going to be another example of trade and its associated dishonesty, he really would have to speak up.

'The mistress at the tavern seemed to think that answers would be found here.'

'She does that.' Wat ran a hand through his hair. 'Did you see Stigand?'

'The dead Stigand? Yes. Some people from the town had come to remove him from the inn.'

'At least Mistress Angel would be pleased about that.'

'And some other people from the town were removing anything of value that Stigand had on him.'

Hermitage tutted at that.

'Which was not much.'

'No coin for buying hawks then?' Wat asked lightly as if he wasn't interested at all.

The Vikings sat and looked expectantly at Wat. Hermitage shifted slightly to get out of the way of an expectant look from a Viking.

'All I know,' Wat began, 'is that Stigand was to buy some hawks from Denmark.' He nodded towards Ragnar and Ulrik indicating that they were as near to Denmark as most people would like to get. 'He was then to supply these to King William who would pay him for them.'

'In a weaver's workshop?'

'Stigand arranged the meeting in Derby.' Wat shrugged. 'And he has family in the area.'

After studying Wat for a moment, perhaps to see if he was to be trusted or not, Ragnar and Ulrik huddled into a private conversation.

Hermitage was starting to think that he ought to make some notes of all Wat's dishonesty, bending of the truth and downright lies. He wasn't sure he'd be able to remember them all when the time came for a thorough review. And the time would come.

'Stigand's death is troubling,' Ragnar said.

'We're all very upset.' Wat got an incoherent groaning noise from Cwen at this. 'But it's just a few hawks, surely?'

'For King William. Trading hawks for silver with the king is an important matter. It's a bit suspicious that Stigand dies in the middle of this business.'

'That's what I said,' Cwen piped up.

Wat looked as innocent as the shepherd on the hill who had no idea what sort of tapestries the wool from his sheep was going to end up in. 'If he'd paid then you could still send the hawks.' He managed to sound as if he knew nothing about how paying for anything worked.

'If he had, we could.'

'Ah,' Wat nodded with only mild interest. He left a pause. 'If there's anything I can do.'

The Vikings looked very doubtful.

'I do have some influence at the court of King William.'

Now it was Hermitage who could not contain a cough.

'Yes,' Wat went on with a firm look at Hermitage. 'In fact, Brother Hermitage here holds an official post with the king.'

The Vikings looked at Hermitage with puzzled expressions. 'Really?'

Hermitage knew that he didn't look very prepossessing and that as a monk it shouldn't matter. Still, these Vikings didn't need to sound quite so surprised.

'What are you suggesting?' Ulrik asked.

'I really don't know. I'm only a humble weaver but if I can bring people together to sort this out I'd be only too happy.'

'Humble weaver?' Ragnar did not sound convinced. 'Wat the Weaver humble? I've not heard you called that before.'

'Ah, you know of me,' Wat smiled but even Hermitage could tell this was rather forced.

'Of course. When Mistress Angel told us to come to the workshop of Wat the Weaver we couldn't imagine what the connection was.'

'Family, eh,' Wat tutted. 'What can you do.'

'Stigand was a relative of yours?'

'Not of mine, no. But someone at the workshop. And as he was in the area, well, you know.'

'No, not really. When our families are in the area they tend to be the ones attacking.'

'Aha,' Wat's smile was getting decidedly shaky. 'He was just passing through. From the king to you, probably.'

Ragnar and Ulrik said nothing but their thoughts looked distrustful, even from the outside.

'Look,' Wat leant forward. 'Let me be honest.'

Please, thought Hermitage.

'Stigand told me of the trade for the hawks and asked me if

I'd like to be involved. Well, with my connection to the king I had to say no.'

There went honesty again.

'Now that he's dead it seems only right that I should step in if I can. Between you, me and the hanging post,' he dropped his voice, 'I'm not sure Stigand had the necessary silver at all. I suspect he may have needed my help to buy the hawks in the first place.'

'Interesting,' Ragnar narrowed his eyes and seemed to carefully consider what to say next. 'So the silver King William gave him as a mark of good faith is not with Mistress Angel?'

'No idea,' Wat replied quickly, masking the very loud grinding of teeth that was coming from Cwen. 'You'd have to ask Mistress Angel.'

'But you'd be willing to make it good?'

'Ah, well.'

'Being so close to the king and all.'

'Be glad to have a word with one or two people, see what might be possible, if it's that important.'

'And how long will that take?' Ragnar was being very business-like now.

'Well, you know how it is. Difficult to find the right people at the right time.'

'You could send word.'

'Oh, yes, I could send word.'

Yes, thought Hermitage, you could send word to the back room of the workshop, that shouldn't take long. In fact, you could introduce the Normans to the Vikings and let them get on with it. He knew that he should not feel satisfaction that the rewards of dishonesty were so close at hand, particularly as those hands belonged to Vikings, but Wat had brought this upon himself. The "I told you so" discussion was going to need careful planning.

'Why don't you send word then,' Ragnar suggested, although it sounded more like an instruction.

Wat gave a smile that looked like it was very hard work indeed.

'We can return to Mistress Angel and see what she has to say about Stigand's possessions.'

'Now that is a good idea,' Wat enthused. 'I'm sure you can sort it all out with her.' He stood to make it clear that the Vikings better go quickly or they might not get the silver that was probably just lying under Stigand's bed.

The Vikings did stand up but only after a few moments. A few moments that loudly proclaimed they were getting up because it suited them, not because of Wat's invitation.

At the door Wat brightly bid them farewell, saying that he would be delighted to see them again should the trip to Mistress Angel be unproductive.

He closed the door, turned his back against it and regarded Cwen and Hermitage. 'Bugger,' he said.

'They seem well informed,' Hermitage managed to say, despite his overwhelming urge to confirm that the practices of trade were turning out to be as bad as he had said, several times over.

'Well informed?' Wat clearly considered this to be some sort of unhelpful understatement. 'Vikings well informed about silver. Just what we need.'

'And Stigand was given silver by the king.' Cwen was on her own track of annoyance. 'Doubtless, my mother has got that already and it's only whet her appetite for more.'

'Or if it was with him before death you can guarantee it's gone now,' Wat complained. 'If Mistress Angel has fresh thatch on the inn this week we'll know where it's gone as well.'

Hermitage was having trouble keeping track of exactly who was deceiving who in all of this. 'If Stigand had the silver, why did he come to you?'

'Get some more.'

'Well, yes, but why?'

'He likes silver?'

'Obvious,' Cwen replied as if this should be obvious to one and all. 'He's a lying, cheating, dung-chewing, scab-faced arse.'

Hermitage indicated with his frown that this was not helpful.

'Could be any reason.' Wat threw his hands in the air and left the door, stomping back to the chamber of little usable furniture. He tried to prop the bits of the chair back together so that they would take his weight but they couldn't even support themselves, let alone a grumpy weaver. He gave, up and slumped onto the floor, resting his back against the wall.

'I heard of a scheme up London way that could be like this.'

'Oh yes?' Hermitage didn't like the sound of schemes up London way. He prepared himself.

'One man has the promise of a good profit. Solid, trustworthy, lots of evidence that it's real.'

'Like a good quality parchment?'

'Exactly like a good quality parchment. Might even have a noble behind it. All legitimate and pounds of silver or gold or anything you like guaranteed. All it needs is ten pounds to get fifty and the poor fellow doing the deal only has five. He'll put his five in, you put your five in and everyone lives happily ever after. And richer, which is more important.'

'Tempting,' Hermitage said, meaning it in a very bad way.

'Absolutely. But anyone can see that the ten pounds really will give fifty, so they hand over their money.'

'And then?'

'And then our man goes to someone else and gets them to put five in. And then to another and another and another.'

Hermitage was lost again. 'But he doesn't need any more.'

Wat bit his lip and spoke in a very stilted manner. 'He's stealing from them, Hermitage.'

'Ah.'

'So, he's gathered say fifty pounds from ten people. He does his deal, which was real all along and gets another fifty.'

Hermitage puzzled the numbers through his head. They weren't his strong point but this should be quite simple. Wat smiled at him and waited while the calculation was done. 'If everyone is expecting fifty pounds to come back and that they will get twenty-five, there won't be enough to go round.'

Wat now applauded Hermitage for some reason. 'I suppose our man could go back to all the people and say that he's so sorry but the deal went wrong. As he's so honest he's going to give them all their money back. Isn't that nice? But he's still fifty pounds up.'

'I suppose it's decent at least. In which case why did he get all the money from them in the first place?'

'Because it's ridiculous.' Wat snapped. 'He simply vanishes and is never seen again having got one hundred pounds in his purse. Each person has only lost five pounds so they might be upset but not murderous if you know what I mean.'

And all this just when Hermitage thought that trade could not get any worse.

'It's a good plan,' Cwen said, seemingly oblivious to the sin involved. 'But a bit stupid to muck around like this with the king and some wandering Vikings.'

'True,' Wat nodded to himself. 'But if our Stigand was going round getting silver from anyone he could,'

'Like you.'

'Thank you, Hermitage. Yes, like me. I'm hardly likely to go complaining to King William that he owes me five pounds. Am I?'

'Or to some Vikings.'

'As you say. Or to some Vikings.'

'Meanwhile, our lying, cheating, dung-chewing, scab-faced arse gives the Vikings their silver, gives William his hawks and we're all five pounds down.'

Wat was considering his own explanation carefully. 'But if William had actually given him some silver, why would he not say so? I'd be even more inclined to go along with it if I knew the king's silver was involved.'

Cwen shrugged. 'Spent it?'

'Ah, yes, could be.'

'Spent it?' Hermitage was in a whole new world of confusion. 'Why on earth would he spend the king's silver when he had to get hawks with it?'

'Lying, cheating, dung-chewing, scab-faced arse.' Cwen explained, carefully.

'I'm going to ask you to stop saying that in a moment,' Hermitage complained.

'Just trying to make things clear. He gets a bag of silver, spends it and so has to get some more. Hence the visit to Wat.'

'And now the Normans have turned up wanting their hawks, the Vikings want their silver and Stigand has gone and died leaving me in the middle of it all.'

'Without a sliver of silver in sight,' Cwen added.

'You two really are the most marvellous help.' Wat's face

was grim.

'It's all the dishonesty that shocks me most,' Hermitage said.

'Take away the dishonesty and there's not much left.'

'Even killers aren't usually this scheming. Yes, they kill, but that's it. They don't kill people for pure mischief. They usually have a reason of some sort. It may not be a good one, but it's there.'

'Jolly decent of them.'

'It's a good job the Normans and the Vikings aren't as dishonest as everyone else.' Hermitage pointed out how the world would go to ruin if everyone behaved like this. 'What if the Normans already had their hawks and the Vikings had their silver and they just wanted more. Where would we be then?' He left this awful scenario to their own thoughts.

He stopped shaking his head and glanced and Wat and Cwen who seemed to be staring at him.

'Say that again,' Wat instructed.

'Say what again?'

'All that about the Normans have hawks and Vikings have silver and just want to get some more.'

'That's about it, really.'

'Like the scheme in London. The Normans get some hawks from Stigand but tell the Vikings that he never delivered so they need some more.'

Cwen took up the awful tale. 'And the Vikings got their silver but claim that Stigand never paid so the king still owes them. Or Wat the Weaver has to make it up as he's so keen.'

'Thank you for the reminder. And what would be the best place for Stigand in all of this?'

'A hole in the ground,' was Cwen's solemn reply.

'So the Normans could have killed him, or the Vikings

could have killed him.'

'Or my mother killed him and they just made use of the fact.'

'Excuse me,' Hermitage tried to bring them down from this fantasy they were creating. 'We don't know that anyone killed anyone at all.'

'No, we don't.' Wat acknowledged. 'But I've got Vikings asking me for silver and Normans expecting hawks.'

'All problems of your own making.'

'Another helpful comment. But there is one thing to our advantage.'

'Oh yes, what's that?'

'We've got the King's Investigator who can sort it all out.'

Caput XI

Let's Go See The Dead

Seldom can there have been such an eager outing to go and see a dead body. It was possible to believe some great parade was in the offing or the town was to gather for a renowned entertainment. Needless to say, the Normans at the back of the workshop were being treated like the naughty children who were not allowed out having committed some misdemeanour, like invasion.

Hermitage had no preparations to make, he was always ready to leave. He would not take the small devotional volume he kept in his chamber as he was pretty confident he would be coming back this time. When the king summoned him to investigate a dead body his confidence was usually quite high that he would die a horrible death of his own in the process.

If there was anything driving him to look forward to his second encounter with Stigand the dead it was just his natural curiosity. Of course, his natural curiosity was a monster of enormous proportions and untameable temper. He was confident that no murder had been committed but it would be intriguing to see how he could prove it.

Wat had also been ready to go straight away. He had a strong argument that when the Vikings came back having not found the silver, his best strategy was to be out. Not being there when Vikings come calling had been a standard defence for much of the country. He now paced up and down the hall, his impatience wearing holes in his shoes.

It was Cwen who seemed to be treating this as a special

occasion. Which seemed odd as it could be her father who was dead. She had instructed them to wait as she was just popping back to her room for something. That had been quite a while ago now and Wat was on the verge of going to demand what on earth was taking so long.

Before he could go and shout for her she appeared down the corridor.

'At last,' Wat turned and headed for the door. 'Perhaps we can go now?'

'Of course,' Cwen waved him ahead and they left the workshop.

Hermitage smiled at her and thought that something looked different somehow. He couldn't put his finger on exactly what it was. It would come to him if it was important. Which it probably wasn't.

Halfway down the path Wat got over his annoyance a little and turned his head to Cwen. He looked back down the track ahead and then quickly back to Cwen again. 'What have you done?'

Hermitage looked now. What had Cwen done? It seemed a strange question to come out of nowhere.

'Nothing,' Cwen replied.

'Nothing eh?' Wat peered at her. 'Apart from putting a fresh jerkin on and it's only Tuesday. Tidied your hair, clean shoes and is that your best belt?'

'Could be,' Cwen didn't seem interested in any of this.

'Oh my God,' Wat said, in a wholly unnecessary manner. 'You've washed.'

'A woman can clean up before she goes out.'

'We're going to look at a dead body.'

'Which could be in the church,' Hermitage pointed out, thinking it was nice to see that Cwen had made some effort.

'And which could be my father.'

Wat looked very thoughtful about this.

Hermitage considered it most appropriate that Cwen should show due respect to the person who may indeed turn out to be her father. She had had little chance to engage with Stigand while he was alive. At least she was doing her best now he was dead. It must be very difficult for her.

'And your mother might be there,' Wat said as if he had reached some great conclusion.

'Could be,' Cwen shrugged.

'So you've put all your finery on to show her how well you've done.'

'One belt is hardly finery. I don't have any finery.'

'Looks finer than anything she's got.'

'We don't know she'll be there at all. She could have cleared off to Arundel now, thinking she's got away with it.'

'Or she really has found that Stigand is here and is dead.' Hermitage tried to bring their thoughts back to the sombre matter of a dead man in the inn, or the church, or wherever it was they had taken him.

'She did it,' Cwen drawled with confidence. 'Of course, we could find her moaning and wailing in the middle of the street shouting about how awful it is that her dear Stigand has been taken from her.'

'That is possible.'

'Of course, it is. They're not going to hand over his possessions to her if she doesn't play the part of the loving wife. The loving wife who killed him in the first place.'

'But you'll be there to put them straight,' Wat said with a heavy sigh and a significant dose of apprehension.

'That I will,' Cwen smiled.

'Until the Vikings and the Normans turn up issuing their

demands. Probably each blaming the other for killing Stigand.'

Hermitage was finding it hard to follow who the latest possible murderer was. His preferred option of no one at all was not finding favour with anyone. 'The poor fellow only turned up in Derby a few days ago and he died soon after. Suddenly we have the place full of potential murderers, one of them your own mother, Cwen?' He tried to make this sound as utterly unbelievable as he found it himself. Unfortunately, the others were nodding at his very sensible explanation.

'And the Vikings,' Wat added. 'Don't forget the Vikings. And the Normans.'

'I haven't forgotten them.'

'They could both want him dead. Silver and hawks and all that. Suit their purposes no end, I shouldn't wonder. And they aren't exactly lacking a reputation when it comes to killing people.'

'That's true,' Hermitage acknowledged. 'But might I suggest that people killed by Vikings and Normans tend not to be found lying comfortably in bed the next morning?'

'People poisoned by mothers probably do,' Cwen explained.

'People poisoned by anyone,' Wat argued.

'And if he just died?' Hermitage pressed his point.

All this got was loud scoffing noises. 'Don't be ridiculous Hermitage,' Wat mocked. 'A dead body with three lots of people who want him dead and half his weight in silver up for the taking?'

Hermitage let his next sentence out before he realised what he was doing. He only meant it as an example of the ridiculous taken to extremes but as he heard the words in the air he could see the trouble circling like crows around a sheep with a very bad cough. 'Cwen said she wanted to kill him, maybe she did it?'

Wat's eyes widened and a look of panic froze his features.

'Never had the chance,' Cwen seemed to think the suggestion entirely reasonable.

Hermitage and Wat breathed again.

'And as you said Hermitage, I don't know if I'd be able to do the deed in real life. Stick a knife in someone? Yeuch. Mind you,' she went on. 'Poison's not so messy, is it? I mean you can give someone poison and then be miles away by the time they actually die. And it wouldn't take a moment.'

'Aha,' Hermitage tried to laugh off the whole idea. 'Where would you get poison anyway? In Derby? Ha ha.'

'Oh, the workshop's got plenty,' Cwen sounded rather knowledgeable. 'Lots of the dyes and the like come from poisonous plants. Be easy to get hold of some. That green you used to use,' she nodded to Wat.

'Oh, that,' Wat shivered. 'Found something else now but it was good stuff.'

'But dangerous?' Hermitage found it very hard to believe that colours could be fatal. Of course, some plants could be deadly, even those gathered for medicinal purposes could be harmful if misused, but in weaving?

'God, yes. Made everyone who touched it sick until we got it into the tapestry and handed it over to Rambon of Nottingham, wasn't it?'

'You know very well it was,' Cwen insisted.

'And then it was all right?'

'It was until the rain leaked on the tapestry one night, washed the colour out into a little stream and killed a dozen mice and his dog.'

'Good heavens.'

'I know. It was terrible. He loved that dog. Had to give him his money back.'

Hermitage tried to take in this new information. He had always assumed that knowledge of such things was limited to physicks and those who practised the healing arts. 'So anyone could get this poison? You wouldn't even need to be a weaver?'

'No,' Cwen agreed. 'But it would be easier. We've already prepared all the plants into their pots and buckets. All you have to do is get a handful of the right stuff and death's on your doorstep, as they say.'

'Do they?'

'They do. And you wouldn't have to go round finding the right plant and picking enough of it and boiling it and grinding it and all that business.'

'And does everyone know this?' Hermitage always liked to hear about new things but this topic was making him very nervous.

'All but the very newest apprentice,' Wat confirmed. 'First job they get is dye work. Hartle knows more than most but he teaches them pretty quick and they get on with it all right. After all, no one else wants to spend hours tramping through the woods getting stung by nettles and picking poisonous plants.'

They walked on and Hermitage considered Cwen, who seemed not in the least concerned that she had just explained how she could kill Stigand, having said that she wanted to.

'This is very sorry news,' Hermitage shook his head as he walked along. The only poisons he knew of left horrible signs of their presence. Although he had never seen any in practice he had read of them. He couldn't bring to mind any that led people to simply die quietly in their sleep. But then he was rapidly concluding that he wasn't the poison expert here.

'And there's mother,' Cwen announced with a happy shout.

'What about her?'

'She'd know all about the poisons as well.'

'How?'

'I taught her.' Cwen seemed to think this was very good news. Hermitage wasn't so sure.

'You taught her?'

'Of course. When I was doing all the work in Arundel I had her go and gather plants for the dyes and so forth. It would have been a waste of my time. I was the one doing the weaving and the sewing and the making.'

'So you both know all about what's poisonous and what isn't.'

'Certainly do. And she said she'd come here to kill him.'

Hermitage glanced at Wat, understood the silent message conveyed and kept his mouth shut. 'That's very interesting,' he managed instead. 'And are there any poisons that would do this to Stigand? Allow him to die quietly on his bed and show no signs of ague or even distress?'

'Hm,' Cwen furrowed her brow. 'They're all pretty nasty from what I've heard. Never actually seen anyone poisoned for real.'

'Rambon of Nottingham's mice didn't look very happy,' Wat said with a shrug.

'Just so.' Hermitage pressed his conclusion. 'Stigand showed no signs of having been poisoned. We have to accept the possibility that he just died. Inconvenient though that be.'

Cwen grunted.

'If there is anything of suspicion about this death it is the parchment. I still maintain that it is too good for the purchase of a few hawks.'

'And fifty pounds of silver,' Wat pointed out.

'I still think it could be poison,' Cwen muttered.

'Let us find Stigand and then we shall know.' He felt as if his confidence that the death was natural was itself being slowly poisoned.

. . .

Why did everything Hermitage said or thought turn out to be so complicated? 'You would think,' he observed as they stood in the street outside the tavern, 'that someone in town would actually know where the body is.'

Mistress Angel had confirmed that some men came to take the body away. She thought they were from the moot and one of them looked a bit like the son of the blacksmith, but she wasn't really paying attention. She just wanted Stigand out.

Hermitage had suggested that paying attention to people who were removing dead bodies from your house was quite normal and indeed might be expected. Mistress Angel retorted that if Hermitage wanted to pay attention to dead bodies that was up to him but that she had more important things to do. And if he did want to pay attention to dead bodies then there was more wrong with him than there was with her.

Purely from the look on her face, Hermitage concluded that an enquiry concerning the details of those more important things would not be welcome. It seemed to involve the tavern being a mess, Ern doing nothing to help as usual and something about a broken bed. Hermitage couldn't really make any sense of it.

She also reported that the "rude woman" had come back poking her nose around and had been sent away with a flea in her ear. Hermitage could only conclude that the nose and ear woman would be Eadgyth. He would be grateful not to bump into her too soon.

There was nothing to do but leave Angel to whatever it was she was doing and start their own search.

'Can't be many places they would have taken him,' Wat said. 'Might as well try the church first?'

Hermitage sighed. He could only hope that Stigand was simply laid out in the church awaiting burial. The thought of making enquiry of the priest filled him with worry. If they could find him at all.

As they left the tavern and headed up the street to the church, Cwen strode ahead leaving Hermitage and Wat to trail behind.

Wat leaned over to Hermitage's ear. 'Wants her mother to spot her.' He nodded toward Cwen.

Hermitage gave Wat a look of surprise. 'They didn't get on very well the last time they met,' he whispered. 'Why should she want to see Eadgyth again?'

'She doesn't want to see Eadgyth again, she wants Eadgyth to see her. And preferably Cwen will see that Eadgyth has seen her but Eadgyth won't see that Cwen has seen that Eadgyth has seen her.'

'Pardon?'

'It's all quite normal, don't worry about it.'

'Worry about it? I can't even make sense of it.'

'It's part of their fight. The part that goes on under the surface. Rather like a molehill? You can see the lump of earth on the top, that's when they try to kill one another.

Underground though there's a whole warren of tunnels and moles going about their business of undermining one another.'

Hermitage shook his head. 'I think I preferred it when they were trying to kill each other.'

'Dead bodies are certainly easier to keep track of.'

Cwen turned and gave them a look that said she knew perfectly well that they were talking about her. They smiled, which seemed to have no effect whatsoever.

It wasn't a long walk to the church and as its simple tower loomed over Hermitage he felt the need to engage with the priest looming even higher. It didn't help that the man insisted on being called Father. Just Father. Not Father this or Father that, "just call me Father", he said. And it wasn't in the friendly manner of a confidante letting you into his personal life, it was more like an instruction; an instruction that extended to any discussion you felt like having with strangers. If you didn't know his name you couldn't spread it about.

As far as Hermitage could tell no one knew the priest's name and everyone now knew not to ask. As he walked up to the building his recent experiences gave him cause to reappraise this priest. Having seen how trade was carried out and how everyone seemed to routinely lie to one another for their own ends, he wondered if Father whatever-his-name-was might have a past that was not entirely ecclesiastical.

These suspicions bubbled along nicely as Cwen tried the door of the church only to find it locked shut. She hammered on it until the lock rattled.

In any other circumstances, in any other church come to that, the length of their wait would lead to the conclusion that the priest was out. Not here. Cwen knocked again. Longer and louder this time.

Eventually, a small wooden shutter opened about halfway up the tower and a cowled shape could just be seen in the shadow.

'What do you want?'

'We want to come in,' Cwen called back.

'Why?'

'Because it's a church and shouldn't be locked in the first place.'

Hermitage silently congratulated Cwen on her argument. It was one that went on loud and clear in his head but never actually made it to his lips.

'Well, it is,' was the not even vaguely theological reply.

'We want to see the body of Stigand.'

'Who?'

'How many dead bodies have you got in there? Particularly ones called Stigand?'

Hermitage felt that the priest had chosen the wrong day to take on the wrong person.

'What's it to you?'

'He's my father.'

Hermitage was surprised to hear loud recognition of this although he immediately realised that Cwen maybe just saying it for effect. The ideal effect being the priest opening the door.

'I've only got your word for that.'

'I can always climb up this tower, kick that shutter out of the way and give you personal proof.'

'She could, you know,' Wat called encouragement to the priest.

'Wait there,' the priest huffed and tutted and closed his

shutter.

After another long wait, which indicated either that the church was exceptionally large or that the priest was trying to delay the inevitable, there were rattling noises behind the door and it opened - if a gap wide enough for one face can be called open.

'Who are you?'

'Who are we?' Cwen simply pushed at the door and brushed the priest aside. 'We are your flock and Wat here is the one who's given quite a bit to your church.' She stopped inside and looked around the simple space. 'Most of which hasn't been spent on the church by the look of it.' She turned to the priest, or rather she turned on him. 'Where's Stigand?'

'Stigand who?'

Cwen went very calm and quiet which Hermitage and Wat knew was not good. Not good for the priest, anyway. She took slow and small steps towards the priest who wisely took slow and small steps backwards.

'Look, Father whatever your name is, you will know, or at least you should know, that I am not generally a patient or tolerant woman.' Wat nodded vigorously at the priest to indicate that the man should take this information to heart.

'And I am having a particularly trying time at the moment. I have a mother who has turned up out of nowhere informing me, for the first time, that this Stigand is my father. We have Vikings prowling around asking for the same Stigand and Normans staying in our back room asking for him as well.' She paused at this and looked very intently at the priest as if she had spotted something of great interest. Rather like a weasel spotting that the baby rabbit in front of it doesn't know about weasels.

'So, Father,' she said and folded her arms.

Hermitage realised that he had never heard the title used as an insult before.

'Perhaps I had better pop back and tell the Normans that Stigand is in the church and that the priest would be only too glad to show them around?'

The priest had backed off quite a way now and was looking around as if for an escape route.

'I'll wager that two big Normans could get you to tell them your name.' She smiled her smile of grim ruthlessness. 'In fact, I'd further wager that your name might be of interest to them.'

Wat took up the theme. 'You know, I've just remembered when the Father here arrived. Just after the battle at Hastings, wasn't it? I wasn't here at the time but people say he arrived in a bit of a hurry. And when he found out the old priest was dead he said that was lucky because he was a priest.'

'You don't think?' Cwen left the question hanging but put her hand to her mouth as if she had just thought of something truly awful.

Hermitage had known nothing of this, having been up to his neck in investigations at the time.[8] He now tried to think what might be truly awful about the Father. Perhaps he wasn't supposed to be in Derby at all and some other parish was expecting him. He frowned his disappointment at such behaviour.

'If we ask the Normans they may be able to shed some light on it,' Wat nodded as if this were the right and proper thing to do.

'He's behind the altar.'

'Behind the altar?' Hermitage questioned the sanctity of

[8] All of which are recorded in Brother Hermitage's interminable chronicles, hence the title: The Chronicles of Brother Hermitage.

this arrangement.

'I'll bury him when I get round to it.'

'You mean when you get someone else to dig the hole,' Cwen snorted as she made her way to the altar.

Wat followed and Hermitage gave a particularly disappointed and disapproving glance at the priest. The man glared back, obviously more concerned about Cwen than he was about Hermitage, which was probably wise. Joining the others behind the altar it was clear that they had definitely found Stigand.

'Ah.' Hermitage appraised the sight before them. The body was laid out on a simple table without even the decency of a cloth to cover him. This did have the advantage that they could consider the dead man in some detail. Not that much detail was required.

Stigand had undergone a change. Quite a few of them, really. Obviously, he was still dead, that much was clear. If anything, it had become even more clear in the short time that had passed. In the tavern he had simply looked dead; a body laying as it had in life only a bit more lifeless. Now there was something about him that screamed death in all its glorious finality. Actually, there were several things about him but the more striking features grabbed the attention immediately.

'Was he, erm?' Hermitage hesitated to ask the question, it sounded very peculiar indeed. 'Was he that big? When we saw him last?'

'No, Hermitage, he wasn't,' Wat confirmed. 'And he wasn't that colour, either.'

'He's only been dead for a few hours,' Hermitage puzzled over what could have caused such a change in Stigand. 'People who've been dead a few hours tend not to swell up and change colour. That doesn't usually happen for a long time.'

'Unless they didn't just die of their own accord,' Wat suggested.

'There you are then,' Cwen was triumphant. 'She did poison him.'

'It seems likely that someone did. And if I was the priest,' Wat gave the corpse a nervous glance. 'I'd bury him quick. Before something really nasty happens.'

Caput XII

Off to Church

Roland and Ralf had grown tired of their back room and sallied forth.

Two big Normans sallying around the workshop made the Saxon apprentices rather nervous and so Hartle had to intervene. He asked if they were interested in tapestry, to which they replied no. He asked if they would like some wine, to which they snorted and said not unless Wat had any better wine. He knew better than to ask if he could get Mrs Grod to prepare them something to eat.

What they did say was that they would like to see Wat. Now.

Hartle managed to get them to sit in the upper chamber while he went to fetch Wat, who was doubtless in the workshop somewhere. Probably working. They pointed out that the only thing he would be working on was getting their hawks so perhaps Hartle had better look there.

After much prevarication and increasingly irritated large Normans, Hartle had to confess that Wat had been called out on business. He had to say this because he had run out of reasons for not being able to find Wat, and because he wasn't paid enough to deal with Normans.

His hurried suggestion that they should wait here for Wat or they might miss one another was dismissed with the astute observation that there was only one path to the workshop and one street in Derby. How hard could it be to find one weaver?

As the Normans strode out through the door Hartle did

consider sending an apprentice, one fleet of foot, to hurry around to the town and warn Wat of the impending arrival. He then reasoned that Wat hadn't warned him that Normans and Vikings and worst of all Cwen's mother were going to turn up in the first place so it was his problem, wasn't it?

He did think that Normans meeting Vikings in the middle of Derby might be quite entertaining, but there was work to do and he would be happy to hear the tale around a fire with a mug in his hand rather than witness it first hand.

...

The Vikings in question had found Mistress Angel. She made it quite clear that Stigand had not left anything of value behind and that if they didn't believe her they were welcome to search the inn. Rather to her surprise they thanked her for the offer and went to it. She was fortunate that it was a small inn and that these Vikings were searching and not pillaging.

Nonetheless, the broken cot caught their attention.

'That was the Normans,' Angel explained, which really interested the Vikings.

'What Normans?' Ragnar asked as he snapped a thick timber of the cot with his bare hands.

'The ones who broke my good cot.' She snatched the pieces. 'And didn't even offer to pay.'

The word "pay" clearly meant nothing to the Vikings.

'Why would Normans break your cot? The cot that Stigand slept in. In fact, why would they be here at all?'

'You know Normans.' Angel shrugged. 'Think they own the place.'

'Must have been quite angry, to smash up a cot like this.'

Angel just shrugged again as if explaining why Normans were angry was like wondering why birds flapped their wings when they wanted to fly.

'And where did these Normans go? After they'd got angry with your cot.'

'Funnily enough, I didn't ask.' Angel had no love for Wat the Weaver, quite the opposite, but there were some things Saxons just didn't do to one another. Sending Normans and Vikings to Wat's workshop separately was one thing; a thing Wat thoroughly deserved. Giving them good reason to do some serious harm was going too far. Only a bit too far but still too far. 'Perhaps they went looking for a stronger cot?'

'You didn't send them to Wat the Weaver by any chance?' Ragnar was starting to sound annoyed.

'Why would I do that?'

'Because it's where you sent us.'

'Ah, but then you were asking. The Normans just wanted Stigand and they found him.'

'Why did they want him?'

'It's an odd thing, that. Two large Normans came in asking for Stigand and didn't explain to the Saxon owner of the inn what they were up to. They didn't knock politely or give a thoroughly good reason for their visit. The topic of why they wanted Stigand didn't even come up. Isn't that shocking?' She folded her arms and looked at Ragnar.

'You, mistress,' Ragnar said with the full force of a Dane striding into a small east coast village with fifty of his companions at his back, 'are asking for your inn to be torn to the ground with no explanation either.'

Angel gulped.

When real, physical Saxon resistance to the Norman invasion fell apart at Hastings the people were left with little choice but to submit. A few pockets of defiance remained in the east, the west and the north but the ordinary people going about their ordinary business simply had to put up with it. That was not to say that their objections to the new overlords simply evaporated. A new form of opposition swept the land, one in which every man, woman and child could engage and one that seemed perfectly suited to the Saxon temperament. Contempt.

Yes, the Normans had won the battle and the crown but they hadn't done it very well. Of course, they were now in charge but a pig organised his mud better than the Normans ran the country. Naturally, they had all the weapons and went around threatening people but any idiot could do that. Which was lucky because the Normans were idiots.

And their haircuts were stupid.

Best of all the Normans didn't seem to notice any of this. Or if they did they couldn't comprehend it. When they sent a small force of armed men to bring order to a village they expected either humble compliance or a hopeless resistance that would inevitably lead to death. Death for all the Saxons. When they got a rather sneering look down the nose and a resigned, "get on with it then", it just confused them. It looked the same as obedience but didn't feel quite right. The Saxons did what they were told but just a bit too slowly and with what could only be described as bad grace.

Perhaps they didn't understand the language sufficiently, perhaps they had spent all their years in battle and strife in France and were not practised in the underhand backstabbing and personal denigration that constituted rule in England. Whatever it was, the average Saxon could get away with the most monumental insults and then brag about them in the tavern afterwards.

The only danger in this was that if the Saxons practised it too often they might get stuck that way. For years to come the natural response to overbearing authority could be simply to talk about it behind its back. The attitude to any leader with the audacity to put themselves in charge would be derision. The whole race would find itself in the position of being able to condescend to anyone, up or down, regardless of position. All of it to very little actual effect.

Mistress Angel could tell that this tactic was not going down terribly well with the Vikings who obviously knew what was going on. She swallowed and tried a smile.

'And then they smashed up his bed?' Ragnar asked.

'Just so.'

'And they didn't ask anything else at all?'

Angel looked as if she was thinking very hard about this. 'Not that I can recall.'

Ragnar breathed deeply and spoke with Ulrik. The language was harsh and guttural and did not sound friendly. When Ulrik spat on Mistress Angel's clean floor it was clear that their conversation had not been a happy one.

Ragnar stared at Mistress Angel with the sort of stare only a Viking can manage. 'I think that everyone in this town is lying to us,' he snarled a very good snarl.

'Everyone?' Angel enquired, worried that these Vikings caught on quicker than Normans.

'All the ones we've spoken to so far. I further suspect that if we speak to any more we'll get some more lies; so we are going to sort this out.' He reached forward and took Mistress Angel by the arm. 'You're coming with us.'

Mistress Angel had been taken by the arm on many occasions and always dealt with it most effectively. All of those occasions had been by drunk Saxons who could barely stand and the taking of the arm was usually to stop them falling over. Seldom had anyone taken her by the arm for any other reason and they certainly hadn't tried it twice. This Viking taking by the arm made it clear that if Mistress Angel didn't go where she was bid, her arm would be going without her.

'Where are we going?' she asked, very politely for her.

'We're going to find some Normans and some weavers and anyone else we want and we are going to bang some heads together until we get at the truth.'

'Is this about hawks?' Mistress Angel asked with a quiver in her voice. 'Only if you want a hawk I've got a cousin over Osleston way who might have one going.'

Ragnar looked at her. 'Shut up.'

Leaving the site of the wrecked cot the three passed through the main room of the inn and arrived at the door just as Ern was coming in.

'Oh, hello,' he said, taking in the sight of his wife being dragged out of the place by two large Vikings.

'Who are you?' Ragnar demanded.

'I'm Ern,' Ern said as if everyone should know this. He looked to Angel. 'Are you going out?'

She looked at him but there were clearly no words to fully express the desired response.

'She is. And so are you.' Ragnar nodded to Ulrik who took hold of Ern and propelled him back out of the door.

'I've got to look after the inn,' he wailed.

Ulrik growled in his ear. 'If we knock it down you won't need to.'

Once out in the street, Ragnar looked up and down the deserted space. 'Where is everyone?'

Angel squirmed in his grip and couldn't resist the natural

answer to this question. 'They're probably indoors, avoiding the Vikings who go around grabbing decent people from their houses.'

'It's not the decent people we're grabbing.'

'Where to?' Ulrik asked.

Angel opened her mouth but Ragnar silenced it with a point of his finger. 'If you say the workshop of Wat the Weaver I shall grab your other arm and splice the two together.'

Angel shut her mouth.

'Where would they gather?' Ulrik asked. 'The great hall?'

'They're savages mostly, I don't think they have such places. Where would they take Stigand? That's the question. These Normans were clearly after him and probably smashed his bed up when they found he was dead in it.' Ragnar turned his attention to Ern. 'Where do you take your dead?'

Ern looked lost. 'I don't have any dead.'

Ragnar nodded to Ulrik who twisted his grasp on Ern producing a satisfying yelp. Satisfying for the Vikings, anyway.

'Where do you people take your dead?'

'Ah, you should have said. The church. The church is the place for the dead, if it's dead you want.'

'Right. Lead on then. Let's go to church.'

...

If there had been anyone left in the tavern to provide information they would have been able to tell the Normans that they'd just missed some Vikings and what a pity it was that they hadn't got here earlier. At least this meant that their search of the place was a short one and did not result in any more broken furniture. There was obviously no Wat the Weaver.

They returned to what had been Stigand's chamber and noted that there was no Stigand anymore. This raised their eyebrows and caused a brief discussion about whether they needed to find a living weaver or a dead hawk merchant. The strong suspicion was that the two went together and finding one would mean finding the other. They could see nothing else of interest so they grunted at one another and returned to the main room.

It took a lot to stop a Norman from going where he wanted but the sight of the room now full of raucously talking and laughing townsfolk was such a surprise that they stopped in their tracks.

They even looked over their shoulders to the back room to make sure that they were still in the same building. There was such a press in the room that they wouldn't even be able to get to the door without pushing half the population of Derby out of the way.

'You,' Roland grabbed the nearest man by the scruff of the neck.

'Oy,' the local resident responded before realising who had grabbed him. 'Oh, aha, yes, hello.' The man smiled.

'What's going on here?'

'Going on?' The local looked around the tavern as if trying to understand what the Norman was talking about. 'This is the inn. The town tavern?' Perhaps Normans didn't have such things. 'It's where we come to meet and drink and so forth.'

'I know what it is. Where did you come from?'

'Outside?' Surely even Normans understood how entering a room worked.

'You weren't here a moment ago.'

'That's right.' The man started to speak more slowly. 'A moment ago we were outside. Then we came in. Now we are inside.'

'Why?' The Norman was getting angry and frustrated.

'Because there's no drink outside.'

Another fellow brushed against them, a brimming mug in his hand. He seemed not to notice that two of the people in the room were Normans. 'This is great, isn't it? First time Angel's left the place unguarded in living memory. Be the last as well.' He gave a hearty laugh and raised his mug.

Roland appraised the room. 'You are stealing from the tavern keeper?'

'No, no,' the first man protested. 'Not stealing. Not really. Just using the inn, that's all. We use the inn all the time. Most of the time Angel is here, this time she isn't. That's the only difference.'

Roland thought about this for a moment but came to the conclusion that he really didn't care what these people did to one another. 'Where is Stigand?'

'Who? Oh, Stigand. He's dead you know.' The man talked over his shoulder as he took his own mug of ale from a generous hand that passed it to him.

'We know. Where is he?' Roland gently took the ale from the man's hand and made it clear that a reply was the only way the mug was going to be returned.

'I don't know, do I? I didn't move him.'

'Who did?'

The man considered his situation for a moment, as well as the fact that his ale was being held hostage. He put his fingers to his mouth and gave a piercing whistle. The hubbub of the inn died to silence.

'Anyone here move Stigand?' he called. 'You know, the dead one? Only these Norman gentlemen would like to know where he's gone.'

'Yup,' a voice called from the back. 'I did. Took him up the church. Of course, that priest didn't want to take him but we said he had to, that being the church and all. But he said that Stigand wasn't no Derby man so there wasn't no obligation. So we said…,'

'Shut up,' Roland instructed.

The room fell to silence once more as the drinkers waited for what was going to happen next. They all took several drinks from their mugs while they were waiting.

The man nearest the Normans took matters into his own hands. 'Out the door, turn left, top of the hill, can't miss it.'

Roland growled a bit.

'And if the priest says he's not in, don't believe him.'

The two Normans stepped purposefully across the room, the drinkers parting before them like Saxons getting out of the way of Normans. At the door, they turned back and one of them pointed a finger at them all but he didn't seem to have any words to go with it. A muttered "bloody Saxons" from the departing backs was responded to with a more lively "bloody Normans." - once the bloody Normans were well out of earshot.

…

The church was likely to get very lively if Eadgyth's knowledge of Vikings and Normans was anything to go by. Her knowledge of them was pretty slight but she had watched from a discreet spot on the other side of the road as two groups of renowned fighting men headed for the same place. Her knowledge of fighting men trying to occupy the same place was much better. She had no idea why they were all going there, the Vikings had been going on about the dead, but then Vikings had some funny ideas. Seeing what they were all up to could only help in the pursuit of her silver.

The list of people she was going to put in their place once she got that silver was starting to get quite lengthy. Obviously, there was her impudent daughter and that weaver she was with. That was disgraceful in its own right, never mind the lack of respect owed to a mother.

Then there was that woman at the inn. Angel, she now knew. Maybe Eadgyth would simply buy the inn and throw Mistress Angel into the street. It was nice to see her being mistreated by a Viking. It was all she deserved. There was another man with her now and he probably deserved to be thrown out as well. He was obviously connected to the inn so it would be for the best.

And a monk. A monk of all things. What was a monk doing in a weavers' workshop with her Cwen? He was obviously no better than he should be. She'd heard all about monks like him.

She left her hiding place and followed up the street, keeping close to the buildings so that she could hide again if the Normans turned round.

The sooner she got Cwen out of this place and back to Arundel the better. She'd never heard of Derby but didn't expect it to be swarming with Vikings and Normans. What a place. Disgraceful. All she needed was her share of the silver, a share that was rightly hers, and everything would be well.

She could set up the shop once more with Cwen working for her this time, as was only right and proper. The girl did seem to have done all right, which was fair enough. After all, it was her who had set her daughter on the path to her current position and so credit where it was due. If Cwen had done very well then she only owed her mother even more.

Stigand was just the same. He had Eadgyth to thank for his current good fortune. It was only her encouragement and inspiration that had driven him to make this trade. It had taken a bit longer than expected but that was only because he was a lazy so and so and didn't have her behind him every day.

And the sacrifices she had made. Don't get her started on the sacrifices she had made. If there was any justice in the world then all the silver would be hers as a reward for the things she had put up with. Being a good wife and mother was a demanding task. All right, she may not have been a wife in the eyes of the church, but what did they know? And she may not have been a wife for very long, but those few short weeks, or was it days, were all it took.

She had given up her own fortune to make sure Cwen had the best start in life. Finding Briston the Weaver to take her on had been the greatest of them all. Seeing her little Cwen taken away had nearly broken her heart. And the money hadn't lasted long either.

After all these years it would come good. It was her just desert. The priests were always going on about just deserts, well hers were made of silver. Despite the denials of everyone in this awful town, she could feel that the deal was close. She was just going to open one door or walk into one building and there would be a big bag of silver with her name written on it. Or a big E for Eadgyth, anyway.

. . .

'Erm.' Hermitage had gone to the door of the church to get some air. Another of the changes wrought upon Stigand was the smell. The air around the body had a very peculiar humour to it and they had all felt the need to step back. 'Vikings,' he added.

'Vikings?' Wat hurried to his side and looked down the road to where the Viking entourage was approaching. 'And they've got Angel and Ern. This is all we need.'

'It doesn't look like Angel was able to sort things out for them,' Hermitage observed as he noted the struggling landlord's wife.

'Right,' Wat clapped his hands. 'Let's be off then.'

'Off?'

'Yes, you know, away from the Vikings.'

'What good will that do?'

'It's always good to be away from Vikings. As a general rule.'

'They probably only want their silver,' Cwen said, casually.

'Even more reason.' Wat bundled Hermitage and Cwen away from the door. 'Is there another way out?' he asked the priest who looked like he really didn't care. 'I mean where is the other way out? There's bound to be one.'

'Don't know what you mean.'

'Yes, you do. I've never seen anyone so twitchy at the mention of Normans. You're bound to have a back door for when those same Normans come in the front.'

'The tower?' Cwen suggested. 'If there's rope we could get out of the window.' She hopped away and stepped quickly up a wooden ladder which led to the window the priest had looked down from. Very carefully peeking out so as not to be seen by the Vikings she could see that it was a pretty long way down. She also thought that the Vikings might notice three people sliding down a rope on the outside of the church tower.

She could also see a long way into the town. 'Ah,' she called down, sounding relieved that problems were solved. 'We'll soon sort everything. Here come the Normans as well.'

'Quick,' Wat called. 'Follow him.'

At the word "Normans" the priest had darted to the back of the church and disappeared into the shadows.

Cwen jumped down from the ladder and they all scurried to the back of the church where the priest had left a small door open that led to the outside and the graveyard.

'I'm not sure this is wise,' Hermitage protested as he was shoved through the door. 'The Vikings and the Normans are only going to find us again. We're just delaying the inevitable.' As he said this he thought that delaying the inevitable actually sounded like quite a good idea, particularly when the inevitable had Vikings and Normans in it.

'We are and they will,' Wat agreed as they ran hunched over across the graves into the woods beyond. 'Which means that we've got between now and then to work out what really happened to Stigand and to show that it's nothing to do with us. Much less do I have to hand over any of my silver. Well, when I say we work out what really happened I mean you work out, obviously.'

Caput XIII

Speculation in the Woods

The street of Derby was going to start getting suspicious itself if many more strangers turned up. The latest arrival seemed to slither through the air somehow, as if afraid to disturb it. There was no fear in the thin and intelligent face though, this face was deceiving the air into thinking no one had passed by at all.

Grey eyes took in everything and gave nothing back. Ears stole sounds and squirrelled them away for some devious purpose. A long nose sucked scents from the surroundings and breathed them out untouched. If anyone was asked to describe the man who just stood watching they'd deny seeing anyone at all and would be sure that they were right.

Those eyes showed very little interest as the church parade began. First, a well-dressed couple accompanied by a monk caught his attention, if a very modest movement of one eyebrow can indicate attention. There was the slightest hint of an inclination towards an intention of movement as the monk passed by but this stranger never engaged in direct action. He influenced and informed and persuaded, what use was he otherwise?

Vikings were next, dragging the proprietors of the inn along with them. A complete lack of engagement with this scene even had the stranger looking down the road to see if anything more interesting was going on.

When the Normans appeared there was a reaction. One foot moved forward two or three inches, just enough to raise the stranger above the personal horizon he hid behind. Roland noticed him and tugged at his companion's sleeve.

They looked over, noted the presence and stopped walking. They then looked up and down the street to check that no one had noticed them noticing anything.

Like men who have decided for no good reason at all just to have a wander over to the side of the street, the men wandered over to the side of the street. Fortunately, most of the population of Derby was enjoying Mistress Angel's hospitality-in-absentia and so didn't see two Normans behaving very strangely in the middle of town.

It was also the case that if any of the townsfolk had been abroad, the effect of Mistress Angel's hospitality was such that most of them couldn't see straight anyway.

Quiet words were exchanged between stranger and Normans but the effect of them upon Roland was not a happy one. He threw his hands in the air, gestured at the stranger and took a few paces to look away. He then returned with a number of hissed comments for the stranger to consider.

He even produced the parchment from inside a jerkin and pointed at various parts of it. This led to a more intense discussion with several chopping gestures from the stranger.

Eventually, it seemed that Roland's resistance was broken and he gave a universal "do what you like" expression and raised his eyebrows in hopelessness to Ralf, who didn't seem to have been following what was going on at all.

The stranger had one more thing to add.

'There's the monk of course,' he breathed into their ears.

'The monk?' Roland sounded surprised and spoke louder than he intended. 'The monk?' he said again, much quieter.

'Of course. He is an awkward presence.'

'Really? He's only a monk.'

'I could kill him,' Ralf offered. It sounded as if he hadn't killed anyone for quite a while and was getting bored.

'No, no,' the quiet man urged. 'Don't you know who he is?'

The killer Norman frowned hard as if he had been asked a particularly tough question about the care of horses. 'Brother something,' he tried.

'They're all called Brother something,' Roland slapped him to silence. 'Hermitage, wasn't it? Something like that.'

'It is. That's Brother Hermitage.' The name came with a knowing nod from the stranger.

It got blank looks. 'So?'

'Brother Hermitage. The King's Investigator.'

Roland and Ralf looked at one another to see if this meant anything to either of them. It didn't.

Roland leant forward to make doubly sure that no one could overhear. 'What the king gets up to in his spare time is no concern of mine. If the monk is a, you know, friend of the king we'll leave him alone. Not a problem.'

The new arrival wiped a hand over his face. 'Idiots,' he breathed. 'Brother Hermitage has been appointed by King William to investigate deaths. Murder and so forth.' He considered the faces looking back at him. 'Investigate means find out who did it.'

'Ah.'

'So, with Stigand now dead...,' he paused to see if either of these two would be able to work out what came next.

Surprisingly, Ralf got there first. 'He could find out who did it.'

'Yes,' the stranger agreed. 'He could if anyone did it at all and the man didn't just die. But that doesn't matter. What does matter is that we don't want any investigating done at all, do we.'

Ralf looked to Roland to answer this one.

'I imagine investigation involves finding out what everyone is up to, who's doing what to whom and why, that sort of thing.' Roland speculated.

'Just that sort of thing.'

'Which wouldn't be helpful.'

'Not helpful at all. So we don't want the monk looking into anything.'

'I can kill him then,' Ralf smiled.

'No, you can't kill him. Didn't you listen to anything I said?'

Ralf looked at the ground.

'This Brother Hermitage is the King's Investigator. Appointed by King William. Do you really want to kill anyone appointed by the king?'

Ralf gave this careful thought while Roland and the stranger looked on.

'Without the king telling you that it was all right,' the stranger added.

'Ah,' Ralf got it now. 'No.'

'No. Correct. Well done. What we do need to do is make sure that this monk doesn't go poking his nose into things.'

'I could cut his nose off.'

The stranger gave up talking to Ralf. 'You explain it to him,' he directed Roland. 'He's your brother.'

'So my father said,' Roland grunted. 'Come on then,' he nodded Ralf to follow. 'Up to the church and see what's going on.'

'They're not there anymore,' the stranger informed them.

'What?'

'They left by a rear door. Probably when they saw you and the Vikings coming.'

'What Vikings?' Roland did not sound very happy at all

now.

'The Danes?' the stranger sounded as if he was talking to an idiot. 'Hawks? Danes? Silver? Ring any bells?'

'I know what's going on, or rather I thought I did. It seems you have information that isn't making it as far as my ears. Information I need. How long have the Danes been here?'

'You'd have to ask them, I only see comings and goings.'

'How very convenient for you.' Roland just gave the stranger a disappointed glare. 'Come on,' he beckoned Ralf once more. 'Let's get into the woods and see if we can find a monk.' He turned back. 'I don't imagine we'll be seeing you again, now that some action is called for.'

'I go where I am needed.'

'And turn up where you're not wanted.' Shaking his head Roland stepped out into the still deserted street with Ralf at his heels. 'Into the woods eh?' the brother said with some enthusiasm.

'Yes,' Roland cautioned. 'But we're not going into the woods to do that. You know what the king said he'd do if he caught you at it again.'

...

The monk in the woods had no idea of the interest suddenly being shown in him, which was, of course, a good thing. If he knew that his name was being bandied about by Normans Hermitage would only worry. Of course, he was already worrying about being in the woods at all, running away from Vikings and Normans, bumping into Cwen's mother behind a tree and having to stay out after dark.

What was worrying him most was Wat's suggestion that he was going to work out what really happened to Stigand.

When he considered that he didn't even know what had really happened to Stigand in the first place it seemed a bit much to expect him to explain anything.

They had taken to the small hill behind the church and rapidly climbed up among the trees, the tower of the building soon vanishing from sight. This was not well-trodden ground but there was a clear path of sorts up and over the top of the slope. Even though it was not regularly used Hermitage reasoned that someone had come this way in the past, or at least had gone to the trouble of keeping the way clear.

His mind turned to the priest who had vanished in front of them and was now nowhere to be seen. It was clear that the thought and mention of Normans had set the man on his path to escape and so perhaps there was more to his story than at first appeared.

It was quite possible that he had been a priest further south somewhere and had run into trouble with the Normans. Perhaps he had even been on the opposing side and was well known. That would explain why he kept to himself so much, and why he ran at the first opportunity.

'No sign of our so-called priest,' Wat complained. 'Not that I should be surprised.'

'So-called?' Hermitage asked.

'Of course. He's shown no sign of actually being a priest since he got here. Now he's run out of the back door and is away over the hills at the first sign of trouble.'

'You mean you don't think he was a priest at all?' Hermitage understood the words but was having trouble with the idea.

'Probably not. Good way to keep out of trouble though.'

'People can't say they're a priest when they're not.' Surely so much was obvious.

'Can they not?' Cwen asked. 'I'm a priest,' she said. 'There you are.'

'Yes, but you're obviously not a priest.'

'I'm a priest too,' Wat added.

'Now you're just being silly. And quite seriously sinful if I may say so.'

'But we both just said we were priests when we aren't, so it can be done.'

'You're just proving a point and a rather frivolous one at that. You're suggesting that our priest has not only said he was a priest but carried on pretending for some time.'

'He never seemed to know what went where in the church.' Cwen said.

'Or who was supposed to say what.' Wat added.

'He kept taking the money though,' Cwen gave a hollow laugh.

Hermitage just shook his head. All around him was deceit and dishonesty. Was it really possible that a man of the church was not a man of the church at all? If such fundamental truths were to fall by the wayside what would be left?

By this time they were over the top of the hill and had come some way down the other side. There was no way anyone would be able to spot them by just looking. There would have to be pursuit and as no one had seen them go that hardly seemed likely.

Wat drew to a halt under a particularly fine oak and stood resting against its trunk.

'So,' said Cwen as she and Hermitage drew up. 'What's the plan?'

'Plan?' Wat asked. 'What plan?'

'The plan for what we do having run away from Vikings

and Normans who want silver and hawks in that order.'

'Well,' Wat said, thoughtfully, 'we've done the running away bit. That's a start.'

'A finish would be nice.'

'Hermitage finds out what happened to Stigand.'

'Yes,' said Hermitage, an unfamiliar irritation sweeping through him. 'About that. What exactly did happen to Stigand? Only it would be nice to know if I'm supposed to work it out.'

'Hermitage,' Wat sounded impressed. 'You're getting irritated, just like normal people. Well done.'

'Absolutely,' Cwen added. 'Well done, Hermitage. And well done, Wat, for getting us stuck on a hillside while Normans and Vikings scour the place looking for us.'

'We don't know they're looking for us.'

'I think we were the ones who promised that we could get them hawks and supply silver. Oh no, wait a minute. That wasn't us. That was you. You're right, we don't know that the Normans and the Vikings are after us. They're probably just after you.'

'Don't forget your mother,' Wat retorted. 'I'm sure she has a hand in this somewhere.'

'She'd have a hand in trying to get at the silver if there was any.'

'Both of you, please,' Hermitage begged. 'The time to review our learning from all of this is later.'

They kept their peace but continued to glare at one another.

'And I think we will need some considerable time for our learning if we get to have any "later" at all that is.'

'We'll sort it out,' Wat sounded confident. 'We always do.'

'We always have up to now,' Hermitage corrected. 'Just so I

can get it straight in my head, why exactly have we run away, at all I mean? Why didn't we just wait for the Vikings and the Normans and explain the situation? After all, we didn't know anything about all of this until Stigand turned up on the doorstep.'

'Because,' Cwen explained with tired resignation, 'Wat here promised that he could sort out their trade for them.'

'I didn't hear you protesting that you didn't want fifty pounds of silver.'

'I didn't hear you offering any of it.'

'You are starting again,' Hermitage raised his arms for quiet. 'As I understand it, and do correct me if I'm wrong, we need to explain Stigand to both parties so that they will go away and forget all about their silver and their hawks.'

'And that Wat promised them both,' Cwen threw in, mischievously.

Hermitage fretted over his own plan. 'Why would they do that anyway? Why would they just go away and forget everything if we show that Stigand just died? They still want hawks and silver.'

'But he didn't just die, did he?' Wat said with some enthusiasm.

'Didn't he?'

'Of course, he didn't. You saw the state of him. That was poison if ever I saw it.'

'Really?' Hermitage felt his last vestige of hope slip down the slope and disappear into the trees.

'Of course. If you know a natural process to make a body swell like that, turn that colour and smell quite so revolting in such a short time I'd be pleased to hear about it.'

'Oh Lord,' Hermitage sighed. 'Another murder then.' While not exactly happy that someone had died, he had been content that Stigand's passing was due to natural causes. Until now. All of the lies and distortions going on around him could at least be put down to venality. Now there was murder as well. And here he was in the middle of it once more. He hadn't even moved away from the workshop and murder came calling.

His unfortunate experiences as King's Investigator had already made him worry that death was attracted to him but that couldn't be the case when he was pulled all over the country to go and look into it. When it actually came to his home he started to feel that it was personal. In this case, the victim had even come in and introduced himself. What next? Would he simply walk down the street and people would drop dead at his passing?

"Oh, here comes the King's Investigator," they would say. "Better get out of the way unless you want to be dead in the morning." Or "if you want someone dead just send for the King's Investigator, it'll happen straight away."

He could appreciate that soldiers would be surrounded by death. To an extent everyone was. Death was commonplace in these times, young or old, fit or feeble, death seemed to have no rhyme or reason. Now it had Brother Hermitage though. Perhaps he should change to a black habit and warn people he was coming.

He realised that he was gazing into the air while these awful thoughts took up residence in his mind. When he dragged his attention away he saw that Cwen and Wat were looking at him with a mixture of concern and anticipation.

'Are you all right?' Cwen asked.

'Have you thought who did it?' was Wat's question.

'No, and no,' he replied. 'It seems that I don't even have to do anything anymore to have someone murdered right next to me. It used to be the case that the king or Le Pedvin would send word and off we would go to find the body. Now they're being delivered. And they even come here of their own volition and then drop dead. What am I going to do if murder victims travel great distances to come and be done just where I'm standing?

'I'd go and live up a tree but I don't want to be surrounded by dead birds. And no I haven't thought who did it, Wat. I'm still trying to take in the fact that it's been done at all.'

'Right,' Wat still sounded hopeful that an answer was close at hand. 'Only I expect the Vikings and the Normans will realise that there's only Stigand in the church and come looking. Not that I'd trust Ralf the Norman to spot a door in a doorway but the Vikings aren't quite so stupid. They could be on their way.'

Hermitage could do nothing but shake his head. 'Then they must find us and we can consider the situation.'

'Aha, right. I'd rather consider considering the situation and then have them come upon us. Be a bit easier that way?'

'Our way is not meant to be easy.'

'And Wat's done his bit to make it so,' Cwen observed. 'But we do know that Stigand was poisoned now. So someone gave him the poison. A killer. Someone who wanted to kill him. Now. Who said that they wanted to kill Stigand.'

'You did,' Wat said.

'Apart from me,' Cwen waved this away. 'My mother. Eadgyth. That's who. She said she came here specifically to kill him and we've already agreed that she could poison him.'

'Have we?' Hermitage asked. 'When did we agree that?'

'Oh, ages ago. When we said she couldn't stick a knife in him.'

'I don't recall...'

'Never mind,' Cwen moved on, enthusiastically. 'If Eadgyth knew all about the silver and the hawks and the Normans and the Vikings she could easily poison him, take the silver and be off.'

'But she wasn't off. She's still here as far as we know.'

'Because she hasn't got the silver. It's all part of her plan.'

'And no one knows where the silver is if Stigand hasn't spent it already. We only have that Viking's word that the king sent any at all.'

'There's still the parchment,' Wat pointed out. 'That's genuine. There's definitely silver at the bottom of all this somewhere.'

'And it will be the ruin of us all,' Hermitage moaned.

Before anyone could say anything else to either add to the conversation or confuse it even more, there was a crashing in the undergrowth.

'Oh, hell,' Wat hissed, looking back up the slope. 'We've tarried too long.'

'You have, Wat the Weaver,' Roland's voice called from the slope below them.

'How did you get round there?' Wat asked.

'Walked,' Roland explained, carefully.

'But how did you know?'

'We will talk with the monk,' Roland ignored the question.

Hermitage knew that there was no point asking what monk. He stood forward and shrugged his meagre shoulders. 'Here I am.'

'Good.' Roland beckoned him further down the slope and with a glance at the others, Hermitage half stepped, half slipped to join the Norman.

'What do you think that's about?' Wat asked Cwen. 'They can't think that Hermitage has got any hawks.'

'Perhaps they want a monk out of the way before they come and chop you up?'

There was little useful discussion they could have, so they just waited while Hermitage took in whatever it was Roland had to say. There wasn't much of it as the Norman soon departed while Hermitage climbed back up the hill.

'Well?' Wat asked, eagerly.

'Well, well,' Hermitage said, wrapped in yet more confusing thoughts.

'What is it? What did he say?' Cwen urged.

Hermitage just repeated the words, he still couldn't make any sense of them. 'He just said that I didn't need to worry about Stigand.'

'Not worry about him?'

'More specific than that, really. He said there was no need to investigate.'

'Investigate?' Wat looked worried. 'Why would he say investigate, unless he knows who you are?'

'Exactly. In fact, he said that I should take this as an instruction not to investigate.'

'Did he indeed?'

'Indeed he did.'

'Just because he's a Norman he can issue you instructions?'

'Well, yes, I think he probably can. But there was more to it. He said that he had received word himself and was only passing the message on.'

'Who from?'

'The king.'

'The king?' Wat and Cwen said it together and both sounded very surprised.

'What's the king's interest in Stigand?' Cwen asked.

'Hawks?' Wat replied. 'It is the king's charter after all and him who wants the hawks.'

'And it's his silver,' Cwen added.

'There is that.'

'But why would the king send word that you were not to investigate Stigand?'

Hermitage sighed heavily. 'That, I think, is the question.'

'Handy though,' Wat noted. 'Being told not to investigate a possible murder instead of being ordered to get on with it on pain of your own death.'

'Well, yes,' Hermitage was hesitant. 'But...,'

'But what?' Cwen sounded worried now.

'Why would the king, who isn't even here, want me to stop investigating an obvious death?'

'Isn't that for him to know.'

Hermitage looked at Cwen askance. 'Yes, it is, of course. But Stigand had his charter and was getting all those hawks and handing over pounds and pounds of silver. What's happened to all of that?'

'Do we care? Maybe he's just gone off hawks a bit.'

'There's an awful lot of activity going on for it to be a simple whim. Never mind the production of a major charter.'

'Maybe he got them somewhere else?' Wat suggested. 'You know. He was going to buy new hawks but then someone gave him some?'

'No,' Hermitage was not having it. 'There's more to it than that. But it's a mystery in its own right. And you know I can't abide a mystery. Now I've got to know why the king wants me to leave Stigand alone. And the best way to find that out is to investigate the murder.'

'Which you were just complaining you didn't want to do,' Wat pointed out.

'Be easy just to say my mother did it,' Cwen grumbled.

'And it's against the king's specific instructions.' Wat insisted.

Hermitage wandered away from the oak tree rubbing his chin as he went. 'We'll just have to be careful.'

'What's this we?' Wat called after him.

Caput XIV

The Body has Visitors

Stigand's condition had not improved by the time the Vikings arrived. In fact, one element of it had got much worse.

'Oh my God,' Mistress Angel choked and pulled at her escort, putting her other hand across her nose as she was dragged into the church. 'What on earth is that stink?'

'I rather suspect that's Stigand,' Ragnar suggested, showing not the slightest discomfort at a smell that could probably drive woodworm out of a longship.

'He wasn't like that at my inn.' Mistress Angel wanted to make it clear that her establishment did not tolerate such malodorous corpses.

Ragnar waved Ulrik to check over the interior of the church for anyone hiding in the shadows. With a pointed finger at Ern that was perfectly sufficient to stop the Saxon from moving anywhere, Ulrik quickly scouted around the building and found nothing.

'I didn't think Christians buried their dead like this,' Ulrik did wrinkle his nose having got a bit too close to Stigand.

'We don't,' Angel complained. 'We put them in the ground, hence the word?' A twist of the arm from Ragnar brought Angel's respect for her captors back.

'So why is this one still here?'

'No idea. You'd have to ask the priest. It costs money to bury people and perhaps Stigand didn't have any.'

'He must have had plenty to pay you,' Ragnar pointed out. 'Where is it now?'

'I don't know what you're talking about. Ow.' Mistress Angel felt the pull of Ragnar's persuasiveness.

'Come mistress. Stigand was staying at the inn, what was he paying you with?'

'Stop twisting my arm. It was just coin. Pennies, mainly.'

'And where did they come from? A chest?'

'A chest? Of course not. He had a small purse, that's all.'

'And where is his small purse now?'

'It's safe, it's safe. I was keeping it for his next of kin.'

'Were you?'

'Yes, I was. And there's no point you fretting over it because it's almost empty anyway.'

'Empty,' Ragnar sounded as if he suspected more lies. He glanced at Ulrik who helpfully grabbed Ern again and shook him about a bit.

'What else did he bring with him? Apart from a small purse?' Ulrik demanded.

'Hardly anything,' Ern reported. 'A small pack and that was it.'

'And what was in the pack?'

Ern looked shocked. 'I'm sure I wouldn't possibly know. It was Master Stigand's pack, I'm not going to go prying into his belongings, am I?'

'What was in the pack?' Ulrik added a twist of his own.

'Just clothes and a spare pair of shoes,' Ern squeaked.

'He didn't have another box? Nothing else at all.'

'No.'

Ragnar looked thoughtful and spoke to Ulrik. 'I think these people could be lying again. If we got a force of our brothers to come and search properly we might find something. You know, take the walls down, that sort of thing.'

'There was nothing,' Angel protested with a heartfelt wail. 'If there was anything we'd give it to you. We've been giving Vikings almost everything we have for years now, we're used to it. If there was a box, you could have it.'

Ragnar just stood and studied her.

'You can have the purse. Take it.'

'Oh, I will. Consider us his next of kin.'

Ragnar and Ulrik now ignored their captives and gathered in a huddled conversation in their own impenetrable language.

They did not appreciate that Ern and Angel had been running a tavern, which until not very long ago at all had been in Daneland. It was all very well kings and such marching up and down the country throwing one another out or letting one another back in again, depending upon their whim, but the ordinary people had to make a living.

In the morning you could have your normal local clientèle and by the afternoon some force or other turned up announcing that they were liberating you from your yoke or something. This was all good business for the active innkeeper. Victorious forces were always keen on celebration and it was important to let them know that they were just the force you'd been waiting for all this time.

Of course, the following day it could all be reversed and a goodly quantity of ale would be required to celebrate being returned to the rule of the first lot. As the life of the ordinary working person was seldom disturbed by these comings and goings it was important to keep in with whoever was in charge.

Obviously, a truly mad army would turn up now and again who wanted to do nothing but leave a trail of destruction in their wake. In these cases, it was important to know how to run away effectively.

Mistress Angel's command of the Danes' language was not extensive, but it was always useful to know what people were saying in case some of their talk turned to trails of destruction after a few too many ales.

She listened now and raised her eyebrows at Ern as the Vikings' discussion focussed on silver. Quite a lot of it, apparently. So much it would have to be in a box of some sort. A box that Stigand might have hidden somewhere. No wonder the wretched man could afford bread and wine each morning. With a box of silver, he could have had the inn.

Angel glared her disappointment at Ern that they'd had no sight of any box at all, let alone one filled with silver. Never mind the Vikings taking her inn to pieces, she'd do it herself if she ever got back there.

After they had spoken without coming to any helpful conclusion the Vikings turned back to Angel and Ern. 'Who brought him here?' Ragnar nodded his head to indicate which stinking corpse he was talking about.

'I don't know,' Angel complained. 'I don't get picky when it comes to people taking bodies out of my inn. As long as they do it, that's good enough for me.'

'I went to the moot hall to get help,' Ern spoke up, perhaps thinking that his wife's talent for abusing everyone she spoke to would be best saved for another occasion. 'There was the blacksmith's son, he's a strong lad.'

'Who else?'

'Just a couple of people who could be gathered at the time and who were interested in moving a body. No one special. Depended on who was free. The headman said just to get him moved to the church.'

Ragnar narrowed his suspicious eyes. 'And the priest?'

'No, the priest didn't come. He was at the church, you see.'

'I realise he would be at the church,' Ragnar's teeth were gritted. 'Where is he now?'

'No idea. He wasn't too keen on taking the body at all but the moot had said he had to. And if I was him with that in my church I'd probably step outside as well.'

'What did he want you to do with it?'

'He didn't say. He doesn't say much at all really.'

'So you just brought it in here and left it.'

'That's it. The priest did say that we had to dig the grave but no one was keen on that so we said we'd come back later.

Ulrik was frowning now. 'How long ago was this?'

'Oh, not long. Not long at all.'

'Then why does he smell so bad. You'd think he'd been dead for days.'

The two Vikings shared curious expressions and wandered over to the altar. Poking their heads around the back they soon reappeared.

Vikings liked their reputation for hardiness, being fearsome, afraid of nothing and leaping in where others would fear to tread, usually with a wild battle cry on their lips.

Ulrik's reputation would need some repair as he ran to the church door and was sick on the step. Even Ragnar looked pale and slightly wobbly. 'Great Odin and all the Gods, what's happened to him?'

'Not nice?' Ern enquired.

'Was he like that when you brought him in?'

There was no way Ern was going to go and look at something that had turned the stomach of two large Vikings. 'I doubt it.'

'He was just dead,' Angel explained. 'Like a normal dead

person. If he had smelt like this I would have had him out sooner.'

'It's not just what he smells like, it's what he looks like as well.'

Ern and Angel took a cautious step away from the altar. Evil humours were a very real threat and could come from anywhere. Obviously, the altar should be some protection, being holy and all, and the church building would protect them, but it didn't pay to push your luck in situations like this.

'Poison,' Ulrik announced when he had recovered.

'No doubt.' Ragnar agreed. They both looked to the Saxons.

'Don't look at me,' Angel huffed. 'I don't go poisoning my customers. It'd be bad for business.'

'Unless there was more money than you're telling us about.'

'If we had money do you think we'd still be working in our inn moving dead bodies about?'

Ragnar didn't look convinced.

'We'd have people for that sort of thing.'

'Someone poisoned him.'

'Well, it wasn't us. And furthermore, I don't want you spreading tales that people staying at my inn get poisoned. It could have happened anywhere. He was right as a right man when he arrived.'

'Where else had he been?'

'All over town. I don't keep track of people.'

Ulrik looked over from where he was still taking the fresh air by the door. 'The weavers' workshop.'

'Yes,' Ragnar nodded with interest. 'The weaver who may be able to help out in this business by putting his hands on some silver.'

Now Ulrik nodded as well.

'Wat the Weaver?' Angel sounded amused by the suggestion. 'He's a wrong one and no mistake but poisoning people? Not him. Too much trouble and fuss.'

'And mess,' Ern turned his nose in the direction of the altar.

'I think we'll decide who the poisoners in Derby are, mistress.' Ragnar said. 'And I still haven't ruled out you two.'

Ulrik reverted to the Viking language, not in the least concerned that Angel and Ern might understand. 'Or the Normans?'

'Could be,' Ragnar replied. 'Sort of thing they'd do but hardly in their interest.'

'Come,' Ragnar said in the Saxon tongue. 'We'll go back to the town where you will stay at your inn.'

'Of course, we will,' Angel said. 'Got nowhere else to go.'

'And Ulrik will stay with you to make sure that's the case.' He nodded to Ulrik. 'Just make sure you don't eat anything while you're there. And have a look around to see what you can find. You know, knock down a wall or two. I'm going to visit our weaving friend. If he has any money I suspect that it belongs to us.'

He directed them all to leave now, which Angel and Ern did with some relief. While they had got used to the odour in the church it wasn't until they got outside that they realised how bad it had got. They took gulps of air and wiped noses.

As they took the first steps towards the town a woman approached at some speed looking fretful and upset. The Vikings and Saxons waited until she drew near.

'Oh, woe is me,' the woman wailed, which got some peculiar looks. 'Where oh where is my dear Stigand?'

'Your dear Stigand?' Ragnar asked.

'Of course, he is my husband, I am the Lady Eadgyth.'

'Lady, ha,' Angel snorted.

Eadgyth ignored her. 'I have looked high and low for my loving Stigand but he is nowhere to be seen. What has happened to him?' She did seem to notice Angel now. 'This washerwoman said she hadn't seen him.'

'It's all right,' Angel spoke before anyone else could get a word in. 'We've found him now, he's in the church. Just behind the altar, why don't you go and have a look.' She smiled the smile of a serpent that's just seen two naked people sitting at the bottom of its apple tree.

Eadgyth turned her nose in the air and ignored Angel with flamboyance. 'I am coming my love,' she called up the church path. 'Never fear, your Eadgyth is here.'

Ragnar just looked at Angel. 'And you reckon you couldn't poison anyone.' He shook his head in disappointment at this behaviour. Which was quite something, coming from a Viking. 'Ulrik, wait here until she comes out again. If she is Stigand's wife she's probably involved in all this like the rest of this wretched town.'

'Aye.' Ulrik gave Angel and Ern the look that told them to stay where they were. They stayed.

. . .

'Where do we go then?' Cwen asked as they walked along through the woods with no destination in mind. 'We're all right with the Normans now but if the Vikings catch up they're probably going to be trouble.'

'Back to the workshop?' Hermitage suggested.

Cwen stopped in her tracks and smiled brightly. 'Of course. We don't need to worry anymore.'

'How's that?' Hermitage thought not worrying anymore was a very good idea but he couldn't see it working somehow.

'The Vikings only want silver. Wat's already said that he's got lots. He simply gives it to them and they go away.'

'Just a minute,' Wat complained.

'If a bunch of real Vikings turned up they'd just take it.'

'Not necessarily. They'd have to find it first.'

'Can't you simply say that you've given it some thought and decided not to go into the hawk business?' Hermitage thought this sounded quite straightforward, particularly as Wat was supposed to be a weaver anyway.

'I don't think Vikings work like that.'

'And they might be quite interested in finding out who poisoned the man who was supposed to have their silver in the first place.' Cwen said, helpfully.

'So when are you going to know?' Wat asked.

'Know?' Hermitage was lost once more. 'Know what?'

'Who killed Stigand,' Wat emphasised each word. 'I thought that was what we were going to do now.'

'Oh, that, yes. No idea really.'

'No idea?'

'No. I can't just sit down and decide right, now I'll work out who the killer is.'

'Can't you?'

'No, of course, I can't. That's not how it works.'

'How does it work then?'

'I don't know that either. It just sort of comes to me when I've got enough information. You should know this from all the other times it's happened.'

'I suppose so.' Wat kicked a stick like a bored child. 'Only when you were going on about it being a mystery and all I thought you had an idea.'

'If Wat won't save us all by giving the Vikings his silver, what's wrong with my mother?' Cwen asked.

'Wrong with her?' Hermitage didn't really know what he was being asked. He hardly liked to comment on the shortcomings of Cwen's mother. He'd only just met her after all. Although that short encounter had given him quite a list.

'For the killer I mean. I know you don't believe it for some reason or other, but she could have done it. Really. She knows about poisons, she'd said she wanted to kill him and there's absolutely no doubt that she wants to get her hands on his silver. What better way of doing that than having him dead?'

'And you?' Wat pointed out, perhaps feeling safe that Cwen's temper was back inside somewhere. Probably resting and building up its strength for another excursion. And perhaps worried that she might decide to hand his silver over to the Vikings without being asked. 'You know all about poisons, you said you wanted to kill him and you had time to do it when you went off on your walk. You could have run down to town, put something in his bread and wine and been back before we knew.'

Cwen had stopped walking again and was now looking at Wat. Hermitage had an unpleasant feeling and hoped that things weren't going to get nasty. If Cwen started to try and break the trees she could do herself an injury.

'And you had that motive thing. Stigand turns up claiming to be your father? We know that made you cross. So cross you murdered my furniture. Why not do the man himself?'

Hermitage found that he was holding his breath as he waited for the response to this idea.

Cwen looked from Wat to Hermitage and back again. After a very long and worrying pause, she tipped her head so that her face looked up to the tops of the trees. She then came down again, bent double and burst out laughing.

Hermitage breathed again.

'I did it?' she managed to get out between her laughs.

'Just a thought,' Wat shrugged.

'And a ridiculous one,' she said when she had calmed a little. 'Yes, I was angry but I'm hardly likely to go and kill my father when we've only just been introduced, am I?'

'You said you would.'

'Yes, but I say I'll kill lots of people. I say I'll kill you quite a lot.' She went over to Wat and slid a hand around his arm. 'It was lovely though.'

'Lovely?' Wat looked very lost. Lost and not a bit worried.

'Yes,' Cwen smiled warmly at him. 'Lovely that you think I really could kill someone. My own father even. I shall remember that.'

Wat's face was a lot paler than it had been, as if a whole new chapter of his life was opening up in front of him and it didn't have a happy ending.

'And what if he is your father?' Hermitage asked. He saw Cwen's mood as a good opportunity to ask. If anything was likely to set her off again surely it would be the death of the father she'd only just met.

'What if he is? Only met him once. He'd never been a father to me before, now he's someone dead who's never been a father to me at all.'

Hermitage couldn't really believe that she would take this so well. He saw some difficult evenings ahead.

'Where do we go then so that Hermitage can work out who poisoned the hawk trader?' She beckoned Hermitage to come over and put a hand through his arm as well. Like some happy troop of blackberry pickers heading for the brambles, she led them along the forest path. 'We'll need somewhere to hide from the Vikings, at least.'

Their happy moment, which was only happy because no one was paying attention to what was really going on, was broken by a piercing scream.

'That came from the church,' Wat turned his head back to the source of the noise.

'And it came from my mother,' Cwen added.

'Oh dear,' was Hermitage's contribution.

Their consternation continued as the screams carried on. There were breaks for the person making the noise to get their breath but it was clear this could continue for some time.

'She sounds in a bad way.' Wat made no movement towards the source of the screams.

'And she is going on a bit,' Cwen noted as the breath-scream-breath-scream pattern continued. 'Do you think she's found Stigand?'

'Ah,' Hermitage saw that this was quite possibly the case, and also a helpful piece of information. 'She sounds, erm, surprised?' he suggested.

'Surprised?' Wat clearly thought this was an understatement. 'She sounds a lot more than just surprised. Surprised people maybe let out one scream, or two. They don't go on and on.'

Still, no one had moved. 'Do you think we should go and find out?' Hermitage's natural sympathy for anyone in distress urged him to try and calm this tortured soul.

'We could do,' Wat agreed, very tentatively. 'Although if my ears are working right I think she may be coming our way.'

They all listened again as if trying to agree that they had

heard a cuckoo in the distance. The screams continued, although the voice producing them was starting to sound a bit hoarse. There was no denying that it was getting closer though.

'We could leave her to it?' Cwen suggested.

'She is clearly in distress,' Hermitage tutted. 'Genuine distress. Which, apart from being something to be comforted, tells us that she probably did not kill Stigand.'

'Really?' Cwen didn't seem happy at this.

'Why would she be so shocked at the sight of him?'

'It is a pretty horrible sight,' Wat pointed out.

Cwen dismissed this. 'She could have put the poison in without knowing what it did. Never having poisoned anyone before. Now she's horrified at what she's done. Serve her right.'

'Or she really has just discovered that her Stigand is dead?' Hermitage posed the question sombrely.

'Ah, right,' Cwen nodded at this. 'You mean she's screaming because she's realised she's not going to get any silver now.'

Caput XV

The Wife Should Know

They didn't have to wait long before Eadgyth came stumbling through the undergrowth. She was still trying to scream but it looked like her voice had run out. Her mouth opened quite regularly but the only thing to emerge was some croaking noises.

She spotted them and headed over, adding some arm-waving to her silent complaint. When she arrived she collapsed onto the floor and sat looking from one to the other. 'Croak, croak,' she said.

Hermitage leant forward to catch the words.

'Have you seen him?' Eadgyth's breathy voice was full of horror.

'Er, yes.'

Eadgyth shook her head. 'That's not my Stigand.'

'No indeed. He is in a bit of a state.'

'What's happened to him?'

'Poison, we think.'

'Poison?' Eadgyth gave them all more looks, this time with wide eyes. 'What sort of place is this that poisons people?'

'We think someone did it to him.'

'I should think they did. No one's going to do that to themselves. Oh, my poor heart.'

Hermitage glanced up at Cwen who was standing with arms folded appraising her mother. 'Not going to be any silver now.'

Eadgyth's mouth tightened. 'Oh, you wicked girl,' she breathed. 'That poor man lying there and all you can think about is silver.'

'It's all you've been thinking about since you left Arundel. Funny how you turn up here looking for your dear husband, the one who was so dear you haven't even mentioned his name for seventeen years.'

'Twenty,' Eadgyth corrected.

'You tell us all that you want to kill him and then he turns up dead. And if there is any silver left I can guess that his loving wife will claim it's hers.'

Eadgyth just sat and shook her head in sadness. 'You've been mixing with the wrong sort I can tell, to be thinking things like that. Him I'd expect it from,' she nodded at Wat. 'But you a monk?'

Hermitage looked at the forest floor. There wasn't the time to explain the role of the King's Investigator and all the devious dealings he had come across. Stealing silver from dead people was quite normal in comparison.

'So you don't want any silver then?' Cwen asked. 'We can give it back to King William if we ever find it.'

Eadgyth did look a bit worried now. 'What's he got to do with Stigand's silver?'

'It's not Stigand's silver at all. We've found out that the king wants some hawks and Stigand was getting them for him. What do you think all the Normans and Vikings are doing wandering around the place? They haven't come to buy tapestry you know.'

Eadgyth said nothing but narrowed her eyes in thought.

'And if we ever do get to the bottom of all this we'll probably find Stigand doesn't have any silver of his own at all. Which means there'll be none left for anyone.'

Still sitting among the leaves, Eadgyth distracted Cwen from her gloating. 'Hawks, you say.'

'Erm, yes, hawks.'

'My Stigand was always interested in hawks. Went on about them all the time he did. Said as how one day he would have a hawk of his own. Course I said he'd have to be a noble or as rich as one, so he said that's what he'd do. Go out into the world to make his fortune and buy his own hawk farm, or whatever it is you keep hawks in.'

'You didn't share his interest?' Hermitage asked. If Eadgyth did know all about hawks she might have more involvement in all this than she was letting on.

'Nah, couldn't see the point. He was going on about breeding the very best hawks you could get. I said he should cross one with a pigeon. That way you wouldn't have to stand out in a field, the bird would come back on its own. Course it would be a bit tricky getting the hawk and the pigeon to do it, what with the one trying to eat the other and all.'

'Shut up,' Cwen instructed this rambling nonsense to stop.

'Stigand was a real hawk expert?' Wat asked.

'Oh yes. He never shut up about them. Knew all the proper words for the little bits and pieces they have, gloves and tassels and such like. Knew where the best birds came from. If you wanted to be bored to death by talk of hawks, you just had to ask my Stigand.'

'That is very interesting,' Hermitage pondered. Stigand certainly hadn't given any indication of being an expert in hawks. Perhaps that was another lie to draw Wat into handing over his silver.

Cwen had some more thoughts to pester her mother with. 'And now that Stigand is dead the king will probably demand his silver back. The silver that's doubtless been spent already. We'd best tell the king to ask his dear wife Eadgyth. You can pay him back.'

'I don't know nothing about any of that,' Eadgyth waved this nonsense away.

'Bit of a coincidence,' Cwen went on. 'You looking for Stigand and his silver and him turning up dead. That's going to take some explaining.'

'I don't know what you're on about.' Eadgyth turned her head away.

Even Hermitage found it hard to believe that the woman thought she'd get away with this blatant denial of everything she'd said a few hours ago.

'Oh, come on, mother. You want his money, you threaten to kill him and then he turns up dead in church.'

'Who has?'

'Stigand!' Cwen turned to Hermitage and Wat. 'Do you think she's going to feign madness now? Claim not to remember anything? Can't see that working with King William.'

'I'm not claiming anything,' Eadgyth insisted.

'You were the one who just came screaming from the church at the sight of his body.'

'Because it was horrible.' Eadgyth sounded bored at having to explain this. 'Like I said at the time, if you'd been listening, that's not my Stigand.'

'Because the effects of the poison have changed his looks,' Hermitage suggested.

'Only if they've changed his height and his age as well.' She stood now and it was her turn to fold her arms as she gazed at the confused looks around her. 'Aha. You think that's my Stigand don't you.' She gave them all a silence to confirm it. 'Well, it isn't.'

'Eh,' said Cwen, followed by, 'What? How? Who?'

'Mistress clever breeches. Not so clever now are we? That

dead man in the church is not Stigand of Worthing. He's too old and too short. My Stigand was a tall young man.'

'That was seventeen years ago,' Cwen pointed out.

'Twenty,' Eadgyth muttered with some impatience. 'He was a lot younger than me then. A lot younger.'

'Mother!' Cwen said with some disgust.

'Mistress Eadgyth,' Hermitage spoke up. 'The man introduced himself to us as Stigand of Arundel.'

'There you are then. Arundel, Worthing, they're different places you know.'

'But he also claimed to be Cwen's father.'

'Did he?' Eadgyth asked with interest. 'And when did this happen? Before I even came and saw you I expect. Keeping secrets from your mother like that.' She shook her head in disappointment.

'It's a shorter time than you kept him secret from me.'

'Why would he do that?' Hermitage didn't want this question diverted by another family argument. 'If he's not her father, why would he claim that he was?'

'You'd have to ask him.'

'Bit difficult, that,' Wat said. 'If he really isn't the right Stigand he could just have been after the money.'

'Lying, cheating, dung-chewing, scab-faced arse,' Cwen spat.

'How would he even know?' Hermitage pressed on. 'If he were a stranger why on earth would he suggest he was Cwen's father?'

'Who knows?' Wat said. 'Could have met the real Stigand on the road and stolen his story, and his silver?'

Hermitage's mind did a little jump at that thought. He didn't want to say anything to Eadgyth, in case she really was involved in all this somehow, but this couldn't be a coincidence. He gave Cwen and Wat his interested look and they gave subtle nods of agreement to say nothing.

A dead man calling himself Stigand turns up to trade hawks when he appeared not to know anything about them. Meanwhile, the wife of another Stigand, one who knows everything there is to know about hawks comes looking for him. What were the chances of that? Very slim, probably.

'I'm confused,' Hermitage said, trying not to give anything away about the two Stigands and their varying levels of hawk-knowledge. Was nothing in this sorry tale going to be honest and true? The traders were constantly lying to one another and now the people were turning out not to be who they said they were.

Perhaps the Normans and Vikings weren't even Norman or Viking? He thought that unlikely, after all, they did look the part. But neither of them had known what Stigand looked like. If this was even the right Stigand? Which one was supposed to be dealing with the hawks for the king, Arundel or Worthing? 'I think I need to get comfortable to think about this,' he said.

'Time to sit down and decide who did it?' Wat asked.

'Time to try and work out who everyone is and what on earth they're all doing. Poisoning seems quite straightforward in comparison.'

'Back to the workshop?' Cwen suggested.

'Probably full of Vikings by now,' Wat said.

'We've got to face them sometime.'

'Don't see why. Leave them alone long enough they might go away.'

'That hasn't happened in the last hundred years or so.'

Wat rubbed his chin in thought, probably hoping to avoid anyone with eyes on his silver having any discussion with him at all. He stopped rubbing when he noticed that Hermitage was staring at a tree. 'Hermitage?'

'Hm, yes?' Hermitage replied vaguely. Several ideas had been passing through his mind, all of them uninvited as usual. There was something about the rough bark of the tree that caught his attention and he wasn't entirely sure why. Wat's call dragged his mind back to the world around him and he slowly focussed on the people, all of whom were staring at him now.

'It's the bark,' he said, which was perfectly clear to him.

'Is he all right?' Eadgyth asked with the tone of someone stuck in the woods with a loon in a monk's habit.

'Perfectly,' Cwen snapped at her mother. 'What's the bark, Hermitage?' She sounded as if she asked questions like this all the time.

Hermitage simply expressed his thoughts. 'The bark is tiny and rough and full of little valleys and indentations. It even has small creatures and growths of its own.'

'Yes?'

'Yet it is a tree.'

'That's right,' Eadgyth said, with increasing caution. 'It's a tree.'

'From the point of view of the tiny creature the tree is invisible. And from our point of view, the bark is invisible until we bend to look at it.'

'Aha.'

'And when we do look at it we lose sight of the tree.'

'That's good then,' Eadgyth now looked very ready to leave. 'We've sorted out the tree and the bark. I'm sure we can do this poisoner later.'

'It's like the lies,' Hermitage went on. Surely everyone could see this, his analogy was so clear. 'The lies show us the bark when actually it's the tree we need to see.'

'Was it tree poison then?' Eadgyth tried.

'I think we do need everyone together,' Hermitage reached his conclusion. 'The Vikings, the Normans, Angel and Ern, even us.'

'Are you sure that's sensible?' Wat asked with some trepidation.

'It's the only way. Every time we talk to someone we just get their view of the bark.'

'Really?' Cwen sounded concerned now.

'I mean events. The whole business is just riddled with people giving us their own version, telling us what they can see and probably lying into the bargain.'

'And you can see the whole tree?' Wat asked.

'Oh, no. I've no idea what it looks like. But, if we get everyone to talk at the same time, well, not at the same time, but you know what I mean, we should get a better picture.'

'What if no one can see the tree?'

'Then we'll just have to draw one from the information we get.'

'You're all mad,' Eadgyth concluded. 'Trees and bark and poison and silver. I should have stayed at home.'

'Yes,' Cwen said. 'You should.'

'Your view will be needed as well, Mistress Eadgyth,' Hermitage explained, wondering why everyone was being so difficult. 'The fact that our Stigand is not your Stigand needs explanation, and could be at the heart of the matter.' He smiled encouragingly. 'Or not.'

'I'm not going with him on my own,' Eadgyth drew back slightly.

'We're all going together,' Hermitage explained. 'In fact, we probably need to go and get the Normans. If they think

Stigand's death is not being looked into they could be leaving.'

'What about the hawks?' Cwen asked. 'We've all gone through a lot for these bloody birds.'

'Who knows?' Hermitage gave a hopeless shrug. 'Who knows anything. The whole situation is a complete mystery. And a shambles. Only when we get everyone together will we have the slightest chance of finding out what on earth is going on. And even then I'm not holding out much hope.'

'So,' Wat said with some resignation. 'We go and find the Normans and the Vikings and Mistress Angel and invite everyone back to the workshop for a chat about silver and hawks and the king and so forth.'

'That's it.'

'Do we need to bring Stigand?'

'Hardly.' Hermitage tutted at this frivolity. 'We have Mistress Eadgyth's word that it's not her Stigand.'

'And we all know that she's as trustworthy as a liar in a lying competition.' Cwen snorted.

'It would useful to find out if he's the right Stigand but I don't think he'll be much help in that.'

'The right Stigand?' Cwen asked.

'The one who is supposed to have the parchment and the silver and be buying hawks for the king. Or should that be Eadgyth's Stigand?'

'Ah, I see,' Cwen nodded. She then looked rather puzzled and was obviously realising she didn't see anything at all.

'I'm not going near any Vikings,' Wat protested. 'They're going to ask for my silver again.'

'Not if the Normans are there as well.' Hermitage reassured him. He felt bad about this as he had absolutely no idea what was going to happen about anything. Still, he felt that most of this was Wat's fault in the first place and so he would have to take whatever was thrown his way. He would just be glad to get all the contradictions and lies out in the open. He only hoped it would help.

'Come on then,' Wat shook his head, perhaps seeing that he really didn't have much choice; unless he wanted to move into the woods permanently. 'You can tell the Vikings I haven't actually got any silver anyway and that I was only trying to be helpful.'

'Trying to be helpful,' Cwen scoffed. 'Trying to be helpful to yourself.'

Hermitage led the way back up the hill towards the church in the hope that the Normans would still be around somewhere. He'd never hoped that Normans would be around before so it was an entirely new sensation.

They arrived at the back door of the church without incident and were all very careful to go round the building this time, instead of through it. Hermitage did wonder briefly about the priest and whether he could have anything to do with this sorry tale. He thought it unlikely as the man had run away at the first hint of a Norman.

He was probably just trying to escape to a new town or village where he could offer his services as priest. The idea that he wasn't a priest at all was plainly ridiculous.

As they passed the main door the body of Stigand made its presence felt.

'I don't think we need to worry about anyone stealing him,' Cwen sniffed and coughed.

'Somebody really should come and bury the poor fellow.' Hermitage was worried about the proprieties of leaving the deceased unattended for so long.

'You're right,' Cwen agreed. 'Someone should.' She hurried

on.

Hermitage had been hoping that he would walk back into the street and the Normans would just be standing there as if awaiting his instruction. Perhaps they would be discussing their next move and he would be able to catch them before they left.

He knew it was a fairly hopeless hope, but then many of his hopes were. Part of him was pleasantly surprised to see that in fact, the two Normans were just standing there. They were just standing there looking at a sight of complete chaos that greeted Hermitage's eyes and which was not even in his list of disappointingly likely scenarios.

It seemed that the entire population of Derby had gathered in one place. Gathered for an argument, by the look of it. People were milling about all over the place with very little rhyme or reason. There was much shouting and a bit of pushing. One or two even fell over and stayed sat on the floor, carrying on their remonstrations from a seated position.

Roland and Ralf exchanged looks with Hermitage and the others that said they didn't have a clue what was going on here either.

He could see no order in any of the activities. There didn't seem to be a leader or a focus of attention. It was as if everyone had been having an argument in their own house and had come out onto the street to carry on.

It was only when a new figure appeared from a doorway that he noticed one thing every member of the crowd had in common. They were all carrying tankards.

'Get out,' Mistress Angel screamed at the crowd as she strode from her tavern. As the crowd were already out Hermitage could only assume that this cry had been going on for some time.

'You're all thieves,' she remonstrated at the top of her voice and with considerable anger. 'I turn my back for two minutes and what happens? I get robbed. Well, you needn't think you're getting away with this.' She tried to point at everyone at once. 'I know each and every one of you and you'll be paying me for everything that's been drunk.'

There were some vocal protests at this but they were largely incoherent and came from people who were clutching tankards as if their lives depended on it.

Hermitage noticed that one or two of those on the ground were now being sick. He nodded and shook his head at the same time in recognition and disappointment at what had been going on.

'I was stolen away by Vikings, for goodness sake,' Mistress Angel's tirade was still going and Hermitage suspected it would continue to do so for several weeks. 'Vikings! And what do my townsfolk do? Come and rescue me? No. They sneak into my tavern and steal my ale.' A fresh idea occurred to her. 'I shall report you all to the moot. That'll see you sorted out. They'll probably hang the lot of you.'

Hermitage glanced around and thought this unlikely as one of the fellows being copiously ill against the wall of the inn was the headman.

Then she spotted the new arrivals. 'Wat the Weaver,' her anger reached new heights. 'I might have known you'd be involved in this.'

'Me?' Wat protested. 'What have I got to do with it? I've only just got here.'

'You'll be at the bottom of it somewhere. You always are.'

'Wat the Weaver?' Ulrik stepped from behind Angel.

'Oh, great,' Wat sighed.

'We're looking for you.' The Viking smiled and beckoned

that Wat should draw near. 'Ah, and the wife of Stigand. This is good news. I wondered where you'd gone. Ran away out the back of the church, no doubt.'

'Oh good,' Cwen smiled. 'Look, the Vikings want to talk to you, mother.'

Wat took a step forward but Hermitage put a hand on his chest. 'I can take it from here.' He gulped and breathed and told himself that this was the right thing to do. Yes, Wat was largely at fault, pretty much most of the time when you thought about it. Even Mistress Angel's problems stemmed from Wat indicating to the Vikings that he had silver in the first place. If he hadn't agreed to dead Stigand's proposal none of them would be in this mess at all. Still, Wat was his friend and he wouldn't really leave him to the Vikings and the Normans if he could do anything about it.

Not that it hadn't done Wat some good to worry about his fate and the wages of sin for a while.

He took his brave steps toward the Viking. He had absolutely no confidence in what he was about to do but just hoped it didn't show.

'Master Ulrik,' he announced. 'Just the person I've been looking for. I am Brother Hermitage and I am King William's Investigator. I am here to find out what is going on and why there is a dead man in the church.'

Hermitage was hugely relieved that Ulrik just looked confused. Confused was better than murderous.

'King William's what?'

'His Investigator. I investigate for him. From vestigare, to track?' He wondered if Vikings knew Latin. Bit late to ask, probably. 'I track wrongdoing and find out what happened. Murders, mostly.'

'You're the monk from the weaver's.' Ulrik clearly thought

this was some sort of ruse.

'That's right. I was resting there before being summoned to my next task by the king. Or Le Pedvin,' Hermitage added. 'Sometimes both.'

That name had an impact and Ulrik frowned. 'Why do you want me?'

'I'm gathering everyone with some involvement in all this so that we can get to the bottom of it.'

'Bottom of it?' That clearly wasn't a Viking phrase.

'Yes. Find out what's going on. Hopefully, who killed Stigand.'

'And where the silver is?'

'Oh, yes. The Silver. That too.'

'Ragnar has gone to the workshop, looking.'

There was a slight squeak from Wat.

'Has he? Excellent. We can all go there then.'

Hermitage turned a questioning face to the Normans. He had to just hope that they would come along. If they didn't want Stigand investigated at all they might simply decide to leave.

'We'll come,' Roland said. 'I'm just doing what I'm told and it would be good to find out why, for once.'

Hermitage nodded his thanks.

Ulrik gave the Normans a very unhealthy look and then seemed to pretend that he hadn't seen them. He concentrated on keeping Mistress Angel moving with as little fuss as possible.

They gathered together again. An odd group, Saxons, Normans and Vikings all following a common interest. Hermitage suspected that the common interest was their own interest, but it was a start.

'Thanks, Hermitage,' Wat patted the monk on his back.

Cwen gave him one of her best smiles, which was always lovely to see. 'It was a brave thing to do,' she said.

'I'm not sure it can be brave when it's the only thing to do,' Hermitage shrugged. 'As well as being the right thing.'

Wat smiled now. 'Doing the right thing usually gets you in trouble, doesn't it.'

They were distracted as Mistress Angel screamed her objection to the proposal. Ulrik had taken her arm and was pulling her along the road once more. 'What do you want me for?' she demanded.

'The king's man said everyone. You're everyone.'

'So are they,' Angel indicated the throng starting to mill around the door of her inn once more.

'One at a time,' Ulrik explained as he walked on with the struggling Angel.

Ern appeared at the door and seemed torn between following his wife who was once more being dragged away by a Viking or staying at the inn.

'You come too,' Ulrik ordered Ern, who followed meekly.

Angel craned her neck back to the crowd. 'You lot stay out of my inn,' she commanded.

The crowd cheered to her good fortune as they fought one another to get back in again, tankards waving.

Caput XVI

Someone will Explain

'I hope you know what you're doing, Hermitage,' Wat whispered in his ear as they approached the workshop once more.

'Me too,' Hermitage replied. It was not like him to go happily into a situation over which he had no control and with no idea what was going to happen. Which probably explained why he wasn't happy. If the weight of expectation could bear down on him he'd probably be buried up to his neck.

As they arrived Hartle appeared at the doorway. 'Aha, there you are,' he sounded very strained and relieved to see them. The reason was soon clear as Ragnar appeared at his back. A battle-axe was in his hand but at least it was the smaller of the two he carried. 'This gentleman was about to start dismantling the workshop to see where you'd got to.' Hartle smiled a thin and fragile smile.

Ragnar surveyed the gathering. 'What are they doing here?' He nodded to the Normans but spoke to Wat.

'They're Normans. From Normandy. They run the country now?' Wat introduced Roland and Ralf.

'I know what they are,' Ragnar ground out. 'And you can think they run the country if you want to. The question was what they are doing here.'

Ulrik left Mistress Angel and quickly joined his companion, drawing his own weapon in readiness.

'We're going to clear everything up,' Hermitage said as brightly as he could manage in the circumstances. 'Hawks, silver, all of that. As I told Master Ulrik here, I am King William's Investigator. This is the sort of thing I do.' As he said this something put him off his stride. It was the Normans drawing their swords behind him.

'We can always clear everything up in a more traditional manner.' Roland said as he hefted his large sword in his hand.

'Gentlemen, gentlemen,' Hermitage begged. 'We are all here because King William wanted some hawks that were coming from the Danes.' He nodded rapidly from the representatives of King William to the Danes. 'How are we going to get anywhere if the people doing the business end up killing one another?'

'We wouldn't all end up dead,' Ragnar pointed out. 'Last one standing wins is how it usually works.'

'Why does anyone want to end up dead at all? The king has silver and you have birds, why bring death into it?'

The Vikings and Normans were at least content to simply growl and mutter at one another as Hermitage ushered everyone into the workshop.

Once they were all gathered around the front door Hermitage felt that a crowd had turned up to hear him. It didn't help his confidence that they were all pressing in on him.

Obviously only the Vikings or Normans were likely to turn to actual violence if they didn't like what they heard, but a room full of people expressing their disappointment at him took him back to many an unpleasant experience in monasteries across the land. Just for a moment, he wondered if a lecture on the post-Exodus prophets might keep everyone entertained while he worked out what he was actually going to say. He quickly concluded that it wouldn't.

Wat suggested the upstairs room for the gathering but

Cwen, on a quick appraisal of Hermitage's pale and nervous condition, whispered that somewhere with a more accessible escape route might be best.

Using the downstairs room at least had the advantage of getting all these people to throw a piece of broken furniture out of the window, saving Wat the bother. With the room clear, people either sat on the floor or stood. The Vikings and the Normans stood.

Hermitage stayed as near to the door as he could without looking as if he was about to run away and surveyed his audience. What a disparate lot. Mistress Angel and Ern were together, although Angel looked as if she would like to borrow an axe from a Viking and do something very Viking with it. Probably to everyone.

Eadgyth sat alone off to one side but managed to look disparagingly at everyone else.

Wat and Cwen were at his side, which helped a little but as he still didn't actually have a clue what was going on here, never mind who had killed Stigand, he feared he was going to disappoint his audience. His plan was to get them all to simply repeat their tales. He expected, well, hoped perhaps, desperately hoped maybe, that through these tellings the truth would emerge. Contradictions and convergences would be revealed and that would be that. Everyone would go home happy. Well, alive at least.

'So,' he said as an opening line. 'Here we are then.'

Everyone looked at him expectantly, which didn't help at all.

'Where shall we begin?'

More expectation.

'How about with the parchment?' If in doubt fall back on a parchment. Nothing more reliable than a parchment.

Parchment didn't lie after all. Words written in black on a fine piece of material could not be corrupted. Even if both sides of the agreement written on said parchment wanted to chop one another's heads off. Which was a bit odd when you came to think about it. Hermitage thought about it.

'Hermitage?' Wat nudged him. 'The parchment? Say something about the parchment then. In fact, say something about anything. Soon would be good.'

Hermitage looked once more at those spread out before him and a simple word came to his mind. A word he'd been using quite a lot recently but one that encompassed everything.

'Liars,' he said.

It was not a good thing to say. Everyone in the room started to speak at once and none of them sounded very happy.

Hermitage held up his arms to calm them all. 'Not you, not you,' he called out. 'Well, not all of you,' he mumbled. 'I was just observing that this whole business has been plagued by liars.'

The Normans and the Vikings seemed happy to conclude that it was the other group that constituted the main liars in the room and that putting them to death would be a pleasure.

'Please, please,' Hermitage said. 'Let me explain.'

The hubbub died a little until he felt that he could begin. He still wasn't confident of his version of events as it was only just forming in his head, but he had enough, to begin with.

'This whole problem started with a lie. Perhaps the biggest of them all. Stigand arrived here, carrying the king's parchment and claiming that he was charged to buy hawks from the Danes.'

There was general agreement to this.

'That's what he told me,' Mistress Angel spoke up with a sideways glance at Eadgyth.

'But we are now told that he wasn't even the right Stigand. If he was a Stigand at all.'

Eadgyth gave a very knowing and somewhat offensive sniff in the direction of Angel.

'Unfortunately, we need to make some assumptions at this point.' His audience appeared not to have any assumptions readily to hand and just gave him blank looks. 'Never a good idea in an investigation but we can always discard them if they prove unhelpful.'

No one showed signs of disagreeing with this proposal or even understanding it.

'So,' Hermitage took a breath and hoped that the first assumption wouldn't start the Norman-Viking war in Wat's workshop. 'Let us assume that our Stigand, Stigand of Arundel or dead Stigand if you will, had already spent the silver for the hawks and tried to get Wat to engage in the business to replace it.'

There was grumbling from the warriors in the room at this but no one actually raised a weapon. 'We can further assume that he claimed to be Cwen's father to give Wat confidence to go ahead.'

'Lying, cheating…' Cwen began but Hermitage waved her to quiet. 'Dung-chewing, scab-faced arse,' she muttered.

'Surely he could only do that if he had met the real Stigand and got the tale from him.'

There was some nodding around the room at this.

'But we are getting ahead of ourselves.' Hermitage calmed his thinking which had just reached a horrible conclusion all by itself.

'Are we?' Ern asked, ahead of himself not being somewhere

he went very often.

'We are, and that would never do.' A few people nodded that they agreed with him on this, but they didn't look as if they knew what they were agreeing with.

'My experience of seeing the business between Wat and Stigand carried out was a revelation.'

Wat smiled.

'Never had I seen such devious, underhand, deceitful and dishonest behaviour.'

Wat kept smiling and even gave a little nod acknowledging his prowess.

'If such men could lie to one another so blatantly and about such matters, what hope was there for the rest of us. Only the parchment was real. The parchment that said William wanted hawks. At least that was a foundation.' He turned to Roland. 'Could we see it?'

Roland looked around the room and seemed content. He gave the Vikings a warning glare that they weren't to touch it and produced the parchment from his jerkin. Hermitage took it and held it open for everyone to see.

There were gasps from the ordinary folk of Derby as they saw the masterpiece unveiled. The colours leapt into the room and Ern even got onto his hands and knees to crawl for a closer look. 'All them letters,' he gawked.

'All them, er, those letters indeed,' Hermitage nodded. 'Letters that say quite explicitly that William has silver, he wants some hawks and there is to be a great trade. For fifty pounds of silver no less.'

This brought even louder noises from the audience. Mistress Angel gave a little whimper.

'A huge amount of money and surely a great boon to those selling the hawks.' He took a breath. 'So why do the two parties want to kill one another?' He looked from the Normans to the Vikings and back again.

'That's just what they're like?' Cwen suggested.

'Ordinary Normans and Vikings maybe so, but Roland and Ralf on the one side and Ragnar and Ulrik on the other are here precisely because of the hawks. They are here to complete a trade. Why would they want to kill one another?'

'They're not very nice?'

'Probably not. The other possibility is that there is another lie at the heart of this. The parchment itself.'

That got no reaction at all from the crowd, which was a disappointment as that had been his grand announcement. He supposed that people generally weren't quite as concerned about the integrity of parchment as he was.

'I thought you said it was the one thing we could rely on.' Wat looked confused.

'I did. And it was. And that was where I was wrong. The parchment is true in that it is a parchment and it records things that cannot be denied, but if people doing trade can lie with their words, why can't a parchment? Faced with so many lies I should have assumed that everything was a lie.'

'So? Cwen asked.

'The parchment is a lie,' Hermitage concluded. Surely they'd all see it now.

'Which bit, exactly?'

'Which bit?'

'Yes, which bit? There's no silver?'

That got the room moaning.

'Oh no, there's silver all right. There are no hawks though, are there?' He turned to the Normans and the Vikings and folded his arms.

Wat was looking at them as well now. 'What do you mean

there are no hawks?'

'Oh Wat,' Hermitage turned his disappointed eye. 'Did you still think that after all we've been through you'd still be able to organise a deal of some hawks for some silver?'

Wat mumbled into his chin. 'Don't see why not.'

'What happened to the hawks?' Eadgyth demanded. 'Where have they gone?'

'There never were any. This exchange of silver was not about hawks at all, that was just a ruse.'

Eadgyth was grinding her teeth and biting her lip at the same time.

'A ruse?' Cwen frowned hard as she tried to think this through.

'If there had really been hawks and silver this would simply have been a trade. The Vikings and the Normans charged with seeing it through would have done the business and been on their way. Instead, they involve someone called Stigand, get him to carry the parchment and move the silver from one side to another. Why on earth go to all that trouble for a trade?'

'What was it then?' Angel asked, paying rapt attention as if to an exciting storyteller.

'King Aethelred,' Hermitage announced with a satisfying nod.

'King Aethelred?' Wat looked at Hermitage as if he had started on an explanation of something completely different.

'I just started thinking about lies. What if the parchment was a lie? What if there were no hawks? Why else would William be giving silver to the Danes? Just as Aethelred paid the Danegeld in pounds of silver so William was to do the same. Pay the Danes to keep the peace and not cause him any trouble while he ruled the south of the country.

'But he made it look like he was only buying some hawks. I did think that the hawks might be a symbol of something else, after all the parchment was too good for some birds. Now I see that the hawks are a symbol. The hawks in the parchment are the Danes.'

Everyone now looked at the Vikings and the Normans. Angel clearly didn't think much of this deceit although Ern was looking hopeful that the Vikings would spread their wings and fly out the door.

'William couldn't be seen to be paying. He wouldn't want it known that he was handing over silver as Danegeld and that he couldn't rule the whole country.'

'Fifty pounds of silver wouldn't go far,' Cwen said.

'It was probably just a token of his agreement. Get the first fifty to mark his compliance and the rest would follow. The Danes would keep to their land and further payments would be made.'

The Vikings and the Normans were saying nothing.

'But we got the wrong Stigand,' Wat concluded with a sigh. 'If he stole the story and the parchment from the real one, he wouldn't know anything about this. And the real Stigand is supposed to have some silver from the king.' He sounded rather wistful as if someone had taken away the silver they had promised he could play with. 'Where's that gone?'

Hermitage sighed. 'That's the next sorry part of the tale. Carried out by some more sorry people who probably never did know what was really going on.

'We have Mistress Eadgyth's word that the dead Stigand is not her husband. He is not the man who knows all about hawks. Dead Stigand said that he had fooled the Normans into believing he was a hawk expert, but the Normans are hawk experts themselves. They wouldn't be taken in by a simple lie like that, particularly when they had already gone to all the trouble of the parchment.

'It seems likely then that this Stigand is not the husband of Eadgyth. Stigand of Arundel did steal from the other. The parchment, the tale and the silver. But I'm not sure even the real Stigand would have been taken into William's confidence. He was only useful because he was someone who knew about hawks. If he were challenged he would simply say that he really was trying to buy hawks.'

'Stigand of Worthing is still alive?' Cwen asked with a slight tremor.

'I don't know, Cwen.' Hermitage had to be honest. 'We have to consider the possibility that he was killed for the silver. Even a small amount would be motive enough.'

'So,' Cwen bit her lip and looked daggers at the Vikings. 'The Danes poisoned Stigand to stop the trade and send a message to William that they didn't accept his terms?'

'No,' said Hermitage. 'Our Viking friends really are looking for the silver.'

'Oh,' Cwen was disappointed. 'Then the Normans killed him because erm, why did they kill him?'

'They didn't kill him either.'

The Normans and Vikings looked a bit smug about this.

'But they did want me to stop investigating.'

'Aha,' Wat said, and then went quiet having nothing to follow his "aha".

'For some reason, they changed their minds about the Danegeld. Word came that I was to stop investigating. That meant they didn't mind that Stigand was dead anymore, which probably indicates that William has decided not to pay after all.'

'He has,' Roland spoke up. 'The message I received is that

King William will no longer pay for any hawks. The fate of Stigand is of no interest.' He did look a bit confused as he recited his own instructions.

'If he will not give silver then he will die,' Ragnar replied in a very Viking manner.

'Our king will doubtless harry the north instead of paying for it.' Roland said these words as a keen fighter who was only too happy to get involved in some harrying.

Hermitage shook his head in sadness. 'So you, Ragnar and Ulrik, you know why you're here and what's going on.'

'Aye,' Ragnar confirmed.

'But you Roland?'

Roland grumbled at his sword. 'No one tells me anything.'

'So they both did it?' Cwen sounded rather lost. 'Just to stop anyone knowing that there had been any Danegeld at all.'

'Not that either, I'm afraid.' Hermitage shrugged an apology.

'What then?'

In all of Hermitage's reasoning so far his original horrible conclusion had not altered. In fact, it had been strengthened. There was nothing for it but to plough on.

'Let us continue with the assumption that dead Stigand is not the original Stigand. Mistress Eadgyth is right in that the body is not her Stigand who doubtless knew nothing of all this. If master Roland here knew only that he was to make sure the trade went ahead, it is unlikely that the trader himself was included in the deceit. He had to be kept in the dark, as it were, otherwise he wouldn't play his part properly.

'That meant that his death was of no benefit to either the Vikings or the Normans. Roland and Ralf clearly had no idea what he even looked like so he was hardly a trouble to their plans.'

'He was kept in the dark?' Roland complained. 'Most of this is news to me.'

'Stupid Norman,' Ulrik spat.

'Do you mind?' Cwen complained, looking at the floor. 'We live here. Go on Hermitage.'

'We come back to the Stigand that arrived here, Stigand of Arundel. He had the parchment and knew about the hawks and the silver.'

'So,' Cwen shrugged. 'As you say, he got it all from the real Stigand who presumably is still out there somewhere. Probably dead in a ditch.' She gave her mother a glare. Eadgyth had got up from the floor now and was resting by the window to get some air.

'But he knew something else as well,' Hermitage said with great weight.

'Which was?'

Hermitage simply looked at Cwen. Surely she could get this bit on her own.

'He thought he was my father,' she breathed.

'Just so. The tale of the parchment and the silver and the hawks he could have got from the real Stigand, Stigand of Worthing. Another assumption is that you were right about your real father. He left before you were born and so may not even know you exist. If that's the case who else could have told Stigand of Arundel about you?'

Eyebrows were raised as folk considered this.

Cwen's were the first eyes to turn to Eadgyth, who wasn't there anymore. 'Where's she gone?' She screamed.

'She went out the window,' Ern reported.

'Well get after her,' Cwen yelled as she turned to the door.

Roland nodded to Ralf who stepped quickly in front of

Cwen and with a courteous nod went after Eadgyth with sword in hand.

In a few moments, a jumping and squirming Eadgyth returned in the grasp of Ralf. The woman made noises of protest and threat but had little coherent to say.

'She did kill Stigand then,' Cwen stated with a little unhealthy satisfaction. 'She said she wanted to.'

'I think she did. And I expect that she thought the opportunity was too good to miss. She doubtless got the whole tale from Stigand of Worthing who was happy to tell her as she's his wife. Or was his wife. He was probably very proud that at last he was to deal in hawks.

'She then stole the parchment and the silver and made an arrangement with the new fellow, persuading him to play the part of Stigand. They have doubtless spent the silver living the good life, thinking that another fifty pounds was just around the corner. In any event, they would be able to use the parchment to persuade someone to put their own silver into the trade.

'Then, when she got here she saw that everything was in place for the deal on the hawks to go ahead. Wat's silver was as good as promised and so why did she need Stigand anymore? With him out of the way, his share of the silver would be hers and he wouldn't be around to tell. She obviously claimed to be looking for him so that she could be here for the trade without raising any suspicion that she was actually involved. She didn't know that there were no hawks and the silver was heading north.'

'And so it is true that dead Stigand isn't her Stigand.'

'Quite so.'

'Why did he call himself Arundel instead of Worthing then?'

'Probably to make you believe his claim to be your father. Worthing would mean nothing to you.' Hermitage felt terribly sorry for Cwen at this point. First, she has someone claim to be her father and eventually, she starts to believe it. Then he's killed by her mother, then he turns out not to be her father after all. He had a vague recollection that he'd read something a bit like this in Greek somewhere. Although in that case, everyone ended up dead.

Eadgyth's expression was hard to read. Her face was constantly twisting about in a combination of anger at being found out, frustration at being held captive by a Viking and annoyance that the whole trade was a sham.

'When did she poison him?' Cwen asked. Finding out that her mother really was a murderess must be an awful shock. She didn't look very shocked though, just sort of grimly satisfied.

'It could have been any time,' Hermitage said. 'She probably started poisoning him as soon as she was sure the trade would go ahead. She put something in his food but it took time to have its effect. We know from Mistress Angel that there was someone else loitering in the area, doubtless, that was Eadgyth who must have been here as long as Stigand. And if the Vikings and Normans were expecting Stigand alone, she would have to keep out of sight.'

'Bread and wine,' Mistress Angel spoke up. 'I told him he shouldn't have bread and wine in the morning. Be the death of you, I said. I was right.'

'And why did she scream so loud when she saw him?'

'That was probably the point at which she truly realised what she'd done. The sight of the body was quite horrible, enough to make anyone scream. But if you knew that you were the cause of such an appalling death, wouldn't you scream?'

'Or she lies when she's screaming as well.' Cwen shrugged. 'So, what do we do with her? Give her to the Vikings?'

Eadgyth did look a bit shocked at this idea. Ragnar didn't look too happy either. 'We don't want her,' he said. 'She's your problem, you deal with her. We've got war with the Normans to organise.' He glared at Roland and Ralf and rested his hand on his sword handle.

'Hand her over to the Normans then?'

'No thank you,' Roland said. 'She's no interest to us. We've got defeating some Vikings to get on with.' He returned Ragnar's glare and added a sniff of contempt.

'What then? We can't just let her go. She killed someone.'

'She did indeed.' Hermitage couldn't immediately think what to do. He had investigated and solved the murder, punishing the wrongdoer must be someone else's job.

'We'll have to take her before the moot.' Wat said. 'They dealt with Stigand's dead body, they can deal with his poisoner.'

Hermitage saw problems with this. 'The last we saw of the moot they were outside the inn falling over and being sick.'

'On my ale,' Angel pointed out.

Cwen dismissed this complaint. 'We just wait until they're sober. In the meantime, we lock her up somewhere.'

Eadgyth had further complaint to make about this proposal but Ulrik's grip tightened and she fell silent.

'She can go in my cellar,' Mistress Angel offered. 'It's horrible down there.'

'Don't you use it for the ale?' Hermitage asked.

'Not since the rats got so big.'

Cwen smiled. 'Sounds like just the place.'

'I'm not going with her,' Eadgyth indicated Angel. 'I don't

trust her.'

'The poisoner doesn't trust the tavern keeper.' Cwen mocked.

Hermitage did worry about this. And there was no way Cwen should be allowed to take charge of her mother, or that Wat would want to. Goodness knew what would happen. Mistress Angel's expression said she was quite looking forward to locking Eadgyth up. Which might also be a bad idea. 'I'll take her,' he offered. 'I mean, I'll accompany her. Make sure she's secure for the moot.'

Eadgyth smiled her contemptuous smile to the others. 'The monk will see I'm treated properly.'

'And perhaps master Roland will help?'

Roland nodded a confused agreement.

Cwen sidled over to Hermitage and whispered in his ear. 'Hermitage, if you lose her I'll lock you in Angel's cellar.'

Caput XVII

What Murder?

It was late the following day before the members of the moot were in any condition to carry out their official functions. They came bleary-eyed and pale to the moot hall, holding heads or stomachs and moaning gently. The only good news they had was that the Vikings and Normans had left at first light. Off to prepare for battle, they said. As long as the battle wasn't in Derby, they were welcome to each other.

The headman, who didn't seem able to open his eyes properly, reported that they had four items of business to consider before they could go and lie down again.

The first was Mistress Angel's bill for all the ale the town had drunk when she had been forced from her inn. She said that the moot should pay for this as they had not protected her from the Vikings, which was supposed to be their job, for goodness sake. She also had a strong case that it was the members of the moot who had led the drinking and so their responsibility was double. She was waiting outside to present her arguments.

The second business was dealing with the stranger Eadgyth, who was reported to have poisoned another stranger, one Stigand of Arundel. Neither of these people was a citizen of the town.

The moot voted that they'd rather deal with a killer than Mistress Angel.

Next was someone called Elpin who claimed that his neighbour had bewitched his geese. The final piece of business was just some ancient old man who had turned up in the town seeking shelter. They'd consider the geese and the old man after the killer and then there might not be time to listen to Mistress Angel. If they were lucky.

Two men were sent to fetch Eadgyth from the cellar and all the other interested parties were summoned.

Unfortunately, the headman hadn't realised that Mistress Angel was an interested party and so before they could do anything about this murder they found themselves promising that Angel would be paid in full. It was the only way they were going to get her to shut up.

Eadgyth was now brought into the hall and looked around her with a confidence that seemed completely out of place. She gazed at Cwen and then turned her nose up and looked away. Cwen snarled a bit and dug Hermitage in the ribs so that he could note how awful the woman was.

The headman lifted his head from the table where he'd been resting it and appraised Eadgyth. It was a few moments before he reached the conclusion that this was the woman they were waiting for.

'So,' he said. Then he stopped and frowned as if his voice were booming inside his head. He looked along the rectangular table that the moot sat behind. The four other members who had made it here at all made sure that they were looking away.

The headman swallowed and forced himself to carry on. He addressed Eadgyth. 'You are erm,'

'Eadgyth,' Cwen called out.

The man held his hand up for silence. 'Yes, you are Eadgyth?'

'I am.'

Hermitage started to wonder why Eadgyth was quite so

comfortable. Surely she knew that the moot would deal with her harshly. Even though Stigand had not been a man of Derby he had still been killed. The weregild for such an act was going to be significant. And with any chance of silver having gone, where would she find the money?

'And you killed erm,'

'Stigand.' Cwen was getting impatient.

'Yes, Stigand.'

'No,' said Eadgyth.

'And even though this Stigand was not a..., Pardon?'

'No. I said No. No I did not kill Stigand.'

'Yes you did,' Cwen shouted. 'We heard all about it last night. You poisoned him so you could get the silver.'

'Prove it,' Eadgyth retorted.

'Prove it?'

'Yes, prove it.'

'We don't have to prove it.'

'Oh, yes you do.'

Cwen looked confused and angry.

'The monk told me all about it.'

Cwen's teeth were clamped shut. Hermitage's knees likewise. 'The monk told you all about what?' She spoke to Eadgyth but looked daggers at Hermitage.

'Investigation. When he took me to the cellar we had a nice chat about evidence and proving things and all that. And you can't prove that I poisoned Stigand. So I didn't.'

'Who did then?'

'How should I know? Could have been anyone. Might have been you. We all know what a temper you've got.'

There was general agreement around the room at that.

Eadgyth pressed her case. 'I didn't even know the man. I told you after I'd seen his body that he wasn't my Stigand.

He's not the man I'm looking for at all. Never seen him in my life.'

'Why did you try to run away when we accused you then? Eh? Tell me that.'

'Who wouldn't run away from a room full of mad people accusing them of murder?' Eadgyth smiled.

'So how did this dead Stigand get the parchment that should have been with your Stigand? Why did you turn up here at all asking for anyone called Stigand?'

'Because I was looking for my Stigand. I wanted to help him with his trade.'

'Ha!'

'And then you lot tell me that my poor Stigand must have been robbed on the road by that awful man who's dead in the church and who I have never seen before. It's just a horrible coincidence.'

'Coincidence!' Cwen shrieked.

'All you've got is cirumstated evidence.'

'We've got what?'

'Not that. What's the word? Circumstantial, that's it. It's circumstantial evidence, doesn't prove a thing. All you've got is some dead man called Stigand who might have eaten some bad mushrooms for all I know.'

'Not in my inn, he didn't,' Angel insisted.

Cwen was now pointing at Hermitage with a very worrying expression.

The headman held his hands up to stop the argument, mainly because it was getting too loud. 'You say you did not kill Stigand?' he said, quietly.

'No, Definitely not.'

'Mistress Cwen, you say she did.'

'I do.'

'Why?'

'Because she did.'

The headman held his head again. 'That's not usually quite enough. How can you show this? Did you see her kill Stigand?'

'Well no, but it's the sort of thing she'd do.'

'Did anyone see her do it?'

No one had anything to offer.

'Is Stigand's family here? Do they claim she did this?'

'He said he was my father,' Cwen reported.

The headman raised his eyebrows at this. 'And was he?'

'Well, she says no but she could be lying about that as well.'

The headman held both hands up this time. 'Enough. If no one saw the act done then we cannot say it was done.'

'What?' Cwen was too stunned to be simply unhappy. Wat was cringing a bit, probably wondering if he could get back to the workshop before she had another go at the furniture.

'Silence!' The headman yelled his command and then held his head in pain. 'We cannot find that this Eadgyth killed that Stigand.'

Eadgyth grinned a very self-satisfied grin.

'Next item.' He breathed deeply. 'I can't face geese at this early hour. Let's just get this beggar dealt with and then we can go.'

Cwen was fuming and boiling and raging all at once. Hermitage knew that this would not be the end of the matter and that he would have a lot to go through before that end even came close. If Eadgyth had any sense she would head back to Arundel at the first opportunity. She was right though. The circumstances pointed very strongly to her being the culprit but there was no real evidence. Could anyone really be considered a killer if there were only circumstantial evidence? Probably not, but in this case, he was strongly inclined to go with the circumstances.

A new arrival in the room distracted him from the worry about what was to come when he was alone with Cwen once more.

He looked and saw an ancient, stooped old man enter the room. Although he had the build and appearance of a beggar he had stout shoes and reasonable clothes. Perhaps he was simply a traveller who wanted to reside in the town for a while before moving on and was seeking the moot's permission.

He was a bit old to be travelling anywhere though. The wrinkled face said the man must be at least sixty. Surely, he should be at home by his hearth.

'Yes?' the headman asked, wearily. 'You want to enter our town and stay for how long?'

'Oh, no,' a quiet and slightly shaky voice barely troubled the room, although Eadgyth's head turned.

The old man addressed the moot. 'I am Stigand of Worthing. I've come to meet some Danes about hawks?' He looked around and smiled at everyone. 'Oh, hello Eadgyth,' he said. 'I say, you haven't got my silver have you?'

Finis

Brother Hermitage will return to deal with

A Murder For Master Wat

Printed in Great Britain
by Amazon

73117790R00156